LITTLE,
BROWN
L B
100 YEARS
LARGE
PRINT

ALSO BY LANE CLARKE

Love Times Infinity

every reason to stay

LANE CLARKE

LITTLE, BROWN AND COMPANY
LARGE PRINT EDITION

Watercolor background by Reinhold Leitner/Shutterstock.com.
Strawberry art by Hein Nouwens/Shutterstock.com.
Stroke divider by Koltukovs/Shutterstock.com.

Cover art copyright © 2026 by Jill De Haan. Cover design by Gabrielle Chang.
Cover copyright © 2026 by Hachette Book Group, Inc.
Interior design by Carla Weise.

Little, Brown and Company
Hachette Book Group
1290 Avenue of the Americas, New York, NY 10104
LBYR.com

First Edition: July 2026

Library of Congress Cataloging-in-Publication Data
Names: Clarke, Lane author
Title: Every reason to stay / Lane Clarke.
Description: First edition. | New York : Little, Brown and Company, 2026. | Audience: Ages 12 & up | Summary: "A teenage girl grieves the loss of her father while acclimating to her new city and family." —Provided by publisher.
Identifiers: LCCN 2025035762 | ISBN 9780759556751 hardcover | ISBN 9780759556744 ebook
Subjects: CYAC: Grief—Fiction | Fathers—Fiction | Adjustment—Fiction | LCGFT: Novels | Fiction
Classification: LCC PZ7.1.C588 Ev 2026
LC record available at https://lccn.loc.gov/2025035762

ISBNs: 978-0-7595-5675-1 (hardcover), 978-0-7595-5674-4 (ebook), 978-0-3166-1076-6 (large print)

every reason to stay

Chapter One

The sound of the whisk hitting the side of the Le Creuset mixing bowl was a bit like music, a favorite melody that got stuck in your ear and wouldn't shake loose until there was a new song to replace it.

I kept time with the echo of the *ting* as metal hit ceramic, and I watched almost in a trance as the dry ingredients were sucked down into the bottom of the bowl, creating something akin to quicksand. I stuck a finger into the bowl—sticky but not too wet. Perfect.

"Mmm, smells great, Sky," Dad said as he sauntered into the kitchen, his guitar case slung over his shoulder like an old leather jacket. In my entire sixteen years of life, I had only seen him without the thing a handful of times. He'd probably be wearing it when he walked me down the aisle. Old reliable.

"It hasn't even gone in the oven yet." I laughed as I set the bowl on our makeshift island, a few pieces of plywood Dad had nailed together to give me some extra workspace in our fingertip-to-fingertip-sized kitchen.

"I smell its potential." He gave two exaggerated sniffs, flaring his nostrils out as far as they could go. He licked his finger and stuck it in the air like he was checking the direction of the wind. "Forecast says it's going to be delicious."

"It's always delicious," I responded somewhat smugly. I'd only ever been good at two things—running and baking. But I was never a natural runner; it was something I had to work at. Hours after school spent beating the pavement until the burning in my chest and knees became almost enjoyable, as full of crap as that sounded. No one was more disappointed than me when my annual physical four years ago led to a suggestion of more physical activity. Because quite honestly, "exercise gives you endorphins" sounded like a scam and a little unhinged. So I joined track, was told I had potential, and worked my way to the top because I was stubborn.

But being in the kitchen was like rolling over in bed and settling into the perfect cool spot, like it'd been waiting for me this whole time. Legend had it that in all the random things Dad and his bandmates would hand me to get me to be quiet during rehearsals, there was nothing that brought me perfect peace like the wooden spoon—a staple in any serious baker's arsenal.

"You know, you're supposed to let other people tell you your food is delicious," he said, attempting to dip his finger into the batter, no matter how many times I'd warned him of the dangers of raw ingredients in cake batter.

"You also always said you shouldn't wait for people to tell you what you already know."

Dad laughed, a deep guttural sound akin to a passenger train coming to a sudden stop. "Who taught you how to be so grown-up?" He picked up one of my dish towels and draped it over my head before pulling me toward him and placing a wet kiss on my forehead. "Don't forget you're still my little girl."

"Gross," I groaned, dragging the inside of my wrist over the wet spot.

He glanced down at his watch, an old Timex with a cloudy face, and blew a breath out of the corners of his mouth. "Gotta skedaddle."

"Gonna be a late night?" I asked. Dad spent most Monday nights with his band, Gastric, at a venue on Congress Ave., a locale he had spent his entire career working toward. It had all finally paid off when he got called up to the big show last fall.

"Hopefully not," he said as he pulled me in for another hug and straightened his guitar to fit through the narrow hallway to our front door. "But whatever the boss wants."

"You're the boss," I laughed as I followed him out to his truck, an old Jeep Grand Cherokee in his favorite color, forest green. He'd had the Jeep my entire life, and in a few months when I passed the test to get my permit converted to a real driver's license, it would be mine. Or at least that was what he'd promised on my tenth birthday, and I planned to hold him to it.

"Then I guess I'll be home just in time for some cake." He gave me a wink before laying his guitar gently in the trunk and climbing into the driver's seat. No matter how old that guitar got, or how often it was accidentally knocked into a wall or doorframe, Dad still treated it like a newborn baby, his hand always cradling its neck.

He honked his horn as he turned out of our small cul-de-sac, each matchbox house smaller and more unusual than the one beside it.

I sucked in the cool air blasting down the hallway as I made my way back to the kitchen. Setting the small white timer on the counter, I poured the batter into two cake pans and slid them into the oven. Despite it being early May, it was already hot in Austin, and I hoped that the heat wouldn't upset the batter. There was nothing worse than dense sponge cake.

The front door slammed just as I finished chopping the green heads off my strawberries. The scent of vanilla and dragon fruit chased the sound.

"Did you know your dad has almost a hundred thousand Instagram followers?" my best friend, Olivia, said as she invited herself into the house and made herself comfortable at our kitchen / dining room table.

"Don't tell him that," I warned her with a grin. "He'll spend the next month DMing everyone individually to 'thank them for their support.'"

"He would not," she said before pausing. "Actually . . . he probably would."

"Day ones, blah blah," I said.

"Show your appreciation, yadda, yadda," she finished. She placed her phone on the tabletop and stretched her arms above her head, exposing just one of her many DIYed belly chains. The rest were on her Etsy shop, going out the door faster than she could make them sometimes. "Speaking of day ones, you going to the track party next weekend?"

"You mean the one being hosted by my ex-girlfriend?" I lifted my eyebrows. Olivia was always trying to get Simone and me to talk, as if we hadn't spent the past two years talking and talking and talking until we realized neither of us usually liked what the other had to say.

"As in, the captain."

"Incoming, she isn't the boss of us yet."

"Even more important to show face. You *know* she doesn't think you're going to show up, which is exactly why you should. Plus, do you really want to go into next season with so much negative energy?"

"There's no negative energy," I said, pushing the bowl of sliced strawberries toward her. She gave me a knowing smile before digging in, immediately getting strawberry seeds under her gel manicure. “We broke up. It was amicable.”

“You sound like a divorcée,” she laughed, using her thumbnail to pluck a seed from beneath her pinky nail.

“As long as I got you in the split, she can keep the house.”

“Ah,” she said, placing her hand on her chest, “I love being fought over.”

I grabbed one of the strawberry stems and chucked it across the kitchen. But not only was Olivia a track rock star, she was also one of the best lacrosse players in the state, so she caught it in midair and popped it into her mouth, grimacing slightly at the taste.

“Doesn’t matter anyway. Dad has a show that night.”

“Not until, like, eleven p.m. The party will be over. In fact, I think Simone mentioned stopping by the show. You know she’s head of the Gastric Fan Club.”

“Don’t remind me,” I responded with a roll of my eyes. “Having your ex be the lead groupie of your dad’s band is so weird.”

“It’s, like, incestuous. There needs to be an equitable division of the assets.”

"Okay, Elle Woods. But seriously, you know I never miss a Saturday night show. It's in my Beloved Only Daughter contract."

"Ugh, why can't you hate your parents like the rest of us?"

"Parent." I shrugged.

Olivia grimaced. "Sorry."

"No big deal. You know I don't even remember her. And you'd basically need to put a gun to Dad's head to get him to talk about her. Hurts too bad, I guess."

"That high school sweetheart shit will mess you up. Still, I am sorry. I know you want to know more about her. But she did marry your dad and have you, so the facts support her being pretty baller."

"Can't argue with cold hard facts like that."

"You're going to cry as soon as I leave, aren't you?" She gave me a knowing look, her eyes clouding over with sympathy. I wasn't super emotional about my mom dying when I was just a baby, in the sense that I didn't have any memories to attach to her. But sometimes the idea of not having a mother for all the big things still to come put a little salt in the scabbed-over wound of only having one parent.

But at least that one parent was like twenty cool parents in a trench coat.

"Maybe a tear or two, drown it out in the shower."

Olivia snorted. "As you avoid putting your face in the water like an infant?"

"Wow. In my own home, no less."

Olivia laughed before slamming her hands on the table to push herself up. "Pray for me," she said as she snuck another strawberry. "Mi madre was very excited about a zucchini brownie recipe when I left this morning."

"Those can be pretty good, actually," I tried to assure her.

"Maybe if you were making it, Rachael Ray." She bumped me with her hip before leaving. "See ya, loser."

As the house quieted again, I made my way up to my dad's room, tripping over his dirty jeans and knocked-over boots on the way to his closet. Guitar picks were scattered across the hardwood, crammed into every empty crevice. The space of a musician who ate, slept, and breathed his work.

I shimmied out a box stuffed into a corner of the overhead shelf, old ticket stubs from shows Dad used for "research" falling to the floor. It was a fabric box, worn around the edges with frayed string in every direction. Inside were pages of old song lyrics on crumpled paper, soft along the seams where they'd been folded and unfolded countless times. Blue ink was settled in deep veins spreading into the cotton of the loose-leaf. I dug to the bottom of the box until my thumb brushed the edge of a Polaroid. In the photo, faded into sepia with time, I was bundled up in a herringbone blanket, my arms tucked into my sides. A scruff of hair sat on top of my head. My face was still bloated from being just a couple of days earthside. My mother hovered over me, the back of her head toward the lens. She had braids, the black of the Kanekalon contrasting brightly with the red of her nearly auburn natural hair in the flash of the camera.

I imagined her face a million times, the smile she probably had as she looked down at me. The glint in her eye as she sang me a lullaby. Or read me a book. Or narrated her day. I imagined holding her fingers in my small hands. This was the only photo I had of us, and I couldn't even see her face. Fitting, really, for the woman I didn't and could never really know. For the love that sat so deeply in my father's heart that he could not dig out even small pieces of her to share with me. But I loved my dad, and I tried not to feel resentful of his grief. He told me about her in his music, in the lyrics he wrote about love and patience and loss.

Dragging my finger over the photo, I imagined the feel of her hair beneath my fingertips. Was it coily like the hair braided in, or straighter? Was it a mix of textures like mine, smooth in the very middle and frizzy all around? Did she have a signature scent like Olivia, or a song that reminded her of home?

Sighing deeply, I slid the photo back beneath the songs and memories Dad kept hidden away. I expertly put the box back in place, fitting it into a gap in the shelf that looked too small for it. For now, I had to be happy with life as it was, sans a mother but with a dad who somehow managed to be more than enough.

Chapter Two

Erin, our usual Tuesday night waitress, sat me and Dad in our usual booth—a solitary bench in the corner of IHOP, past the kitchen and as far away from the bathrooms as one could get. Despite the fact that I could make melt-in-your-mouth pancakes with my eyes closed and both hands tied behind my back, there was just something unbeatable about an IHOP short stack. Maybe it was the fact that it was consistent? I found comfort in knowing exactly what I was getting, no surprises. Or maybe it was the fact that Dad and I had been coming to IHOP every Tuesday for as long as I could remember that made the fare especially good.

Either way, I relished the predictability of it all as I perused the menu, already knowing what I'd come for. Short stack, a cup of whipped cream, strawberry syrup (vastly underrated), a side of sausage links, and a large orange juice that never seemed like enough no matter how slowly I sipped at it. Dad read the menu more seriously than I ever did, hopping around the listings every week and taking a chance on the specials. He wasn't nearly as into predictability as I was. It was only when I noticed the too-offbeat tempo being stomped out with the steel toe of his work boot that I realized his eyes had not left the descriptions of the onion rings.

"Dad?" I asked, kicking him in the boot, which only served to startle me more than him. For a guy who lived in Converses, it was always weird when he wore his contractor job garb—the "real" job he was forced to work to support us. He managed to do pretty well as a musician, but "pretty well as a musician" still didn't quite cover our mortgage, much less my frequent trips to Williams Sonoma. He had picked up the job in order to get me a much-coveted KitchenAid stand mixer for my thirteenth birthday, and had managed to hold on to it ever since. I suspected he liked being creative, even if it was with kitchen cabinetry instead of music.

"Dad?" I kicked again, this time being careful to aim for the soft, exposed part of his shin.

"Hmm?" he said, as if noticing me for the first time.

"You good?"

He grunted again and returned to studying the menu.

If there was one thing my father wasn't, it was a man of few words. He could talk an automated machine into complete silence. "Dad?" I said, louder this time, as Erin dropped our drinks off at the table. She took out her notepad to write down his order, mine already scribbled across the top. Ah, IHOP. You just couldn't get that kind of service everywhere.

"I think Mother's Day is coming up soon," he said finally, taking a big gulp of his fountain Coke, no ice.

"Uh, okay," I responded, confusion laced in my tone. In sixteen years, we had never even acknowledged Mother's Day. On account of, well, no mother being present. Dad didn't speak to his parents, a falling-out occurring prior to my birth that he had never bothered to explain. Which was kind of his MO, pretending things in the past weren't worth a mention. "Does that mean something to you?"

"We should do something," he said. "Take a trip, see the East Coast maybe. New York, Boston, DC."

"For…Mother's Day?" I asked tentatively. "And you hate the East Coast." I didn't know much about Dad's childhood other than the fact that he'd grown up in Virginia and hated it. Stuffy people. Stuffy summers.

"I hear it's a lot cooler now."

"Cooler than here?" I wasn't a stan for my city or anything, but it was an objective fact that Austin was pretty legit. "Should we also go see a Civil War reenactment? I hear they're all the rage."

"Don't be a smartass," he said with a small laugh.

"Well, you're being super weird, Daddio." I took a more aggressive sip of orange juice, starting to relax into the worn pleather beneath me.

"Just some things I've been thinking about. Feeling like maybe I ran away from talking to you about your mom and feeling some type of way about it, is all. Maybe a trip back home would shake some things loose."

I shrugged, even though I had been waiting for him to say that for years. There wasn't a real way to tell him to get over losing her and talk to me about her without sounding like an ass. "If that's how you're feeling. Took long enough, I guess."

"You mad at me for it?" he asked, grabbing an onion ring off his plate before it was even fully on the table. He gave Erin a smile. She was a college student at Baylor already home for the summer, and Dad had always been fond of her—she'd been our waitress for years now. "Nice kid," he said as I mouthed the words alongside him with a laugh.

"Not mad, per se," I said, jumping back into this admittedly weird conversation. "I definitely wish I knew more about her, but I get it." Even though I definitely didn't. If you loved someone and had nice things to say about them, wouldn't you want to share them with anyone who would listen?

He gave a deep sigh and cleared his throat, bringing his fist to his mouth. "There's just a lot that's hard to explain."

"Like what?" I asked. She was here one day

and gone the next, an apparent labor complication that went unnoticed for days before causing absolute chaos, and pretty much the reason I never wanted to have children. Not ones I birthed, at least, though I could totally see myself fostering kids in need of a good home. Though saying that made me feel like I was talking about puppies and not actual human beings.

"All of it, really."

Maybe it was hard to talk about pregnancy and labor with a teenager. Especially as a man, who only really went through it on the periphery. Maybe he didn't want me to be afraid of it when I was older, even though I already was.

"We made a lot of decisions, your mom and me. Decisions that just feel less and less like the right ones."

"Like having-a-kid sort of decisions." A knot settled into the pit of my stomach. He finally started talking about her and it was to tell me I was a mistake?

"No, definitely not," he said with an adamant shake of his head. "You were the best thing we ever did. I just wish we'd thought more about you growing up without her, when we…well, like I said, it's hard to explain."

I swirled my fork in the whipped cream before draping it over my strawberry-syrup-laden pancakes, but my appetite had left the premises.

"Was she happy? When I was born?" I asked. This had always been my biggest fear—that somewhere on the other side, wherever people went when they died, she wished she was here instead of me. I mean, that was the truth, wasn't it? If it wasn't for me, she'd still be alive.

"Absolutely," he said. "No regrets from either of us ever."

"How do you know? It's not like you can ask her."

"Because I know your mother," he said.

"Knew her."

"Hmm?"

"You knew her."

He stared at me for a moment before a sadness settled behind his eyes.

"Yeah. I knew her."

I draped an old T-shirt over my head to dry my hair, a trick I learned from TikTok. Shaking my head like Lassie in from the rain, I wrapped a towel around my body before sliding into my postshower shoes and yanked the bathroom door open. Steam spilled out into the hallway like dry ice.

"We never should have done it this way." Dad's voice floated from his room. He was louder than usual, and his typical jovial tone, something akin to Santa Claus if he wasn't so burly, was gone. I inched toward his cracked door, pressing my ear as close as possible to the gap between door and frame.

"It was asinine then and it's asinine now. It was selfish on my part, and it was selfish on your part."

I held my breath to hear better. Maybe if I was really silent, I could hear who he was talking to. Dad rarely spoke to anyone in a way that didn't display his incredibly charming Southern upbringing. Whoever was on the other end of the call must have royally messed up.

"I'm going to tell her the truth... Well, I don't care how you feel about it. You're not raising her."

My back straightened. Was he talking about me? With who? I could only guess he was talking to his parents, who he never mentioned and who I didn't even know he still had phone calls with. But I was shocked that he would use that tone with his own mother, regardless of how he felt about her. It just wasn't him.

I leaned even farther forward, trying to peek into the gap with one eye. If I could just see his body language...

My toes pressed on a soft spot in the hardwood floor, letting out a long, loud groan.

Dad stopped talking instantly and quiet filled the hallway. There was no way to back up without making even more noise. I was stuck.

"Skylar?" Dad called.

"Shit," I muttered under my breath. Full name, too, which meant he wasn't pleased I was snooping. Best to commit. I slammed into his room like I had been on my way the whole time. "I had a shower thought."

He held his phone to his chest, like he was on FaceTime with someone he didn't want me to see. "Can I come hear about it in a minute? Just wrapping up a call."

He shifted uncomfortably, which was odd for someone usually so relaxed. Everything about him the past few days had been odd, to say the least.

"Oh, who you talking to?" I asked, trying to sound as casual as possible and not like I had been eavesdropping only moments before.

"Just trying to sort out our Verizon account; shouldn't take too much longer."

I bristled but tried to recover quickly. Whoever he had been talking to, it was *not* Verizon, which meant he had just lied to me point-blank. I couldn't recall a single time he'd ever lied to me before, at least not a time I had figured it out. My dad was almost painfully honest, even to his own detriment. Whatever was going on, whatever he was keeping from me, was serious.

"Oh, okay," I said, trying to hide the concern in my voice. "I'll be in my room when you're done. Have to pick out my outfit for your show Saturday."

"I'm sure it'll rock," he said, though his voice sounded strained.

I turned on my heel and got the hell out of there, slamming my door behind me and falling into bed.

Pensive during IHOP Tuesday. Weird phone call. *Lying.* Something was going on and I didn't like it one bit.

Chapter Three

I felt the speaker vibrate beneath me as Dad's band hit the crescendo in their first song of the night. I watched as Dad transformed into someone else beneath the spotlight. The chains hanging from his black cargo pants shimmered like stained glass. The pants themselves, shredded along the hem, were one spin cycle away from complete annihilation.

Hopping off the speaker, I dug out my earplugs from each ear. Ronnell, behind the bar and hustling to keep up with orders, had a Dr Pepper with no ice ready for me on the bar top. I brought the straw between my teeth as I bobbed my head to the music. Dad's rock was a far cry from the movie soundtrack instrumentals that were frequent fliers in my Spotify Wrapped every year, but I still relished Saturday night shows.

"Hey!" A shout came from my left. I turned to find Simone, my ex-girlfriend, standing in a cropped top that stopped just above her belly button, showing off the piercing she had gotten last summer and was still keeping secret from her parents. I guessed she made it here postparty after all.

"Hey, Sim!" I shouted over the drums, which were keeping a steady beat for the rest of the band. I could almost smell the sweat coming off them, knowing I would have to endure what I called postshow funk from the passenger seat as Dad drove us home tonight.

Simone dragged her arm over my shoulders, a gesture of familiarity that made me a little uncomfortable. She had always been the more touchy-feely one in our relationship, a fact that I was pretty sure had contributed to our demise. Her love language was physical touch and boy, did she like to show it, even if the constant skin-to-skin contact made me want to crawl out of mine.

"Funny meeting you here," she joked. But we both knew that the only local show I had ever missed was during the great hostile flu takeover of 2023. We had just started dating, followed quickly by nursing each other back to health as we each fell to the chills and nausea of the common flu in quick succession. But now we were over.

"You missed my party," she said, glancing at me from the corner of her eye as she scooped a piece of ice from her nearly empty cup into her mouth. I watched her lips as they worked over the ice cube, stopped myself from catching the melted water as it slid down her chin. It was that exact train of thought that would lead to nowhere healthy. I was generally of the mind that once people broke up, they should *stay* broken up. But Simone had good lips, a cute chin, the kind of features that made you want to write poetry, and that was the kind of spin-the-block mentality that was bound to get me into trouble.

"You mean the end-of-year track party," I reminded her.

She rolled her eyes in response. "It's bad karma to blow off your captain like that."

"Tiff is still the captain, at least for three more weeks." I turned around to face her properly, placing my elbows on the bar top behind me.

"Oh, come on, Tiff checked out at regionals. Once she knew we weren't making state, she was pretty much already on a plane to Wesleyan. Hence why you should have been there. It was me and the boys stuck in a room with the Shrill Team."

The Shrill Team was the nickname for the group of long-distance track girls who spoke in an octave only suitable for dogs and spent every second of practice gossiping about which boys on the soccer team they were currently hooking up with. They would squeal, well, you know, shrilly, at every new development. They got their name honestly, not that they even knew what Simone and I said about them behind their backs. To them, we were just the token lesbians. Which wasn't even totally fair, because I wasn't a lesbian. I liked who I liked. Simone, though? Lesbian poster child, so they had us there.

"Well, you've *really* made me regret my decision to miss it," I said with a smirk. "But be so for real, did you really think I was going to show up? I mean, after everything?" I swung my thumb between us in illustration. "If anything, *I'm* pretty surprised to see *you* on these old stomping grounds of my father's, and thus mine, by biological extension."

A group of men much larger than either of us moved toward us like a swarm of locusts, so I grabbed Simone by the belt loop and pulled her toward me. Her eyebrows twitched upward in response. I told myself it was simply to make sure she wasn't trampled, and so that I could hear her properly, but it surprised us both. In our relationship, she was hands. I was, well, mouth.

Simone shook her shoulders with a jolt, attempting to regain her composure. "Why? Just because we broke up doesn't mean I'm going to abandon my love for Gastric." She gave me her signature crooked smile, her slight overbite causing her top teeth to settle softly into her bottom lip. All of her features were quirky and noticeable, giving her the kind of imperfections that made "interesting"-looking supermodels, like Coco Rocha.

Simone's love of Gastric was what had brought us together in the first place. It was impossible not to speak to each other during track practice when we kept bumping into each other at shows—Simone there for the experience, me there out of daughterly commitment.

Now I stood beside her for two more songs before it got too awkward to continue. Simone's perfume was making me dizzy, which sooner or later would make me stupid, which sooner or later would have us making out in the small cramped bathroom behind the stage. Plus, every time she took her phone out, I could see that she was Snapping her new situationship, which made me feel hot behind the ears. I was the emotionally unavailable cause of our breakup, but that didn't make it hurt any less that she had moved on before the ink was even dry.

"I gotta go find Naomi," I said, putting as much distance between me and Simone as I could before she could stop me. Naomi was Dad's manager, the only female mainstay and influence I had ever had in my life, even though she never seemed to have more teen-girl insight than Dad, despite being a woman her whole life. Finding out she had never even attempted to use a tampon as I struggled for the first time was truly the point at which I knew I'd be doing this whole girlhood thing alone.

I pushed my way through the crowd, which was only getting rowdier and drunker as the night went on. But Dad's band had already done most of their set, which meant they'd be gearing up for the encores and then calling it a night.

And you wanted to be in the greenroom when that happened, because the stampede to get out the door—and catch an Uber before the interstate became a parking lot—was real.

"Hey, kiddo," Naomi said as I entered the greenroom and sat beside her on the makeshift couch-that-was-really-a-futon shoved into the corner. Naomi had been in charge of Gastric since I was too young to even sing the lyrics of the songs. She was a staple backstage and in the Morrison household, serving as a sort of somewhat clueless, somewhat wise, way older sister. "Enjoying the show?"

Talking to Simone had, to be honest, left me a bit rattled, so I shrugged in response. I took a battered book out of my backpack, which was stashed in the coat closet masquerading as the greenroom. The table of snacks listed in the band's rider was nothing more than a few cardboard boxes with a Party City tablecloth thrown over them. The plastic bowl of Chex Mix Bold Party Blend looked like it had been overturned, with half the pretzels scattered across the tabletop. I pulled my knees up to my chin as I settled down to read in the almost-soundproofed room, only a hum coming through the walls. Finals were in a couple of weeks, followed by the sweet, sweet release of summer vacation. The only thing standing between me and trying to re-create every recipe on *The Great British Bake Off* was a trigonometry standardized test that would serve as our final exam grade, a chemistry lab, and the unabridged *Les Misérables* currently sitting on my lap.

No offense to Mr. Victor Hugo, but I had already started to doze off twenty pages in when I was woken up by Dad's usual parting words on the stage, airing live on a TV screen jammed into a corner: "And that's all for Gastric, thank you and good night." Just like a real rock star. I heard the crowd explode, as if Kurt Cobain had just risen from the dead onstage. It was pretty cool sometimes to know how much people loved my dad and his music. He put so much of himself into it, and his fans gave it back in spades night after night, tour after tour. I was proud of him, even if I never really told him.

The door to the greenroom flew open as the band filtered in, bringing the raucous cheering behind them like a gust of wind pushing leaves across barren ground. The sound of plastic cups being abandoned on the floor filtered through before the sound was instantly cut off by the slamming door.

"That was awesome," Tony, the bass player, sang. He swung his sweaty locs off his forehead in a fashion that would make the Little Mermaid jealous. I tried to hide my laugh at the thought, but a snort crept through anyway. Having previously had the discussion about his uncanny resemblance to the Disney princess, he tossed a sweaty towel that he had just dragged across his forehead at my face. I escaped the towel itself, but the odor was a complete assault. I made a gagging sound before nudging it farther away from me with the toe of the vintage Doc Martens I wore to every show. That they were vintage was important, because new Docs were basically made out of public bathroom toilet paper and a dream.

"Leave Tony and his gadgets and gizmos aplenty alone," Dad laughed, smooshing his hand into the top of my hair. I jerked away in almost more disgust than I had toward Tony's sweaty towel. These braids were fresh, and despite the headache they were giving me, I didn't want my roots loosening up too early. I was not about to spend another ten hours in a chair anytime soon, and that would only be after fighting for my life for an appointment with Instagram braiders on a race to the bottom of hospitality. I was still bitter that my mainstay had retired, a seventy-year-old Dominican woman whose fingers moved so fast it looked like watching real life in fast forward. But she had finally had to close her shop when the arthritis got too much to handle. I understood her reasons, but I was still bitter, because the new options I could find on IG weren't exactly giving "customer service."

"Quit, Dad," I mumbled, running my hands over the crown of my head and through the still-slick and oiled parts between each braid. Still tight. I flexed my eyebrows up and down to loosen my scalp at the front. I never understood why anyone would get Botox when they could look just as startled with a fresh set of braided-up edges.

"You hear that?" Dad asked the other guys and Naomi. "She turns sixteen and suddenly she's too good for her old man."

I rolled my eyes before fading into the background as the band members did their Saturday night postmortem, going over what they each had done well and what they could do better next time. It was the part of the night that I really hated, because inevitably someone would get their feelings hurt and then all of a sudden the best friends would be engaged in a fight that would be forgotten about by the time they each got home. But until the storm passed, being in a room with upset Black dads and uncles was a special kind of uncomfortable, because not a one of them had any chill or statute of limitations on what they would drag you for. Prom date stood you up in high school? Hope you can laugh about it now. Wife cheated with the deacon? Welcome to the party. The only thing that had ever seemed completely off the table was my mom. But I guess dead wife and mother was a bit of a trump card in terms of boundaries, especially since I was usually around.

Tonight was no different. It didn't take long for Tony to take offense at Felix, the drummer, scolding him for being off beat during their signature song, "Tear Me Down." The snide comments spoken from the corners of their mouths became a full-blown argument, complete with Felix calling Tony a mama's boy and Tony responding by shoving Felix clear across the room, almost making him stumble into my lap.

"Hey, hey!" Dad yelled over them, squeezing between their chests to separate them. Despite his smaller stature, Dad wasn't the kind of person anyone wanted to get physical with. The man was scrappy, a bit like a bulldog—he didn't look like he could fight but God forbid if he just decided to sit on you or something. "You about stampeded my little girl—now, relax. What's gotten into the two of you? We're brothers." Dad pinched the center of his nose and took a deep breath before turning to Naomi.

"Nay, do you mind driving Sky home tonight? We have to sort out a few things and she's got track practice in the morning."

I groaned inwardly and let my head fall back. Even though track had grown on me, Sunday morning practice never had, especially when the season was basically over. I had considered it some sort of hazing tradition for the varsity-bound newbies. But I had paid my dues—two years of dues, in fact. I was over waking up at the butt crack of dawn every Sunday just to run down each side street in our subdivision. The major plus of track was supposed to be that I could run anywhere, that I didn't have to *go* to practice in order *to* practice.

"Of course," Naomi responded. It wouldn't be the first time she had been tasked with driving me home at the end of a show. In fact, despite her being the band's actual manager, Dad acted more like the *band* manager, while Naomi acted more like *my* manager. She had always been in charge of making sure I got to and from shows okay and was safe at each venue, away from what could be some seriously creepy glances, and she made sure my face didn't appear in any of the public Instagram and TikTok reels the venues would post for marketing. She was like my five-foot-six bodyguard and nanny wrapped into one person. "Come on, Sky."

Dad stretched out his arms for me and I jumped out of his reach with a laugh. "No more hugging, Dad. Too much hugging."

"You'll miss me when I'm gone," Dad said before waving to us and turning his attention back to his still-fuming bandmates. "And try not to fall asleep too quick, Sleeping Beauty. I want to talk when I get home."

"Talk about what?" I asked, thinking back to the half conversation I'd heard earlier that week. I hadn't brought it up and he seemed to be pretending not to know I'd been listening in.

"Guess you'll have to stay up and see," he said with a wink.

"Mkay," I muttered, once again dodging him as I leapt out of the room.

"Don't play him like that," Naomi said, bumping me with her hip. "He just loves you, is all. You know he's a big ol' teddy bear."

"He loves me too much," I said as I waved to Ronnell, huddled around the snacks as he watched the argument go back and forth like a tennis match, and followed Naomi out of the venue and to her truck. Leaving now meant we wouldn't be stuck for an extra half hour trying to get out of the parking lot.

"No such thing," Naomi said, hitting the key fob twice to unlock the doors. Her Chevy Silverado stuck out far past the other cars, and like I did nearly every weekend, I wondered how she was going to get out of the small spot without decimating the cars on either side of her. Though one was a Cybertruck, so I was totally okay with it getting Hulk-smashed by Naomi's truck. "My dad wasn't a hugger and sometimes we weren't even sure if he loved us. At least you know without a shadow of a doubt."

“I guess.” I shrugged, stuffing my backpack in the space beneath the glove compartment.

“All right,” Naomi said, turning the radio to the Hot 100, a station my dad would have protested against. He despised mainstream modern music. But I loved it, especially since right now music was almost completely dominated by badass women. I reached to turn up the volume on the newly released Sabrina Carpenter.

“Let’s get you home.” Naomi shifted into gear and, as shockingly as ever, practically whipped the massive truck out of its parking space.

✧◇✧

It was a small shake that became more urgent. I jerked awake, catching myself from the vertigo that makes you feel like you’re falling. Naomi came slowly into focus, perched on the edge of my bed, her hand firmly gripping my shoulder. I shook off the fogginess of my last dream, the pieces of it quickly escaping my mind like sand blown in the wind.

“Sky?” Naomi prodded. She couldn’t see my eyes barely open in the dark bedroom. “Skylar, I need you to wake up.”

“I’m up,” I muttered, my speech slurred with

sleep, but noting the urgency of my full name. "This better be good." I pressed the heels of my hands into my eyes, rubbing them roughly. It felt like I had just gone to bed, before I realized I had been waiting up for Dad. Wait, what time was it? I never fell asleep before he got home. Usually, I couldn't. Which meant it must have been really late.

My eyes adjusted to the dark and took in Naomi's face, backlit by the curtainless window. Her mascara ran down her face in black rivulets, carving a jagged pattern into her thick foundation.

"What's wrong?" I asked her. I could feel something dark twisting in my stomach and slowly climbing up my throat. A taste of bile filled my mouth before Naomi even opened hers.

"It's your dad," Naomi's voice croaked, like her tonsils were swollen, her throat scratchy. "He's in the hospital."

"What?" I couldn't understand her. I grabbed my phone off the nightstand, the time flashing across the screen as I raised it to my face. It was nearly three a.m. We were supposed to talk, but he must have found me asleep and shelved it for later. Now Dad would be in his room just across the hall from mine like he was every night. He had to be. He would've been exhausted from tonight's show, collapsing into bed with his outside clothes on.

"No," I told her. "I'll go get him."

I moved to rise out of bed. I would go get him and then Naomi would see. But she grasped my hand and tugged me back down before I was out of reach. The sheets were still tangled around my ankles, and I fell back easily.

"Skylar," Naomi said, louder now, her voice a little more assertive. "There was an accident."

I yanked my hand from her grasp and stumbled out of the room, kicking the sheets from around my legs as I went. I pushed Dad's door open with a force so strong it bounced against the wall and back toward my face with alarming speed. Dad's sheets were rumpled like they always were, but the bed was empty. I felt Naomi's breath on the back of my neck, she was standing so close behind me. Her hands hovered by my shoulders as if she was afraid to touch me. I turned and fell into her chest. Finally, her arms wrapped around me.

"It's going to be okay," Naomi hummed, smoothing her hands over my braids. "It's all going to be okay. It was just an accident."

"What kind of accident? He's okay?" I asked her.

"They didn't give me much information," she said, holding me against her. "But you know your dad's hard head could survive anything."

I laughed involuntarily, the sound almost a choke.

"Get dressed," she said. "We'll go together."

The next twenty minutes were a blur as we climbed back into Naomi's truck and took the express lanes to the hospital. I shuffled the stack of coasters Naomi kept in her cup holders from each venue Dad's band had ever played. Naomi pulled into the first open spot and I was out of the car before she had even changed gears. My too-long pajama pants caught beneath my sneakers, scraping along the pavement.

Unlike the silence of the car, the hospital was bustling with noise, despite the time. Wailing family members in a crowded waiting room, beeping machines from farther down the hall, and an avalanche of voices greeted us as we passed through the automatic front doors. Naomi led me to the front counter.

"Excuse me, we're here for Theodore Morrison," she said to the woman in scrubs sitting behind a massive computer screen.

"Are you family?" the woman asked. I took in her name tag. *Nurse Vicky.*

"I'm his daughter." I had to practically yell to be heard above the cacophony of sounds.

Nurse Vicky nodded before typing something into the computer. Any other time, the clacking of her acrylics against the keyboard would have scratched my brain in the best way, but right now it made me want to scream. Nurse Vicky's formerly cheerful face took on a stony expression before she looked at us again. My stomach dropped to the floor.

"I'll page his doctor," she said stiffly, avoiding eye contact. "Can you have a seat over in the waiting room? She'll be right with you."

"Can you at least tell us his status?" Naomi asked. "The police mentioned he was being taken into emergency surgery and we could receive an update when we got here."

"Surgery?" I asked. She hadn't mentioned that he had gone into surgery. I had tried to convince myself it was nothing more than a bump on the head, but clearly that wasn't the case. I swallowed down the vomit rising up my throat, a staple of my anxiety.

"The doctor will have more information,"

Nurse Vicky said, looking past us to the next person. Whatever the problem was, Vicky had about the worst poker face in the world.

"He's not okay," I said to Naomi as we sat in the poorly cushioned chairs in the waiting room. "I can feel it." Was this what Dad had felt the night my mother died, sitting in a hospital waiting for the worst news of his life? Was the world that cruel?

"Don't talk like that," Naomi said, wrapping her arm around my shoulders. "Everything will be fine. You know how strong your dad is."

I did know. But my gut didn't seem to be aligned with my heart. I could feel it in the way the air of the hospital felt heavy on my shoulders, like I was Atlas expected to hold up the weight of the world. A world where Dad was okay felt lighter than this, gentler.

"I'll call the guys," Naomi said after a few minutes of waiting. "You going to be okay for a minute?"

I nodded, not taking my eyes off a crack in one of the floor tiles. In my short-lived stint as a ten-year-old gymnast, the instructor had taught us to find a spot and focus on it when we spun in order to keep ourselves grounded, to fend off the spins. Well, the room was spinning now, and I felt the need to stare at the crack to keep myself from toppling over.

I didn't know how long we sat there after Naomi returned before a soft voice finally called Dad's name. The woman was dressed in blue scrubs and a white coat with an embroidered label that spelled *Dr. Lisa Edwards.* She was a Black woman who looked way too young to have worked on my dad. But then again, Black don't crack. She could be thirty-five or sixty, there was no telling.

I had been waiting for her for so long, but now that she was here, I didn't want her here. I wanted to delay whatever bad news she was bringing with her. But Naomi nudged me softly with her elbow, so I raised my hand meekly. Dr. Edwards came over, dropping into the seat across from us. The waiting room was nearly empty now and much quieter.

"How are you doing?" she asked.

I almost wanted to laugh. Bad. We were doing bad. Wasn't that obvious?

"Is my dad okay?" I asked, cutting to the chase. It was subtle, but the doctor's shoulders stiffened like she was preparing herself.

"Your father had serious injuries and went into surgery right away. There were . . . complications."

"Is he okay?" I asked again.

"We did everything we could."

"IS HE OKAY?" This time I screamed it, thankful that the waiting room had cleared out. I just wanted a yes or a no. I could only handle a yes or a no. Directness, I craved it.

Dr. Edwards looked down at her hands for just a second before looking back at me intently, like she had practiced this one hundred times in the mirror. "I'm so sorry. We lost him."

We lost him.

The floor fell from beneath my feet. I could already feel Naomi shaking with sobs beside me as she pulled me closer to her. But all I wanted was space, to be far, far away.

Dr. Edwards stood up and beckoned to a police officer hovering near the wall. He was scrawny and short—I was surprised there was no height requirement to be a police officer. That there were people who couldn't ride certain rides at the theme park but could be a cop. I recognized the guitar case in the officer's hands immediately. Dad's stickers nearly eclipsed the black of the leather. The doctor had said it, but it wasn't until then that I believed it. Dad would never be caught without his guitar.

The officer cleared his throat. "We extracted this from the vehicle," he said.

It sounded so clinical. *Extracted. Vehicle.* Like Dad had ceased being a person and had become something like a science project or a mathematical equation. A problem to be solved.

"Extracted?" I repeated with a loud swallow. *Extracted* meant it had been hard to get him out, that he hadn't just opened the door and freed himself, that he had been hurt. Really hurt.

The officer handed me the guitar case and I saw my arms reaching for it though I couldn't feel any part of my body. Everything had become detached, someone else controlling me like a Sim. I wished someone would stop gameplay and start over, all the way back to my creation so they could leave out my heart. A heart that now hurt so bad I was sure I was having a stroke.

"The driver who caused the accident has already been charged with a DWI and, likely, vehicular manslaughter, but we'll have an accident report ready in a couple of days and will be back in touch. Is there a number I can reach you at?"

I didn't like that he was talking to me so formally, like I was an adult equipped to deal with something like this. But just like Dad was all I had, I guessed I was all he had too. Sure, he had friends who were like family, but when it came to the real thing, we were it. The thought made tears burn behind my eyes, and I squeezed them shut to cast them away like scary dreams.

"Miss?" the officer asked.

I cleared my throat, fighting off a full meltdown. I said our landline number mechanically, almost robotlike as I tried to remove myself from my body and the weight of everything it was feeling. The police officer wrote it down in a pocket-sized notebook he then tucked into an open pouch on his belt before snapping it shut, like our number was precious cargo.

"Thank you," he said when he was finished, smoothing over the snap to ensure it was closed. "I'm really sorry for your loss." He avoided eye contact as he said it, before leaving with his partner, who was hovering by the sliding front doors. I wondered how many people he had told their life was over just today, much less in his entire career. He looked somewhere in his forties, so if he'd been doing this awhile, probably dozens, maybe even hundreds of people. How did it feel to ruin hundreds of people's lives in just one short conversation?

Dr. Edwards turned to me and Naomi and told us that there was paperwork. I tuned her out, along with the rest of the noise in the room. It felt wrong to leave here without Dad, now just a body beneath a sheet. Naomi took the paperwork. I glanced over the requested information—Dad's Social Security number, our health insurance information. It was a small thing, but this one piece of paper with too many spaces to fill out sent me over the edge. The tears started slowly and then fell all at once, settling into the space between my nose and upper lip. I didn't know how to answer any of these questions, and I wasn't supposed to know how. But here I was, alone, and in charge. This was how it was going to be now.

"Just fill out what you can," Naomi said, rubbing my back as she read my mind. "They'll call us for the rest."

So I answered the most important parts—our, my, address, and my phone number. I added my school email address despite how silly it seemed. Surely they would realize they were asking a teenager to pay a hospital bill. And did you even have to pay the bill if the patient died? Was it like being refunded for flowers that got delivered already dead? Was there some kind of performance guarantee or was it just adding insult to injury? *Sorry we didn't save your dad, that'll be a million dollars, please.*

Finally, I was placing the clipboard and half-completed form back on the countertop and Nurse Vicky was handing me a box of Dad's "effects," whatever that meant. For what it was worth, they might as well have called it the Fuck You box, because everything in it was designed to make me ugly cry. The leather bracelet he always wore on his left wrist. His Ray-Ban sunglasses, usually tucked into his car visor. The frames were cracked, one lens sliding loosely. His wallet, tattered and soft along the middle seam where it folded. And his signature boots, now orphaned in the box. I stared at his belongings, most of which I had never seen separate from him. Nurse Vicky gave me a sad smile as I hugged the box against my chest. This couldn't be all that was left of a man who was larger than life. Right? This box and the guitar case over my shoulder?

Naomi turned me gently and guided me

away from the desk and back outside. I felt the ground beneath my feet and little else as we left the hospital. Hours must have passed, because the sky was already turning the pewter color of early sunrise. It had started to rain like it had been doing all early summer. I closed my eyes and lifted my face, letting the rain mix with the tears I could finally let fall freely. I shrugged from beneath Naomi's arm and curled my body forward over the box, trying to protect the things inside. Raindrops pinged against Dad's guitar case. I laid both the box and the case on Naomi's back seat, as if they were the most fragile of things, and closed the door as quietly as I could. They had been rattled enough tonight.

"I think I'm going to walk," I told Naomi as she paused while putting on her seat belt.

"Are you sure?" she asked. "It's, like, six miles."

"I'm sure," I told her, zipping my hoodie up to my chin. Despite the rain feeling pretty warm against my skin, I couldn't help but shiver, cold settling deep into my bones from within.

"Okay," Naomi responded, though it was clear she felt like she should protest. "I'll take his"—she paused and cleared her throat—"I'll take his things home. Come find me when you get there, I'll be at the house still."

I nodded, unable to put words together into anything coherent. And then, before I could think any more about it, I shut the passenger door and took off. The pants legs of my pajamas whipped around my ankles, threatening to take me down, but I pushed through, lengthening my stride to keep from tripping. There were trails that would shave a mile or two off the run, but I needed to feel the burn in my lungs, in my shin-splinted legs. I didn't worry about breathing techniques, and I was pretty sure my coach and captains would drag me for filth about my form, but I just wanted to hurt in a way I could control.

Because if I hurt all over, maybe hurting just on the inside wouldn't feel so awful.

Chapter Four

The sun was starting to fully crest the horizon, turning the sky from purple to orange, when I finally made it home, drenched to the bone. My ankles and shins ached, old injuries reignited from having run in my Vans instead of my beloved spikes, but at least it distracted me, even if momentarily, from the tightness in my chest.

Naomi stood from the couch as I burst through the front door. She was rubbing sleep out of her eyes, clearly having crashed on the sofa. Dad's guitar case and box were set against the wall leading to the stairs. Without thinking, I reached into the box and pulled out his boots, placing them by the shoes at the front door. I stared at them, placed neatly, and tipped one over with my toe, remembering how he would always kick them off. I could almost convince myself that he had just stepped out for a moment and that a big mistake had been made. I practically willed my phone to ring, imagined myself picking up to hear his laugh on the other end after he'd pulled off the biggest practical joke that ever was, cruel as it might be. I could forgive some cruelty if it meant he was still here.

"What can I do for you?" Naomi asked as I wandered around the room, lost in my thoughts. "Whatever you need." Her face was clean of mascara now and her eyes were swollen red. She might have crashed on the couch, but it didn't look like she had gotten much sleep in the hour or so it had taken me to run home.

"I don't need anything," I told her as I stripped off my sweatshirt and wet pajamas and dropped them into the open washing machine, only half full of dirty clothes. We weren't a household that used hampers, instead simply stashing clothes in the washing machine until it was full. I didn't mind being in my underwear and sports bra in front of Naomi.

"Sky, there are some things we need to figure out."

"And we need to do that right now?" My voice cracked. I didn't need reminding of how much there was to do, how much needed to happen when a life ended.

"Well—" Naomi began. She twisted her fingers nervously. Dad called her Swan because she was usually so graceful. But she had none of that grace now. She was angsty, fidgeting, and it was unsettling.

"I really just want to go back to bed." It was six in the morning and I was starting to shiver again, now from the air-conditioning cooling the warm rain against my skin. All I wanted was a hot shower and to settle between my blankets. Sleep would not come, but at least I could lie down. Hey, maybe I would wake up and this whole night would just be a terrible nightmare.

"Right." Naomi nodded. "We can talk about it later. Go get some rest."

I bounded up the stairs silently, the only noise the steps creaking beneath my feet. Dad's bedroom door was still open, his sheets and comforter still disheveled. I grabbed one of the dirty sweatshirts off the floor and put it on, burying my nose in its sweaty collar and inhaling Dad's scent until I was nearly dizzy. Then I climbed into his bed and pulled the covers over my head. Enclosed, his smell assaulted my senses, a scent like a candlewick right after you blow out the flame. A sob hiccuped out of my throat before the tears flowed, sleep chasing mercifully close behind.

I woke up groggy, with a headache that could challenge the worst migraine in the world. For a moment, my brain had not yet caught up with the day. But my whole body jerked out of bed as the realization smothered me once more. There would be no Sunday morning jumping-into-Dad's-bed-and-scrolling-through-TikTok ritual, arguing over who had the funnier algorithm, until I finally got up to make Belgian waffles with a scoop of Talenti gelato while Dad pulled off his best Padma Lakshmi judging impression. And if he was feeling particularly inspired, he might contribute some concoction of foods that he would call breakfast. If there were eggs in it, it was breakfast, regardless of what else it was made of. But now, Sunday and every day after would never be the same.

Dad was dead. My best friend was gone. And

all I had left of him were unwashed sheets, a mostly empty box, and an old guitar. It felt silly to be upset about not getting his Jeep—scrap metal now—in just a few short months, but my brain was latching on to every little thing I had lost in a matter of hours.

Rotating until my feet hit the carpeted floor, I pressed my fingers into my temples, trying to put as much pressure on my brain as I could. Maybe that would make it stop banging against my skull like Felix in the middle of a solo. The floor creaked beneath my feet, breaking the silence that had fallen over the house.

"Skylar?" Naomi called from the bottom of the stairs. "Are you up?"

Obviously. There wasn't anyone else in the house. Not anymore. I winced at the use of my full name. No one ever used my full name, everybody preferring to call me Sky instead, because according to Dad, I was boundless. Corny for sure, but that was just how Dad was. Now it meant little, not when life had just shown me how limited it could truly be.

"Yeah," I mumbled, stopping in my room for a dry pair of pants to pull on under Dad's sweatshirt. I needed a shower something fierce, but I didn't trust myself to stand beneath the hot water without collapsing.

The kitchen was silent as I sat at the table shredding a piece of unbuttered toast. Naomi sat across from me, a cup of coffee cradled in her hands.

"How are you feeling?" she asked, then cringed. She could probably guess: really fucking bad. She cleared her throat to try again. "There's someone stopping by in about half an hour. A lawyer."

"A lawyer?" I asked. "Do they want us to sue or something? Is someone suing us?" I thought about the ambulance chasers in the Hulu ads that always came on before and after an episode of *Grey's*, and I couldn't imagine a person I wanted in my home less. The person who caused the accident had already been arrested and charged and, as far as I knew, Dad hadn't done anything wrong but be in the wrong place at the wrong time.

Naomi was silent, her body stiff as she took a sip of her coffee. I couldn't understand how she was drinking anything. Just the thought of putting something in my stomach right now made me want to hurl.

"There are... things," Naomi said. "The lawyer will explain everything." She took a deep breath when she was done, her chest rising dramatically. The deep breath you take when steeling yourself to say something uncomfortable, but Naomi didn't add anything. She stared at a spot over my shoulder as she brought the cup to her lips again, though she didn't drink this time.

She was trying not to cry, for my sake, afraid it would set me off again. But I didn't think I had any tears left. My whole body felt dry, parched, my mouth like beach sand far from the shore.

I wanted to ask her more questions. Why would a lawyer be here? What was there to explain? But I couldn't get the words to form. Everything felt like alphabet soup, the letters mixing and settling into nonsensical formations.

Maybe the cops had more information about the drunk driver who took my best friend away, or even better, they were coming to tell me they had made a mistake entirely and my dad was in a hospital room cracking jokes with the nurses. I was usually anticop, and tended to reject prison as a concept, but it was shocking how quickly personal pain could make hypocrites of us. Because I would bury that person under the jail if I could. I'd make them pay for every day they stole from me, stole from Dad. If I lived the average lifespan of an American woman, I would live another sixty-five years without my dad. Someone had to pay for that and it couldn't just be me.

"I'm going to try and shower," I told Naomi. My skin was starting to itch with dried rain and sweat. I rubbed at the tears crusted into my bottom eyelashes.

The water was hotter than usual as I stood beneath it, but I barely felt it on my skin. My arms turned red beneath the steam, my feet shone bright pink. I held my braids up in a high ponytail as I avoided putting my head under the water. With my free hand, I washed the rest of my body. It wasn't thorough, but it was enough. Enough was all I was capable of right now, maybe all I would be capable of ever again. A bath would probably help, so I could just soak last night away with minimal effort, but I didn't trust myself not to sink into the water and never come back up for air. I was in shock that Dad was dead, but I was even more shocked by how much I wanted to be dead with him. I could wish him back all I wanted, but joining him was the only chance I had of seeing him again. It was scary—I had never been someone who thought about dying, and now it was the only thing on my mind.

My face looked bloated when I glanced into the mirror, and that set me off again, tears sliding down my face with surprising speed. The fact that no one poked their head into the bathroom as I cried only made me cry harder. Dad was always nosy, sticking his nose in my business at the smallest sign that I was upset. His absence was everywhere, in every nook and cranny of my life.

A body slammed into mine as I pushed open my bedroom door.

"Oh, baby," Olivia crooned into my neck as she pulled me into a hug. Six inches shorter than me, she still managed to make me feel completely engulfed. "I'm so sorry."

I didn't get out a single word before I started crying again, dropping my head into her shoulder. She stood there silently, her arms tightening every few breaths until I was unable to inhale fully.

Finally she pulled away, her eyes finding mine. Despite how silently she had supported me, her eyes were glassy, as if she had been crying as well.

"Who told you?" I asked, dragging my hand across my face. A sound escaped my mouth that could only be described as a blubber.

"Naomi called me this morning," she answered. "And the band already made an announcement on IG."

"What?" I was surprised they had done that without talking to me first. I grabbed my phone from its charger. There were several missed calls and texts from Dad's bandmates. Dad was the front man and they did have several shows lined up this week, so maybe for business purposes they needed to get ahead of it, but it didn't seem right that they had already closed that part of Dad's life. I mean, he hadn't even been gone six hours yet. And didn't they need confirmation from me first, as his next of kin or something? I didn't like how final everything around me was becoming, how many parts of Dad's life I was already feeling locked out of.

"Some of the tributes are really amazing," Olivia said, sitting back on my bed and patting the space beside her. "Did you know your dad knew 'Weird Al' Yankovic? And Bono?"

"Yes to 'Weird Al.' No to Bono." I sat beside

her and leaned my head against her. She grabbed my hand and pulled it to her face, tucking it beneath her chin.

"I keep waiting for someone to tell me this is all some big joke," I told her.

"I know," she said. "I can't imagine. I feel like the world stopped turning, and he wasn't even my dad. I mean, not for real, though sometimes he felt like he was. Gonna miss dad chats."

"God, but if we had to hear about ants being the real apex predators one more time..."

Olivia snorted loudly before slapping her hand over her mouth. "It's not funny, but yeah."

We both sat quietly, each listening to the sound of the other's inhales and exhales in the silent room.

"So what happens now?" she asked.

"I don't know." I shrugged. "What happens to people without any parents? Orphanages?"

"I don't think orphanages are real anymore," Olivia said. "Foster care, maybe?"

"Even worse."

"You know my parents would take you in a heartbeat. Pretty sure my mom loves you more than me."

"That's not true," I told her. "Don't take it for granted."

"Yeah," she said. "Sorry."

"That's okay."

"Maybe you can live with Naomi?"

"Would they let me? I mean, she's not actually my mom or anything, more like my handler."

"You're sixteen, almost seventeen. Surely you get some say in this whole thing."

I shrugged again and exhaled out of my nose. "She said there's a lawyer coming."

"For what?" she asked.

"Whatever it is lawyers do, I guess." Even though I had no idea what lawyers did other than argue with people and say "Your Honor" to some guy in an oversized and overstarched robe.

"You want me to stay for it?"

"No, that's okay. Plus, I'm sure your mom needs help with the gremlins." Being a teenager with toddler twin siblings meant that Olivia spent a lot of time as basically a coparent, which was probably why she had decided that she absolutely did not want children.

"When life doesn't suck so bad, I'll tell you about their end-of-year progress reports. I swear we're raising actual Neanderthals." She stood from the bed and pulled me into another hug. "But I'm here if/when you need me. And don't try to be all strong or whatever. I think you get full license to mope and cry and just generally be a fucking nightmare."

"Thanks," I told her. "I'd lead you out but I'm naked." I glanced down at my still-toweled body.

Olivia rolled her eyes but the sass didn't reach her smile, which looked sad and perfunctory. I listened to her make her way downstairs and exchange muffled words with Naomi before I closed my bedroom door. She'd said it would be okay if I moped as long as I wanted, but I knew sitting in a cold towel was only going to make me feel worse, if that was even possible. So I got dressed quickly, pulling on a fresh pair of pajama pants before raiding Dad's bedroom for another worn sweatshirt.

My phone's lock screen lit up what felt like every few seconds as the news got out. There were more notifications than I could count or keep track of, and I got several texts just telling me my voicemail was full. That wasn't particularly surprising, since I had never erased a single voicemail from Dad since I had first gotten a phone six years ago, a practice that I was now incredibly grateful for as I sat on the floor next to my bed and listened to each one again and again.

Dad's passing was already all over the news and going viral on Twitter (I would never call it X). Headline: Lead singer of local Austin band killed by drunk driver. When I'd had my fill of Dad's voicemails and the notifications became too overwhelming, I turned the phone off. I didn't know how anyone wanted me to perform grief, and I didn't have the energy to try. They wanted to hear that I was okay, or that I would be okay. But I didn't know if that was true. Right now it didn't feel like I'd ever be okay again.

I had been lying on my bedroom floor all morning, and it was nearly noon when three sharp knocks sounded on the front door. Too light to be the police, but too sharp to be someone familiar with our open-door policy.

"I'll get it," Naomi called down the hall as I made my way downstairs. I peeked my head into the living room as she made her way past me to the front door. With one hand, she nudged me forward. "Why don't you wait in the dining room?"

"Why?" I asked, suddenly suspicious. We were living room people. For family time, for meals, for homework. The dining room was reserved for Thanksgiving dinner and important conversations. I would normally have asked who died whenever we had a Dining Room Conversation. But that joke, while fitting, wasn't really funny anymore.

"Please," Naomi said without further explanation. We were both hanging on with the strength of dental floss, the cheap Dollar General kind, not the good stuff you got at the dentist. So I followed instructions and took my usual seat closest to the French doors that led to Dad's office, which he only used about four times a year, when filing his quarterly taxes. I looked everywhere but at Dad's empty chair at the head of the table. It was slightly askew, like he had bumped into it before leaving the house.

A tall man in a blue suit and glasses followed Naomi into the dining room. His smile was as stiff as his white button-up. His tie was the perfect kind of Windsor knot that made you question if it was a clip-on.

"Are we being audited?" I whispered to Naomi.

Dad was a musician who was mostly paid in cash, and he often joked about being audited because there was no way he ever did his taxes right, but I never thought it would actually happen. And so quickly after he was gone. Didn't the IRS give you a grieving period before trying to arrest you for back taxes?

"Sky, this is Mr. Matthews. He's an estate lawyer," Naomi explained, taking her usual seat to the right of Dad's.

Mr. Matthews pulled out Dad's chair.

"You can't sit there!" I blurted out.

He looked at me like I had grown additional heads like the Hydra, but he simply nodded, squeezed between my chair and the wall, and took the seat on the other side of Naomi.

"Yes," he said, though no one had asked him a question. "As your—" He glanced at Naomi like he wasn't sure how to characterize her. "As Ms. Gellar has said, I am, was, your father's estate attorney."

I snorted. Dad was a responsible guy, but he wasn't estate-planning responsible. He always went to the dentist about two years late, and he couldn't find a bill he needed to pay if a million dollars was on the line. There was no way he had an *estate.*

Mr. Matthews stared at me with a serious expression and I clamped my mouth shut. Yesterday, nothing was funny, and today, everything seemed like pure comedy. He waited an unsettling amount of time to ensure that he had my full attention. Finally, he snapped open his briefcase and pulled out a packet of documents.

"Your father left very clear instructions on your care in the event of his death," Mr. Matthews said. He spoke matter-of-factly, emotionless, like death was an everyday occurrence in his life, which I guessed it was. I wanted him to care that my father was gone, but at the same time, it was nice to talk to someone who didn't look at me like I was irreparably broken. Even if I was.

"In the event of his death," Mr. Matthews started, "your care should be transferred to . . ."

"Naomi," I finished for him. Or Olivia's parents. Basically, anything but foster care. I was not trying to be like Bow Wow in *Like Mike*, or Little Orphan Annie. I had people who cared about me, even if they weren't family.

I glanced at Naomi, whose face went blank. She was avoiding eye contact at all costs, which made me nervous. A stone dropped to the bottom of my stomach like an anvil. What did she know that I didn't? Did she not want me?

"...a Mrs. Mona Morrison," Mr. Matthews finished, ignoring my interjection completely.

I heard Naomi's gulp from clear across the table.

"Mona?" I said, not understanding. "I'm a Morrison—Skylar Morrison. My dad is...was Theodore Morrison. There's no Mona."

"Actually..." Mr. Matthews nodded again. He pulled out a document I had never seen before. My birth certificate. "There *is* a Mrs. Mona Morrison. Your mother."

Now I stared at him like *he* was the one with Hydra's heads. I was surprised Dad would hire this guy. His information was about sixteen years out of date. I bet he was a Groupon find—you really did get what you paid for.

"My mother died when I was a baby," I told him. That fact didn't hurt nearly as much as Dad being gone. How could you miss someone you never really knew? Especially now that I knew what it was like to lose someone real and not just an idea of a person.

"Well, that's highly unlikely," Mr. Matthews said. "As I just spoke with her this morning."

“Naomi,” I sighed, waiting for her to confirm and get this dunce out of my house.

But Naomi stared just past my shoulder and waited. Waited for me to piece it together.

“Naomi, my mother is dead.” I didn’t know if I was asking or pleading for her to agree. “She’s been dead for sixteen years.”

“I’m so sorry,” she muttered, dropping her head. “I’m so sorry.”

“Naomi?” My voice was little more than a whisper. I was waiting for someone to start laughing or for a camera to be revealed. My eyes shifted around the room in anticipation.

Finally, Naomi lifted her head, but she turned to Mr. Matthews instead of me.

“Could you give us a moment?” she asked him.

Mr. Matthews stood wordlessly. Surely, he knew the bomb he’d just detonated at our dining room table, but he moved around the room as if he was feeling none of the discomfort and disappeared into the kitchen.

Naomi clasped her hands on the table. “Ask.”

“My mother is dead. Right?”

Naomi seemed unable to speak, so she gave a nearly imperceptible shake of her head.

“No,” I said.

"Sky."

"No." I banged my fists against the table. The R2-D2 salt shaker and C-3PO pepper shaker wobbled, clinking together. "No."

"Sky."

"Stop." My voice was rising. I had never yelled at Naomi, or anyone, really. But something was moving through me like a tornado. "This isn't funny."

"Skylar," Naomi said now with a sob in her voice.

"My mother is dead," I repeated through gritted teeth, willing it to be true because all of my life it had been. Could one thing just make some goddamn sense right now?

"No," Naomi answered. I could barely hear her. Even she didn't seem to believe it. "Your mother"—she hiccuped—"is not dead."

I was up from the table before Naomi finished her sentence, and I sprinted through the kitchen and out the back door. Mr. Matthews's suit was a blur of blue through my eyes, thick with unshed tears. Naomi called behind me, begging me to come back as she tried to keep up. But I was fast. I had always been fast. And Naomi did not have an athletic bone in her body.

I skirted around the house and back toward our driveway. The gravel dug into the bottoms of my bare feet but I didn't stop. I ran and ran. Past the high school, which seemed abandoned in the summer. Past the park where Dad had taught me how to ride a bike. Past our favorite record store and IHOP.

My mother was alive. My father had lied. And everyone knew it but me.

Chapter Five

The church looked like something out of *The Princess Bride*, a stone building leaning with age.

I had never set foot in a church. Religion had never been anything more than a far-fetched idea to our family.

"Come, sweetie," Naomi said. She grabbed my hand as we crossed the street like I was a wayward child and not sixteen. But I didn't pull away despite how much I wanted to. It was nice to be treated like a child again, even if just for a moment. And while Naomi couldn't possibly be taking Dad's death worse than me, she was still really struggling. Sometimes it felt like she was holding on to me more because *she* needed it.

It was even more solemn inside the church than outside it. The lights were dim, candles flickering on steel chandeliers. The room was thick with the smell of smoke and vanilla, like a Bath & Body Works candle had been melted into the stained-glass windows. At any moment I expected a group of friars, my only retained knowledge of *The Canterbury Tales* from AP English, with ropes tied around their waists, bald heads gleaming, to pop out from behind the columns reaching to the wood-beamed ceiling. The whole aesthetic was giving *Da Vinci Code*. Dad would laugh if he was here. The thought nearly cracked my tear-solidified face into a ghost of a smile. Nearly.

Naomi led me to the first pew. I avoided making eye contact with anyone, and wished more than anything I could make my ears as senseless as the rest of my body. I could escape the pitying stares to some extent, but the whispers surrounded me like unwanted cigarette smoke from a stranger standing much too close.

But I didn't think the whispers would ever stop. Not as long as I was the girl whose dad died tragically, a thing still somewhat noteworthy to my high school peers who hadn't left town for the summer. I imagined myself telling my college roommate and the first partner I might want to marry—why, yes, I am a member of the Dead Dads Club. Talk about baggage.

"Hey." A tap on my shoulder.

I nearly leapt out of my skin. But I didn't even have to turn around. I was enveloped by the scent of jasmine and citrus. Simone.

"You holding up okay?" Simone asked. Her fingers massaged that small crescent swoop that fell from my ear and stopped at my collarbone. She knew me well.

I jerked my head quickly from side to side instead of speaking out loud. I hadn't spoken in full sentences in days, not since they had released Dad's body to the funeral home. They had advised me not to see him before he was cremated due to "damage" caused by the accident, like he was a stereo on the side of the road. Part of me was grateful that my last image of him wouldn't be that, but another part felt like I could never really accept that he was gone without seeing it for myself. Was I just supposed to believe everyone around me regarding something so utterly unbelievable? It was easy to imagine he had run off to Cuba or something for a well-earned vacation and would hit me up as soon as he landed back in the US. I was ping-ponging every few minutes between the worst grief of my life and a naïve belief that this was all a mistake. I wasn't sure if seeing him would have helped, but maybe it would have brought some closure.

"Excuse me," another voice said, more forcefully but cloaked in sweetness, like a chocolate-covered beet. Olivia nudged her way past Simone and squeezed into the space between me and the end of the pew. She gave Si-mone a sideways glance that caused the much taller girl to scurry away, and then smoothed her electric-blue bangs down against her forehead. Before the breakup, Olivia had always been Team Simone, but seeing as this was the first time Simone had approached me since Dad died, not even a phone call or text prior, I didn't think she was feeling too gracious. I had been surprised myself. Simone wasn't only my ex and the first girl I ever loved, but she was a genuine fan of Dad's band. If she didn't feel anything for me, didn't she at least feel grief as a fan, like when we both spent the night crying after the Chadwick Boseman or Chester Bennington news?

"Who does she think she is?" Olivia asked with a suck of her teeth.

"She was being nice," I muttered, smoothing my palms over the bottom of my staticky black dress.

"Humph," Olivia responded. "Should've been *nice* a week ago, innit?" She reached into her small, fashionable clutch (trust Olivia to be the best-dressed and -accessorized person in the room, even at a funeral) and pulled out a pack of Orbit gum. "So you don't grind your teeth," she said knowingly.

I shoved the gum in my mouth and smooshed it between my molars.

Naomi grabbed my hand again as the priest, pastor, whatever, stepped up to the lectern. I hadn't bothered to look anywhere besides my feet, but now that my eyes were drawn to the front of the church, bile rose up my throat.

Dad's urn, a silver monstrosity that looked like it belonged on a shelf in an antique store, sat in a sea of awful white roses. The smell slapped me in the face like a breeze off the Gulf Coast. Truly the gaudiest shit I'd ever seen, like Lady-Gaga-in-a-meat-dress horrendous. It didn't look anything like what I had picked out from the funeral home's catalog. He would've been happier in an old coffee can.

If Dad was here, *really* here, he'd die on the spot.

The thought made me giggle, a small thing at first that grew into a lion's roar. Soon I was doubled over, my stomach aching. The laughs turned to hiccups and then I was certain I was going to vomit. It was a bit scary, the hysterics and hyena-like quality of the laugh coming out of me, but also a bit comforting—I hadn't thought I would ever be able to laugh again. Olivia and Naomi rubbed my back, each of them laying claim to the side closest to them. If this was as frightening to them, they didn't show it. And no one else seemed to be reacting either. I guess you got a bit of leeway at your dad's funeral.

And just like that, the laughing broke like shattered porcelain, into a sound found in dark places. What could only be described as a banshee wail, ugly and broken. My face was wet with tears, with sweat. My skin still sickly from a few nights of crying myself to sleep.

I stood and the pastor, preacher man, went silent. The whole room was silent. Even the flickering flames of each candle seemed to still. I stormed up to the front of the room and snatched

Dad's urn from among the flowers, giving him room to breathe.

I thought of his allergies going wild, and wondered if his ashes, the pile of dirt left of him, felt the tickle of a sneeze that would never come. He was choking in here. Couldn't they hear him wheezing? I wanted to put my finger beneath his nose, chase the sneeze away. But there was no nose. There wasn't even enough left of him for a real coffin, not that he would want to be stuck in the ground like a tortured Barbie doll buried by a mischievous puppy.

Couldn't they see how wrong this all was? To talk about Dad in the past tense, to read scriptures he didn't give a fuck about and didn't even believe in?

I made my way back down the aisle, ignoring the glances falling on my shoulders as I passed each pew. Dad's urn was cold in my hands, a vast contrast to his warmth. The way a hug from him felt like July. This wasn't how we should say goodbye to him. We should be standing on a trailer like in Eddie's last moments in *Stranger Things*. Hell, give him a campfire with shitty campfire songs and marshmallows burnt to a crisp.

Anything but this, because God wasn't bringing my dad back. Scripture wasn't going to turn back time and make that drunk driver call an Uber. And we could sing hymns until the cows came home, but it would never be the music that made Dad feel alive.

A face at the back of the church stopped me in my tracks. The woman made eye contact with me and stood halfway from her seat so that she was hovering above the pew. She looked familiar, but I couldn't place her, like when you see a face in person that you remember vaguely from a dream. We stared at each other until I felt a hand on my shoulder.

"Let's get out of here," Naomi whispered. She led me to the front steps of the church.

I wheezed as my breath stalled, Dad's urn held close to my chest.

"Just breathe," Naomi said.

Olivia sat down beside me, having followed us out, the scent of her Billie Eilish perfume floating through the wind. She wrapped her arm around my shoulder and pulled me in to her. I dropped my head onto my knees, cradled Dad's urn against my thighs, and hugged my legs.

The tears didn't come, and the heat was seeping through my dress, but still, I shivered.

Despite it not being the end of the service, the church started to empty. Hands squeezed my shoulder or pressed gently into the top of my head as each person passed by, but no one stopped to talk. Dad's bandmates each bent down to give me a long, silent hug before they left as a group, holding hands. I was proud that Dad was the kind of guy to surround himself with men who didn't feel any shame or embarrassment about showing their male friends affection. I absorbed the *I'm so sorry*s and *Let us know if you need anything*s, but I felt like a sponge with too many holes, too porous; nothing seemed to stick. Until suddenly I felt a presence hovering behind me.

"Skylar?" It was a raspy female voice that sounded like it'd been gargling gravel.

I lifted my head from my knees and twisted around. The woman I'd seen at the back of the church stood behind me. Her textured hair was cut close to her scalp, and her long legs made her tower over us. The black leather jacket she wore stopped midthigh, and I couldn't help but compare her to a female Shaft. The woman wrung her hands together as she slowly descended the steps.

Naomi moved to step in front of me before seemingly changing her mind, a look of indecision etched into her face. She avoided my questioning stare but seemed nervous.

"Yes," I said, placing Dad's urn beside me on the step before standing up.

"You don't know who I am, do you?" the woman asked. She was standing so close now that I could see the sparse spattering of freckles across her nose, nearly invisible on her dark brown skin.

"Should I?"

Olivia stood up as well, her body half in front of mine.

"I guess that's to be expected." The woman eyed Olivia's protective stance before giving us a shy smile. "My name is Mona... Morrison."

Her familiarity suddenly hit me in the face like a slap. Her face was familiar because it looked so much like mine.

"I'm your mother."

Chapter Six

"So don't panic," Olivia said as she sat on the edge of my bed, folding her black dress beneath her. "Like, really, don't panic."

"I'm not panicking," I said, pinching the bridge of my nose.

"Oh, well, I'm definitely panicking on your behalf then, because what the actual hell is happening?"

"Nothing's happening," I snorted. "It's obviously some very intricate joke my dad planned in the event of his death. It's the only explanation. And it *is* kind of funny, don't you think?" I pressed my back against the wall and slid down until I was cross-legged on the carpet.

"Okay, fair. But she looks just like you," Olivia said.

"She does not," I retorted.

Olivia stared at me and raised her eyebrows. "Spitting image, babe. You stole her whole face."

"We have, like, the same eye color, along with half the human population."

"And hair. Remember when you shaved it all off freshman year? It looked just like that for months. And that mole below your bottom lip. And you're both built like a beanpole. I bet she runs."

"Olivia, stop," I begged.

"Even her voice kind of sounds like yours. And her eyes? It's like the OB said 'Copy and paste' when you were born."

"Olivia, STOP," I repeated, slamming my hands on the floor and clutching the fibers of the carpet between my fingers.

"Sorry," Olivia said, falling backward onto the bed. "It's just kind of crazy."

"If she is my mother, and I really mean *if*, because what the fuck were they thinking, we have literally nothing in common, I can tell you that much. I mean, she can't be. My dad told me she died. He never mentioned her in the present tense. So we have a similar mole—so do a lot of people. And hair? I mean, you could cherry-pick half the Black population and they'd have the same hair type and look with a TWA."

"Okay," Olivia said, sitting back up. "But what if... she is, though?"

I leaned my head against the wall, tapping it just hard enough not to cause brain damage but with enough force to hopefully knock me out so I could either wake up from this nightmare or enter a mini-vacation-like coma.

"If she is, then I really don't know," I said finally, squeezing my eyes shut. I glanced at Dad's urn on my desk. Part of me was almost angry enough to toss it into a wall.

"So what does your mother not being, ya know, dead mean?" Olivia asked.

"I guess it means she calls the shots."

"And what are those shots?"

"Well, she wants me to move in with her and her family. In DC."

"As in *Washington,* DC?"

"The very one."

"Absolutely not. Not happening."

"Not sure we have much of a choice. She's my legal guardian and I don't have anywhere else to go."

"I'm not accepting the fact that my best friend is moving halfway across the country the summer before our senior year. Is she even fit to parent? I mean, there's got to be some questions on fitness for a woman who *faked her own death*. That's all kinds of crazy."

"I don't disagree," I responded. "But it seems that it is what it is."

"Why are you being so blasé about this? Aren't you angry AF?"

"I want to be angry, but honestly, I don't feel anything right now. I feel so drained it's like my brain went on permanent vacation."

"I get it," Olivia said. "But we can't just let it happen. When does she want you to go?"

"When she heads back in a couple of days. To her wife. And her"—my stomach turned—"kid."

"You're shitting me."

"I wish." I wondered what it was about her new kid that she loved so much more than she had loved me, enough to at least stay a part of his life. I was almost nauseated by the idea that I would have to be cordial with the person who had basically replaced me in my mother's life, who knew versions of her forever lost to me.

I shrugged and closed my eyes, laying my

head back against the wall. Olivia was right—I shouldn't just take this lying down, and there probably was really an argument to be made that Mona had given up all rights to command my life. Sounded more like someone should have put her in a padded room. But I was the kind of tired that went bone-deep.

"So what do we do about it?" Olivia said when I failed to respond to her disbelief. "I mean, she's trying to make you move to Washington, DC, in, like, two days. Which is crazy. Your dad's funeral was damn near thirty seconds ago. And this is your home. She can't just uproot you like this, especially to the political armpit of America."

"It's Alexandria. Northern Virginia, technically," I corrected.

"Whatever. Don't you want to do something? You're not just going to let this happen, are you?"

"I don't know. I'm so tired. So, so tired. I don't really know what recourse I would have anyway."

"Right. You're totally right. I know this totally sucks." Olivia stood from the bed and dropped down in front of me, touching our knees together. Then she grabbed my hands in hers. "But there has to be a solution. And I'm going to figure it out. Because I'm not letting you leave me here with those simpletons we go to school with for our senior year. This is supposed to be our moment. You, track star. Me, overall amazing. You can't break up the Dream Team."

I let out a small laugh before shaking my head in disbelief. "This just can't be real. My dad wouldn't have lied to me like this."

"Maybe it wasn't a lie," Olivia said. "Maybe it was just a strong misinterpretation of the truth."

"So, a lie?" I asked.

"Yeah, I guess." Olivia blew out a deep breath. "But it's your dad. There had to have been a good reason."

"What good reason could there possibly be for telling me my mother was *dead* for sixteen years? That's diabolical."

"I don't know what said good reason would be, but I know your dad, and you know your dad. There just had to be one. Because otherwise this would just be cruel, and your father and *cruel* don't belong in the same sentence."

"You're talking about him like he's still here. He's not. And maybe he wasn't who we all thought he was."

"He is still here, kind of. All he did was pour into you, and sometimes even me, so of course he's here. And I refuse to believe he would do something this major for shits and giggles."

"Whatever." I flexed my toes until I felt the pull in my calf muscles. Then I flexed even further, until it hurt.

"Well, just know I'm going to be visiting so much that your . . . Mona will be begging for you to move back to Austin and live with my family. I can be a lot, as you know."

"Indeed. But those airplane tickets are going to stack up."

"Let me worry about that. I have hella free babysitting points to cash in with my parents. I was going to save it for a graduation trip to Europe, but desperate times call for desperate measures."

"I know this is going to sound super forced and like I don't mean it at all, but I love you," I told her.

"Oh, I know." She grabbed a fallen pillow from the floor, throwing it at me, and while it didn't get me to laugh the way it normally would, it did make me smile. And for now, that had to be enough.

"Now let's get you packed," she said, hopping up from the bed. "Failing to plan is planning to fail, and I don't want to be harassed every day because you forgot to pack your favorite ironic Ms. Rachel T-shirt or some shit."

"Before I go, though, there's something we need to do."

"Burn the patriarchy?"

"No. Well, yes, but no."

"Bummer, but I'm in."

We parked farther down the shopping center for plausible deniability, Olivia's VW Bug kicking back as she changed gears.

Dad's urn was tucked beneath my sweatshirt as we crossed the parking lot to the IHOP. Its neon sign shone brightly, advertising that it was open twenty-four hours. It was a service worth offering, because even at eleven p.m., the restaurant was still busy. I looked through one of the windows to see a couple at our usual booth, and I knew that Dad and I would never sit in it together again. And now that I was leaving, I probably would never sit in it alone either. In fact, the chances I'd ever set foot in an IHOP again were pretty slim.

I stooped under the neon sign, pressing

my knees into the dirt. Olivia dropped down beside me.

"Is this legal?" she asked.

"Probably not," I answered. I untucked Dad's urn from my sweatshirt and placed it between us before starting to dig.

"Awesome," Olivia said cheerfully. "Definitely going to up my street cred." She rolled up the sleeves of her cropped sweater and began digging beside me, putting her hands together like a shovel.

It didn't take long to dig a hole deep enough. Dad's urn made a metallic clanging noise as I unscrewed the top.

"Are you sure you don't want to take them with you?" Olivia asked.

"I'm sure," I told her. He belonged in Austin. Even more, it felt right to make this his final resting spot. This was our place, where we had shared the most laughs and deep conversations over pancakes and scrambled eggs.

I tilted the urn with both hands, pouring the ashes into the freshly dug hole. Then Olivia and I pushed the upturned dirt back into the hole. We banged the dirt down when we were finished, making sure it was packed in tight.

"I'll stop by once in a while and check in on him," Olivia promised with a sad smile. She gave my hand a squeeze. "Grab a short stack and eat it with him."

I gave a small laugh, more than I thought I could muster. "How are you going to explain eating pancakes under the IHOP sign?"

Olivia shrugged. "It's not the weirdest thing anyone around here has seen me do."

"You're not wrong."

"Hey," a voice called from the restaurant's back door, which banged against the open trash bin beside it. "What are y'all doing?"

"Nothing!" we yelled as we raced back across the quiet parking lot and fell into the Bug.

"God, I'm going to miss you," Olivia said through her laugh.

I looked out the window back toward the sign and where we had left Dad's ashes. Yeah, I was going to miss a lot.

Chapter Seven

"Welcome to Reagan Washington National Airport," the pilot said over the intercom. "Temperature on the ground is eighty-two degrees and the local time is one thirty-five p.m. We here at American Airlines want to thank you for sharing the friendly skies with us this afternoon."

"You ready?"

I glanced away from the window, where I could see the ground crew gathering the luggage from the cargo hold. Despite the pain in my shoulder from hauling it through security and the terminal, I was happier than ever that I'd stowed my KitchenAid in my carry-on as I watched them toss bags like they were full of air rather than people's valuables.

Mona was standing in the aisle waiting for me. She yanked my small suitcase out of the overhead bin and set it on the floor. I followed her off the plane and through the long tunnel that would deposit us in the airport terminal. As Mona had come to expect from me, we walked in complete silence.

Just as we had since Mona introduced herself on the steps of the church.

Just as we had since she followed me, Naomi, and Olivia home, where Naomi and Olivia had discussed what would happen to me now, like I was a piece of antique furniture or an orphaned pet. Ever since Dad died, I'd been shuffled around like a game piece. I'd completely lost control of my own destiny.

"I have someone coming to pick us up," Mona said, breaking the silence. "He's going to meet us at baggage claim."

For a moment, I wondered who *he* was. All I'd gathered from Mona was that she had a wife named Gaby and a kid named Frankie, and she was the type of person who could unceremoniously remove herself from her own daughter's life. What else did you really need to know about a person?

I nodded and continued to follow her wordlessly. Once at baggage claim, I dropped into a seat by the luggage carousel as we waited for the rest of my bags to come down the chute. I had only packed my small carry-on and two large suitcases, with Naomi promising to ship the rest of my stuff in the coming weeks. Dad's things would go into storage, paid for by the huge sum of money I got from his savings, which had come as quite a surprise. Dad had never been the type to seem like a saver, very much a "why save for tomorrow what you can spend today" kind of guy.

"Do you know anything about the city?" Mona asked as she stood beside me like the emoji of the guy standing awkwardly with his hands by his sides, despite there being two empty seats next to me. "Anything you're dying to do?" We both winced at her choice of phrasing.

Again, I acknowledged her questions with silence. Mona had had my whole life to talk, to even exist in my world. It was too late now, even if the courts and Dad's will said this was where I was supposed to be.

Mona sighed deeply, accepting my silence, and moved closer to the bags spinning around. She picked each one up and inspected it, even though none of them looked like the bright neon-green luggage we had checked that morning. I took her in from a distance. She was tall like me—like Olivia had pointed out, we shared long torsos and even longer legs. Where my hair was in braids down my back, Mona's was cut close to her head, just the beginnings of curls starting to sprout from her scalp like recently cut grass bending in the wind. I couldn't tell yet if she had just done a big chop or she preferred to keep it this length. Her skin was a deeper mocha than mine, which was more akin to Dad's caramel color. Her nose was slender, unlike my wide one, and her eyes were closer together, but they favored mine, so deep chocolate they almost looked black. I disagreed with Olivia that I was an exact replica, but the resemblance was there. There was no mistaking that we were related, and I could imagine having received "You look just like your mother" comments growing up if anyone had ever seen us side by side.

Finally, my bags landed in front of Mona and she yanked them off the carousel. They were filled with all my summer clothes and shoes, my immediate needs. I doubted Northern Virginia got as hot as Austin, but I had read enough Reddit comments describing it as swampy to stick to tank tops and shorts.

"Hey, Mrs. Morrison," a voice called from behind us. I spun around in my seat to see a boy of average height, maybe the same height as me, barreling through the crowd heading out of the sliding glass doors to the taxi lanes.

Mona turned and smiled. I guessed this must be our ride. The boy appeared to be about my age, his hair cut into a fade that looked like he should tip his barber especially well. He had the beginnings of hair growing into a mustache above his top lip. His skin was even deeper than Mona's, such a deep brown that I could nearly taste it on my tongue.

"Hi, Cameron," Mona said, rolling my bags toward him. "Cam's our next-door neighbor," she said to me in explanation while skillfully avoiding eye contact.

I stood up and placed my duffel bag back over my shoulder at the same time that Cameron reached for it.

"I can take that," he said with a smile. His

teeth were slightly crooked in the front, overlapping just so.

"I got it," I insisted. My voice came out in a croak—it was the first time I'd let words spill from my lips in Mona's presence since I'd met her. I cringed at the unexpected sound.

"No, really," he said, grabbing the strap off my shoulder. "All these people will think I'm not a gentleman if I let you carry your own bag. And I'm definitely a gentleman."

I let him place the bag on top of one of my suitcases before wheeling them both around to pull behind him. Mona shook her head with a laugh, and for a moment we caught each other's eyes. Whatever laugh I was working up to died in my throat. I wasn't sharing anything with Mona, not even a single solitary chuckle.

"Thanks for picking us up," Mona said to Cameron. "I know your parents probably forced you, but I appreciate it. These Ubers give me a headache with their stopping and starting."

"No problem." Cameron veered around a couple standing in the middle of the sidewalk and headed toward a larger building across the street. "I'm right over in the parking garage."

The garage was only a couple of levels and

he'd parked near the back of the second, a black Bronco's lights flashing as he clicked a button on his keys. I climbed in behind the driver's seat as Cameron gently placed each bag in the trunk. He earned some points for not throwing my KitchenAid around, not that he knew what was in the bags. So I guess he just earned points for being considerate generally.

On the passenger side, Mona tucked her small backpack at her feet. It seemed she had packed just a couple of shirts and, hopefully, underwear, because she'd been wearing the same jeans, shoes, and leather jacket for the past few days.

"Where's your sister?" Mona asked him as he turned the ignition. Nipsey Hussle spilled from the speakers and I grunted in appreciation of Cameron's music taste. Mona reached to turn the music down, which, in my opinion, was a huge party foul. Yeah, we were definitely not going to see eye to eye. "I rarely see you two apart."

"She's helping Mom with the competition," he answered. He searched me out in the rearview mirror and I blushed when his gaze found mine. He wasn't really like any of the people I'd dated in the past, but he was cute—there was no denying that. He picked up on the question in my eyes. "Our parents own a bakery and host a competition every summer. They pay for the winner to travel to Paris to study in a patisserie owned by our aunt. It's kind of a big deal, and it's a hell of a lot of work, but it's pretty cool."

My interest was piqued. I loved baking, even more than running, but I'd never won any competitions for it. Not that I'd ever entered any, though I never got anything but rave reviews from the band for the desserts I left in the greenroom for after a show. And I had never been out of the country, but getting to study baking in Paris like Marcus did in Copenhagen in the second season of *The Bear* would be more than an amazing opportunity.

Still, I stuffed down the questions rising up my throat. I wasn't going to let myself get excited about anything here. This was not a move I wanted, and I wasn't going to let anyone convince me that living here could ever make me happy. Besides, half the fun of baking was Dad trying all my new recipes, and he wasn't here to do that. My KitchenAid was my prized possession, but who knew if I'd ever even touch it again? Too much of what I enjoyed about baking was gone.

"When is it?" I asked, my curiosity getting the better of me, though I told myself it was just that—curiosity and not genuine interest. Mona seemed surprised to hear me speak voluntarily and she turned to answer before Cameron could.

"It's over the course of the summer. Ends in August."

I grunted in response, irritated that Mona had taken my question as an opportunity to talk to me.

"You bake?" Cameron asked, attempting to end the awkward silence that had befallen the car.

"A bit," I said. I wanted Mona to know as little about me as possible. She didn't have the right to know who I was or what I enjoyed. Not like a real mother would.

"Cool, you should check it out then." Cameron searched in the center console with one hand and pulled out a flyer, then reached behind his seat to hand it to me.

The first round was in two weeks, when contestants would submit their best cookie recipe, along with a batch of said cookies. I immediately thought of my snickerdoodles, so good they should be criminal, according to Olivia. My brain shot in all different directions on how to make them really stand out for a competition. Maybe a hint of ginger or key lime.

"I'm an honorary judge, so maybe you'll have an in." He winked into the mirror.

"And by honorary judge, he means he's not allowed anywhere near the judging table but will be tasting all the submissions," Mona explained.

"For quality control purposes," he said. I rolled my eyes with a smirk and folded the flyer into a small square, which I stuffed into the front pocket of my jeans.

Cameron turned the car into a cul-de-sac with houses that all looked similar but not identical, like they'd rolled into a development from someone with an actual soul.

"Ta-da, we're home," Cameron sang.

"This isn't my home," I mumbled. Mona stiffened in her seat.

Cameron stopped in front of a house with a Pride flag flying above the door. In fact, most of the houses in the cul-de-sac had Pride flags, BLM flags, or Palestinian flags. Some houses had a combination of all three. It was like nothing I'd ever seen in my neighborhood back home, and it instantly calmed me down. A place with people like this couldn't be all bad, right? For a moment, it made me think there was no way Mona was the monster she was in my head, but I couldn't reconcile the person who would live in a neighborhood like this with the mother who would fake her own death. Was there room for both people in one body?

Despite my height, I still had to leap down from the Bronco, scraping the backs of my calves on the doorframe. This guy needed to carry around a complimentary step stool or something for this behemoth; they didn't even do it this big in Texas.

The neighborhood was quiet as we made our way to the front door, the only noise the sound of my suitcase wheels against the pavement.

"Um, actually," Cameron said, dropping the bags at the steps to the porch. "Do you mind waiting a second?"

Mona looked at him with raised eyebrows. "And why is that?" she asked him. Her tone was knowing, like they were in on the same secret.

Cameron tried to hide a smile. "Just a second, please?"

Mona sighed before lowering her hand from the doorknob. "Cameron..."

"Be right back." And with that, he disappeared around the house.

"I told her not to do this," Mona said under her breath. Before I could ask what she was talking about, or could even decide if I wanted to ask what she was talking about, the front door swung open.

I could only assume that the woman standing in the door was Gaby. She was a small Latina woman with dark brown hair that fell down her back and a smile that seemed to stretch all the way down to her toes. Her picture should appear in the dictionary under the word *bubbly*, if the way she was basically bouncing on her toes in excitement was any indication of her overall demeanor.

"Hi, sweetheart, welcome home!" Gaby ushered us into the house, from whose ceiling beams hung a long banner. *WELCOME HOME SKYLAR* was painted in neon-green handwriting. Cameron stood at the back door with a conspiratorial smile on his face.

"Hi, Skylar," a small boy—Frankie, I presumed—called from his place on the steps. Mona had mentioned him, but now, seeing him in person, I was unprepared for the feelings that came along with meeting the child she'd chosen long after she'd abandoned me. Was it because he was a boy? Was it because he wasn't Black? Both options felt too nefarious to be true, but I didn't have much to go on. Why was she happy and ready to be his mother and not mine?

"Yes, hi!" Gaby pulled me into a tight hug. Her scent of daisies and something sweet filled my nostrils. "We're so happy to have you with us. Well, not happy per se, because of the circumstances, but . . . happy, you know."

I stiffened at the contact as Gaby swayed me from side to side. I knew Dad would hate it if I was rude to her, and if he was looking down I didn't want him disappointed in what he saw, but man, did I want her to let me go expeditiously.

"Gab," Mona said, reaching for Gaby's arm. "Maybe we can give Skylar some space so she can get adjusted."

"Oh," Gaby said. "Oh, right, sorry. I'm just so excited you're here. Well, not excited per se . . ."

"I get it," I said, throwing her a bone. If she was going to qualify everything she said from here on out, every conversation was going to take twice as long. I could tell she wanted to hug me again and I wondered if it was her nervous tic, like how Olivia blew air kisses to her ex-boyfriend because she was never really sure how to interact with him anymore.

I almost wished Gaby would hug me again, because now that we were all standing arm's length away from each other in silence, I was starting to hate all the eyes that were on me at once. Cameron, Mona, Frankie, Gaby—I felt like an exhibit at the zoo.

"Um, where's your bathroom?" I asked. "I need to pee." TMI, but nothing like the mention of bodily fluids to get you out of a sticky and uncomfortable situation.

"Oh, there's one in your room," Gaby explained before pointing up the stairs. "Right at the top of the steps."

"I'll bring your bags up," Cameron offered, hurrying across the room to meet me at the bottom of the stairs.

"And then come right back down," Mona added. She gave Cameron a knowing glance, to which he shrugged. I didn't want to be a part of any silent conversations that went on between neighbors, so I hurried up the stairs to distance myself from Cameron, who struggled as he carried all three bags up at once behind me. Clearly, a one-trip-or-bust kind of guy.

The room at the top of the stairs—my room, it seemed—was spacious and painted in shades of yellow and green, like spring threw up on the walls. The bed was bigger than the one I had at home, and a small bathroom was off to the side. I'd always had to share a bathroom with Dad and already I missed his singing in the shower when he thought I was still asleep.

"Here you go," Cameron said, laying my two suitcases on the floor. "So," he said, inviting himself to sit on the bed. "What's your story?"

"My story?" I asked.

"Yeah, I mean, that permanent sneer on your face looks like someone ran over your dog or something. But you also don't seem like someone who lets themself get emotionally attached to a dog, so I'm just wondering what your story is and why you showed up here out of nowhere. Everyone's been crazy cryptic about it. My parents called you a visitor, like you were E.T. or something."

"Didn't Mona tell you?"

"She asked my parents whether I could pick

her up from the airport and that there'd be two of you. It doesn't take a rocket scientist to tell that you're related," he said, echoing Olivia's earlier thoughts. "And the only people I could have this much disdain for are my parents, so I assume you're her daughter that somehow none of us ever knew about?"

"You're astute," I told him, unzipping one of the suitcases and grabbing the neat stack of T-shirts that Olivia had color-coordinated.

"So you *are* her kid?" he asked, his eyes lighting up like he'd learned life-changing news.

"That's what they tell me. And no one ran over my dog, though someone practically ran over my dad, so close enough."

Cameron's eyes widened in shock. "Wait, Mona has a teenage daughter and your dad got... huh?"

"He died," I elaborated. "Drunk driver. So now I'm here."

"Oh, shit." He frowned. "I'm sorry. I had no idea. About Mona having a kid or your dad, you know..."

"Dying?" I finished for him.

"Yeah," he admitted.

"I can tell," I told him.

"Well, seeing as you have actual reason to be pissed off at the world, I'll give you a pass. Besides, I'm pretty funny. I'll get a smile eventually."

"You think so?" I asked, pulling out one of the empty drawers and dropping the shirts into it.

"I do," he said with a smirk. "But I'd hate to use all my persuasive powers at once so I'll see myself out." He stood from the bed and straightened out his gray joggers. I glanced quickly away from the bulge in the material. That was so not what I was supposed to be noticing right now.

He crossed the room in about three steps and stopped at the door, turning back to me. "I really am sorry, about your dad. Losing people sucks."

"Yeah," I said. "It does."

I watched as he left the room and closed the door behind him. Then I fell onto the bed, exhausted. I felt like I had been playing house, except instead of pretending to be the doting housewife, I was pretending to be the somewhat okay, somewhat orphaned daughter. I already had to adjust to life without Dad forever, and now I couldn't even do it in the home where so much of him still lived. Which meant the only way to keep him close to me was through my own memories, which were already starting to feel murky after just a couple of weeks. Could I trust that his laugh sounded exactly like the one I could conjure? Or that his smile lines were where I could imagine them to be?

My phone vibrated in my back pocket.

How is it? Olivia texted.

I reacted with a thumbs-down.

It'll get better, she responded. *I promise.*

I put my phone face down beside me and closed my eyes, willing myself to sleep, where Dad was easiest to find.

Chapter Eight

The room was pitch-dark when I woke up, with a small sliver of moonlight shining through the open window. The curtains blew slowly in the breeze, and an owl must have lived in the tree right outside the bedroom, because its hoot made it sound close enough to touch.

The house was silent.

I tried to convince myself to go back to sleep for at least another twenty minutes, trying to find cool spots beneath the comforter. I flipped the pillow over, settling myself into the silk. A part of me considered the thoughtfulness of making sure there were silk pillowcases, but the rest of me was too stubborn to give Mona any credit at all. It was probably Gaby anyway. She seemed like a thoughtful person. Gaby probably hadn't even known I existed.

I wondered what that conversation had looked like. Was Gaby angry that Mona had kept something so important from her? Or maybe she had known about me, and never bothered to convince Mona that abandoning her kid was a shit thing to do. I could never love someone if I knew they were capable of so easily throwing people away. If Gaby had known, I had no choice but to hate her too. Willful bystander, or whatever Mr. Calhoun was talking about in that sociology elective I took last year.

Smacking my hands against the bed, I gave up on sleep. My body still felt like I had just finished an Ironman, and my eyes were burning with unshed tears that I wasn't sure would ever dissipate. I was pretty sure I would spend the rest of my life ten seconds away from my next sobfest. But my brain was wide-awake and full of thoughts, mostly about Dad and how he could've kept something like this from me. I didn't want to be angry with him, especially since he wasn't here to settle it over a shared Choco Taco sundae, but I still couldn't help but feel hot with fury.

I disentangled myself from the sheets and got out of bed. Grabbing my phone off the nightstand, I scrolled through my favorite dessert Instagrams. Baking was the one thing that always made me feel better. One of my favorite bloggers had posted a classic molten chocolate cake recipe to her story. I scanned the ingredients and instructions, even though I'd made it a million times, and it didn't look like I would need anything that I couldn't find in an average kitchen. Even if their kitchen wasn't particularly well stocked, I should be able to make this happen. I'd had to improvise a recipe a time or two when we ran out of unsalted butter or semisweet chocolate (Nutella for the win).

My duffel bag was still on top of one of my suitcases. I unzipped it roughly and everything but my KitchenAid, too heavy to just fall about, spilled out onto the floor. There was only one pair of sweatpants I'd saved from Naomi's rush to pack my nonsummer things into boxes and I stuffed my legs into them, pulling them high up my stomach and double-knotting their string. I breathed in deeply, inhaling the smoky smell that clung to them no matter how many times they were washed. The fingerprints of Dad's late-night shows were imprinted in the fibers, the smoky cloud that followed him even though he had never even touched a vape pen, let alone a cigarette.

The hall was even quieter than my temporary bedroom as I made my way down the stairs. The house was sturdy, none of the wood creaking beneath my feet like the floors at home. It wasn't a house with stories to tell in its bones, holding up its foundation. Just a nothing house, still waiting for something to make it quake. Well, house, here I was.

The kitchen was organized and spotless. I couldn't help but compare everything in Mona's life to my own. Wooden spoons sat in a ceramic container painted a bright red that almost glowed in the dark. I opened all the cabinets and pantry, finding the pots and pans in every color of the rainbow stacked by size. The definition of organized chaos. I didn't need anyone to tell me that Gaby was responsible for the explosion of color thrown around the house like paint splatter and Mona was the parts of the house that remained lifeless, still.

I scanned the kitchen for the rest of what I

needed. I pulled a bag of milk chocolate chips from the pantry. They wouldn't cook as well as semisweet chips or sticks of baking chocolate, but they would have to do until I could get to the grocery store. The sugar was in a bag behind dog treats. I looked around. I hadn't seen a dog, not even a rogue dog hair, but I'd only walked a straight beeline to the room upstairs and back. I didn't want to wander. Wandering indicated interest, and I was not interested in the goings-on of this house. I didn't care to know anything about this house other than how Virginia humidity moved through it. Humidity always affected baking success.

I gathered the rest of the ingredients around the kitchen—flour, eggs, salt, and butter. The oven dial turned to 450 degrees smoothly, like it was used often and well loved, greased up. You could tell whether someone actually used their kitchen or lived off DoorDash. It was a small grace that it wasn't electric. Baking in an electric oven was like throwing rice in the air and hoping a camera could catch the word *surprise*. It was a little bit of intent and a whole lot of luck.

Then I went searching for the one thing I really needed, for which no substitute would do.

I searched every drawer, tossed aside every glass, utensil, pot, and pan.

"Come on," I muttered to myself. "Every adult has a ramekin." It was one of the random things that would find its way into your Target haul because it was (1) super cheap in the dollar section and (2) way too cute not to purchase.

"What's a ramekin?"

I leapt into the air, dropping a container of raw spaghetti from the topmost pantry shelf. It burst open on the floor, sending spaghetti snapping in every direction.

Frankie was standing by the kitchen island, large headphones around his neck. He hadn't grown into his skin yet, bones sticking out at every angle as they tried to find where they fit.

"What are you?" I asked, surprised to see him.

"Um." He pondered my question. "Ten?" He was even smaller than his age suggested.

"My condolences," I responded. I dropped to my knees and started collecting the spaghetti. I wasn't too worried about germs; it would get boiled.

Frankie dropped to his knees as well, collecting the spaghetti wedged in the crack between the floor and the island. I felt his eyes on me and could hear the Fortnite home screen music playing through his headphones.

He handed me his collected spaghetti and I slid it back into the container. Despite my height, I had to stand on the tips of my toes to slide it back onto the top shelf. Mona must have been in charge of fetching it—Gaby was much too short. Which meant that Mona probably did the cooking. That was typically how kitchens were organized, with items placed where the person who used them most could get them. The pieces of their lives started to fit together in my head like a jigsaw puzzle.

"Can I help you?" I asked, feeling Frankie's eyes on my back.

"No," he responded.

"Well, then stop staring and make yourself useful. Y'all got ramekins?"

"What's a ramekin?" He repeated his question. His voice was high and small, like a parakeet peep.

"It's a small dish." I put my hands together to create a small circle. "For soufflés."

"What's a soufflé?"

I sighed. "It looks like an upside-down chef's hat for a doll baby?"

His eyes brightened in acknowledgment before he disappeared down the hallway without a word and ran back up the stairs.

"Okaaaay." I found a large glass bowl under the sink and set it on the counter. I would have to make pudding instead. Small consolation but better than nothing. It would hit the spot nonetheless.

I turned to wash my hands and nearly choked on my tongue. Frankie was standing beside me, an unopened box in his hands.

"Holy shit!" I screeched. "Announce yourself or something."

"Sorry." Even in the moon-cast dark I could see his cheeks deepen with color. He gently set the box on the island beside the glass bowl. For a ten-year-old boy, he was way too quiet. Too demure, too cutesy.

I grabbed the box. A ramekin set of four.

"Mama's boss gave that to her," he explained, watching as I ripped the box open with the grace of a bull in a china shop. If they weren't even in the kitchen, I doubted anyone intended to use them. Either way, this was a dessert emergency.

"Thanks," I said.

I washed the ramekins quickly and then set

them upside down to dry before grabbing a stick of butter.

"Can I help?" he asked, stepping closer. His breath was wheezing, and I noticed that his chest was rising and falling a bit more violently than it should. Probably from his sprint up the stairs. I recognized it immediately—asthma. A lot of my track teammates had it as well, ironically. Apparently cardiovascular exercises made it better, also ironically.

As much as I wanted to be a bitch to the kid my so-called mother chose over me, he was ten and I wasn't a monster. I handed him a ramekin wordlessly and set the second stick of butter down in front of him. He grabbed it and repeated my actions, peeling the paper back like a banana peel, just enough to expose the butter, and then pressing it against all the sides and the bottom of the dish.

"So, you're Skylar?" he asked, starting in on a new ramekin.

"That's what they say," I answered, beginning to combine the dry ingredients. "And you're Frankie."

"Mama said you're my sister." His tongue poked out of his mouth as he concentrated.

"That also seems to be what they say." I turned on the stove and filled a small pot with water. Then I put a bowl on top, creating a double boiler. I dumped the rest of the butter and the chocolate into the bowl and let it melt, stirring it every other minute.

"Mama said your dad died."

I handed him the spoon and he took it greedily. I remembered that feeling, just wanting to make myself useful and still my mind. Dad would read a book quietly at the counter while I worked out the recipe, giving praise even when I messed up and used salt instead of sugar or burned a pie crust.

The precision required for baking quieted my mind. Being there to support me quieted his.

I hand-whisked the eggs, extra egg yolk, salt, and sugar in a separate bowl. My KitchenAid was still in "my room" and I didn't want to risk a trip back upstairs to get it.

We worked in silence but in rhythm. Frankie was a pretty decent sous-chef, much better than Dad, who I'd spent the entire time trying to keep from eating all the raw batter. Now the fan over the stove whirred, and I lost myself to a place where Dad wasn't dead or alive, where the only things that existed were me, my whisk, and the bowl in my hands. My mind was blank for the first time in days. That was what baking had always given me. Quiet. Peace.

"This is finished, I think." Frankie's voice broke through my brain fog like a crack of thunder, rattling me back into this new kitchen in this new house that was supposed to be mine but felt like another planet.

I brushed him aside, folding the egg mixture and flour into the chocolate quickly.

"Get those for me." I nodded at the buttered ramekins.

Frankie hurried, holding one in front of me, his hands cupped beneath it.

I poured the chocolate halfway to the top and Frankie dutifully switched the full ramekins out for empty ones until we were out of batter and all four ramekins were full.

Frankie pulled the oven open and I placed the ramekins on a larger cooking tray and slid them onto the top rack.

"Gently," I warned as Frankie closed the oven door.

He heeded my warning with maybe a little too much caution as he moved in what felt like slow motion.

"All right," I sighed, climbing onto one of the island stools. "You have twelve minutes to ask your questions."

He dragged a stool to the other side of the island and sat in front of me.

"So you're really my sister?" He seemed to come alive with the permission to speak.

"I guess." I shrugged. "Loosely."

"Mama says you're Mom's daughter," he elaborated.

"I guess," I repeated. "Loosely."

Frankie huffed with frustration. I decided to go easy on him. You can't be mean to an elementary schooler, I reminded myself.

"Your...mom," I started, trying to keep his titles straight between Mona and Gaby, "is my mom. I guess *birth mother* would be the best descriptor."

"Birth mother?" he asked.

"It means someone who gave birth to you but didn't raise you or wasn't otherwise a part of your life."

"Why not?"

I snorted. "Isn't that a question for the ages. I don't know."

"But you lived with your dad?" he continued.

"Yep," I answered, swallowing the lump that rose in my throat. I sniffed the air, checking on the cakes baking in the oven with the best sense a pastry chef could have in their arsenal. Especially when dealing with a new appliance. Not all ovens were created equal.

"But your dad isn't my dad." I wasn't sure if he was making a statement or asking a question, so I answered it anyway.

"Nope. I mean, no, I don't think so. That would be a little too *Parent Trap*–esque for me."

"*Parent Trap*?"

God, what were they teaching Gen Alpha these days? Was appreciation for cinema a lost art?

"Don't worry about it," I told him.

"Why didn't you come to visit?" He picked at a hangnail, his nerves so obvious that they practically took corporeal form.

I didn't know what Mona and Gaby had told him. I didn't know if he was aware of the fact that until a few days ago, Mona was a ghost.

"I guess I didn't know it was an option." If he was going to know the truth, it wasn't going to come from me. I knew what it was like to have the reality of who your parents were thrown in your face like ice water.

"My dad died too," he said suddenly. "When I was four."

"I'm sorry," I said. Okay, so he definitely had been making a statement before about our dads not being the same person, not asking a question. Which meant the *Parent Trap* reference going over his head could be forgiven, a little bit. "Do you remember him?" I couldn't imagine not having Dad around for so long.

Sometimes I was unsure if having memories of Dad was worse than forgetting him altogether. Would it have been easier if he'd been a shadow in the background, a fuzzy outline of a person rather than one completely filled in with colorful life, so bright that he burst out of the lines in every single one of my memories?

"Not really," Frankie muttered. But he wiped at his eye like he did. "I have a photo of him, but he looks like a stranger."

I nodded. That was kind of how I felt when I looked at Mona. Like she was both familiar and an image my mind had conjured from a combination of old faces to create someone totally new. Even the parts of Mona that were me felt foreign.

"And your mom?"

"Mama's my mom—birth mom?" he asked, trying to use my terminology. "But Mom adopted me when I turned seven, so they're both my parents." He shrugged like it was the most normal thing in the world, and despite how I felt about Mona, I was happy that her home seemed to be the kind of place where there was nothing unusual or unacceptable about a nontraditional family.

I took another deep inhale, pulling it all the way into my stomach, filling it with the chocolate decadence of the aroma in the air. The cakes were nearly done even though the timer I set still had four minutes left. So, a hot oven. I would need to be careful not to dry things out. Higher heat didn't always mean a better and faster bake. Ten minutes in Austin, you'd be as dry as unused linens. Ten minutes in DC and you'd be slick with sweat. Baking was the same way.

"Mama was married to my dad, but then he died, and Mama married Mom because she's—" He thought about his next words carefully. "She loves boys and girls."

I laughed a little as I stood to take out the trayful of ramekins. *Like me.* The cakes had risen beautifully. I set them carefully on top of the stove to cool off. The tops jiggled just so, waiting to set.

"Bisexual," I filled in for him as I opened every drawer for the utensils. I finally found them in a corner drawer and pulled out two forks.

"Yeah," he said. "Bisexual." The word sounded clinical on his tongue as he tested it out. "But Mama doesn't like labels. She says she loves people for however they come."

I was probably going to like Gaby, even though I was still unsure whether I could trust her, if she'd known about me all along. Time would tell.

I started washing the bowls and spoons I'd used. The cakes were already beginning to harden, a satisfying crust forming on top. Not too bad for ingredients scrounged together in the middle of the night.

Frankie stood to help, wiping down the island with a spritzer of bright pink cleaning solution and a paper towel.

"Mom likes a clean kitchen," he said as he

scrubbed already hardened chocolate off the granite.

I grunted. Yeah, Mona seemed like the type of person who liked things neatly sorted. Pots. Pans. Daughters.

When we were both done, I carried two ramekins to the island with the tips of my fingers. I barely felt the heat on my skin—I'd probably long ago destroyed any nerve endings there, since I'd started baking at the age of nine. Sometimes my brain was moving too fast to remember not to grab a hot pan directly out of the oven.

Frankie's eyes lit up as I set his cake in front of him. It probably wasn't a good idea to give a kid chocolate late at night, but I certainly wasn't going to tell. I demonstrated how to eat it, knocking my fork on the top of the cake to crack it open. Frankie followed my lead and gasped when his fork broke through the top layer and a small geyser of chocolate seeped out. Molten chocolate cake was tricky—trying to cook the outside while leaving a gushy middle that didn't overbake. I spent two months of the summer between middle and high school perfecting it. It was one of Dad's favorites. The memory of how much he'd enjoyed it made me grind the cake into something indecipherable between my teeth.

For the first time, my theory that sugar covered in chocolate and baked just right could solve any problem was being disproven, because each bite only seemed to make me feel worse. But maybe Dad put all the sweet in the world, just like he did with all the color. And maybe dessert wasn't the cure-all I'd always believed it to be. It didn't seem to do much at all for a broken heart.

"You like?" I asked Frankie, hoping he was enjoying it more than I was. That always made it worth it, when my food was loved by someone else. I couldn't trust my senses to tell me if it was any good. Lately, everything tasted like sawdust.

"It tastes like a shooting star." Frankie smiled before shoving another bite into his mouth.

"Then you have to make a wish," I laughed. I put my fork down. No use wasting perfectly good cake on grieving taste buds.

"I wish that you would be happy living with us," he said, eyeing me skeptically as he chewed.

"We'll see, kid," I said, though I highly doubted it.

"What do you wish?" he asked, his cake nearly done. I inched my unfinished one toward him and he dug in.

"I don't think I have any wishes," I said.

I couldn't wish Dad back.

And I wasn't sure anyone was listening anyway.

Chapter Nine

It had taken a while to fall back asleep, a combination of missing Dad, sleeping in a new place, and too much refined sugar. I reached under my pillow for my phone, feeling it vibrate beneath my head.

Olivia's name and picture flashed on the screen.

"Hello," I said, the word coming out in a mumble from the side of my mouth as I pressed the speaker button.

"Good morning, my dear," Olivia sang into the phone. The reception crackled. She was probably in her basement art studio. I imagined splatters of paint across her face, too-large pants snagged from Marshalls with the bottoms cuffed three times to accommodate how short she was.

I imagined her fingertips covered in charcoal like she'd run them through a fire pit. "You didn't call me when you got in."

"I'm sorry," I told her. "There was a lot going on. Did you know it's kind of hard and time-consuming ignoring someone you have to travel with all day?"

"I'll take your word for it," Olivia said. I could hear the swirl of a paintbrush in a cup of water in the background, the tap-tapping on the cup's edge to get rid of the excess. "Obviously, I know it mostly sucks since I'm not there, but anything you like about it so far?"

"Um," I said, pulling myself up into a sit. "Their kid, Frankie, he's pretty cute. And one of the neighbors seems decent, think he's my age."

"Oh?!" Olivia said.

"Calm down," I told her, reading her mind. "It's nothing."

"I don't know, sounds like potential," she said.

I rolled my eyes. She was almost too much of a lover girl sometimes. "You know people can vibe with each other without wanting to be in a relationship, right?"

"So y'all were vibing?" I could hear the laugh in her voice.

"Oh my God, shut up." I groaned and kicked my phone off the bed, letting it tumble to the floor with a loud *smack*.

"Don't kick me, bitch," she said, probably hearing the commotion through the phone. "No, but for real, is it super weird with Mona?"

"Not *super* weird," I told her. "She's left me alone for the most part, which I guess I appreciate."

"It's good to give her a chance," Olivia advised.

"Well, let's not go that far. Someone needs to come up with an explanation and they need to come up with it quick."

"Heard," Olivia said. "I wish your dad had at least written you a letter or something. It still just doesn't make any sense to me."

"No sense at all, actually," I agreed. I slid off the bed and shuffled through my clothes to find something to wear.

"Are you going to ask her? Try to talk to her about it?" Olivia asked.

"No way in hell," I answered.

"But you're not going to let her talk to you either?"

"Correct."

"Sooooo how exactly are you going to get answers if you won't talk to her and you won't let her talk to you?"

"Stop trying to be reasonable, I don't like it."

"I know, I know," she said. "But something's gotta give. And it seems like she's respected your boundaries and isn't trying to push all that kumbaya shit."

"At least." My stomach let out an egregious growl as I pulled on a pair of socks.

"Damn, well, I'mma let you go; hunger sounding like a tectonic plate."

"I really hate you sometimes."

"You don't, but call me later, okay?"

"Aye, aye, Captain," I responded.

"I can't hear you!" she sang.

"Aye, aye, Captain," I repeated.

"Ohhhhhhhh, who lives in a pineapple under the sea?" we sang together. This was why Olivia was my best friend, because this was inarguably the worst period of my life and she still, somehow, made me laugh.

"All right, bye, bitch," she said before my phone beeped three times, indicating she had hung up. And then she was gone. I took a deep breath as I stared at my closed door, trying to mentally prepare for the day, my first full day in Virginia.

There was commotion going on in the kitchen as I descended the stairs but nothing like the ruckus Dad usually caused in the mornings. Another jolt of missing him dropped in my stomach like a lead pipe.

"This is delicious," a voice moaned. I turned into the kitchen to find someone who looked creepily like a female Cam sitting at the table. She had one of the lava cakes on a plate in front of her, a large bite taken out of it, and slammed her hands on the table as she spotted me in the doorway. "Compliments to the chef."

"Thank you," I mumbled, heading toward the electric teakettle, which looked as if it was still half full of water.

Mona was standing by the sink, a hot mug of tea cradled in her hands. She turned to take another mug from the cabinet behind her, placing it on the counter with a small smile. So we had tea instead of coffee in common. The thought almost made me not even want it anymore.

"But seriously, this is, like, monumentally good," the girl said as she polished off the rest of the small cake. "You know our parents own a bakery, right?"

"I think your brother mentioned it," I told her, pouring hot water into the mug Mona set out for me, tea bag already hanging from the side. "Your twin brother, I assume?"

"What gave it away?" she asked, giving me the same smile Cameron had yesterday. "But of course he mentioned it already. I swear he's like those cars covered in advertisements in human form. But yeah, we have an opening on the pastry team for the summer if you're looking for a job."

I hadn't considered getting a job, but it would get me out of just moping around the house for the next few months.

I dunked a spoonful of sugar into my tea and stirred, the spoon making a sharp sound against the ceramic that filled the kitchen.

"Maybe," I told her.

"Well, let me know." She got up from her chair and pushed it back beneath the table. "I'll put in a good word for you with the hiring committee."

"Hiring committee?"

"It's me," she laughed. "The entire committee is me."

"Ah," I said.

"Taylor, by the way," she said, offering her hand across the island.

"Oh," I said, surprised at the formality of a handshake but taking her hand anyway. "Skylar, Sky, whatever."

"Do you have a preference?" she asked.

"Sky, I guess."

"Cool," she said. "Sky it is. Well, I have to skedaddle. Pastry isn't going to puff itself." She winked at me, acknowledging that she'd drawn from me a hard-to-come-by smile. "Think about stopping by the shop. If everything you make is as good as that," she said, pointing to the small ramekin, which looked as if it had been licked clean, "then we'd love to have you on the team. And Mrs. Gaby, let me know about the cake design, okay?"

"Will do, Taylor, thank you." Gaby, sitting at the kitchen table, barely took her eyes off the pile of bridal magazines in front of her as she waved goodbye. Each looked to be tabbed about a hundred times, neon-colored Post-it notes sticking out of the pages like twisted branches.

I stepped toward the table and slid one of the magazines toward me. "Are you a wedding planner?" I asked her.

"Oh no," Gaby said, taking a newly unpackaged red Sharpie and circling a French-blue-and-gold table arrangement that covered the center spread. She went around and around the page until it looked like a circular cranial incision. "I can barely plan my own wedding."

"I thought you were already married."

"You sound just like your—" Gaby stopped midsentence as her face settled into a cross-eyed puckered-lip combination. "Yes, we're already married." She cleared her throat. "But you know, after Obergefell we did what so many of our friends did—hurried to the courthouse before they changed their minds. You should've seen the place that first month. Like a Pride parade with even more taffeta. The plan was always to have a larger wedding, but . . . life." She smoothed her hand over Frankie's head as he passed, earning a groan of disapproval. "But we've finally caught our breaths and I'm ready for a wedding. Especially since who knows how long we'll have the chance with all that's going on in the courts."

I tested my tea, now cool enough to sip slowly. Frankie settled into the chair in front of me, digging his spoon into the bottom of a large bowl of Frosted Flakes.

"How many is that?" Gaby asked him as he brought an overloaded spoon of already soggy cereal to his mouth.

"My first one," he muttered as he chewed.

"Only one more, tops," she semi-scolded as she stood from the table. "So anyway, I want to have a real wedding with real guests and a real band and real flowers before the orange man tells me I can't."

"Mood." I wasn't even sure I wanted to get married, but it did scare me that as I got older, I seemed to *lose* more rights than I gained. Who knew if I would be allowed to marry whoever I wanted? I worried about what kind of world we would be living in when that time came. So I could support getting in while the gettin' was good.

Gaby gave me a small smile before turning to a new magazine that had not yet been tabbed to hell. Frankie stood up and laid his head on her shoulder.

"Can you take me to the skate park, Mama?" he asked her. He already seemed like a sweet kid, but he was laying it on hella thick. Seemed he had a little more grit in him than I thought.

"Are you trying to manipulate me, my sweet

boy?" Gaby asked, leaning her cheek on the top of his head. "Because normally it would work. But Mama has a client today. Maybe Mom?"

"Mom has a conference call she's going to be late for if she doesn't leave this minute," Mona chimed in. "I'm sorry, kiddo," she followed up as Frankie's face fell.

The way she interacted with him made my face hot. If I'd been a mere bystander with no knowledge of these people, I would have thought her the doting mother. But I *did* know her, and I couldn't reconcile the woman who'd abandoned me and roped Dad into lying about it with the wife and mother standing in front of me right now. The dissonance almost made me itchy.

"But you promised I could go today," Frankie groaned.

"I know," Gaby said. "But you know how we feel about the whining. No whining. I really am sorry, though. Maybe this weekend?"

"I'll take him," I offered, the words leaving my mouth before I'd had time to really think about them. But my only plans today involved sulking and scrolling through Instagram stories to see all the fun my friends were having without me, and this just, frankly, seemed like a better use of my time. Besides, it was a little sketchy, but maybe I could pump the kid for some Mona intel. Who was this woman the universe had brought back from the dead?

"Are you sure?" Gaby asked, though I could already see the relief on her face.

Frankie tugged at my arm. "Really?" His smile was so big I could practically see his molars.

"Sure." I shrugged. "Nothing better to do." The sulking and doomscrolling would still be viable evening activities. And it would make the day pass faster anyway.

"Oh God, thank you," Gaby said. "You're a lifesaver." She grabbed her purse from the countertop, digging to the bottom in search of something, finally pulling out a polka-dot wallet I could identify as Kate Spade only because of the thorough history lesson Olivia had given me upon Kate Spade's passing. Gaby slid an Amex toward me. "You can use this for anything. There's lots of cute lunch spots by the park. Ooh, you have to get a lobster roll from Chickadee. Weirdest name ever for a seafood spot but I swear it's the best lobster roll on the East Coast, and I grew up in Maine."

I grabbed the card awkwardly. I didn't really

want to accept anything more from them, but without my re-up of allowance this week on account of, well, Dad dying, and his estate tied up into a trust until I was eighteen, I didn't have any cash, and I really did want to try the lobster roll. But it was mostly for Frankie anyway, I reasoned. I slid it into the pocket of my joggers along with my phone.

"You ready?" I nudged Frankie with my elbow. He drank the rest of his cereal, soggy Frosted Flakes and milk in one gulp, with a nod.

"I'll get my board." He hurried from the table, the sound of his feet running up the stairs echoing through the house.

The silence that remained was so thick, I had to sit down again beneath its weight. Like gravity increasing at too high an altitude, but oxygen failing to keep up. Gaby continued to flip through her magazines while Mona and I looked everywhere but at each other.

"I'm ready," Frankie called down in mercifully short order.

I gave Gaby a weak smile and waved as I met Frankie in the foyer.

"Let's go," I told him as I stuffed my feet into my most reliable pair of Vans.

He was wearing a similar pair, just as scuffed up, with laces hanging loosely. I smiled to myself. I'd never wanted a sibling, but there was already a tug in my heart that felt a little like attachment. I draped my arm over his shoulder as he led me out of the house.

A shadow passed through the hallway as I shut the front door, so quick that I'd probably imagined it.

I heard the sound of wheels hitting pavement and turned to find Cam doing kickflips in his driveway. Frankie ran over to join him and I followed close behind.

"Good morning, sunshine," he called, gripping his skateboard by the front edge.

"Sure," I responded.

He let out a long whistle. "You know, I was just thinking, I sure do wish Skylar was around, she really does brighten up a room."

I gave him my best scathing glance.

"I'm just giving you a hard time." His laughter was like bells ringing, harmonic and loud. "Y'all going to skate?"

"Yep," Frankie practically squeaked. He looked at Cameron like he idolized him.

"Not that I have anything to use while there."

I had tried roller-skating for a hot minute during that fad a few years ago, but one too many falls on my tailbone had sent that hobby packing almost as fast as it had started.

"You can use Mom's bike," Frankie offered before running toward the garage door. He hit a small button on the side paneling, making the door rise slowly in front of us.

The garage was a mess of overturned boxes and plastic containers filled with what looked like seasonal decorations—Thanksgiving, Christmas, Easter, even Valentine's Day. Three bikes were stashed near the back corner. One, which I presumed was Frankie's, was much smaller than the other two. And another had a flat tire. That left a sapphire-blue bike clearly meant for an adult. I blanched a little. I hadn't ridden a bike in a decade and while they say you never forget, I was pretty sure I was about to disprove that theory.

I followed Frankie and Cam between stacks of boxes to get to the bike. Cam lifted one of the boxes sitting in front of it as I tried to shimmy the bike out of the corner, a string of Christmas tinsel laced between the spokes of its back wheel. A box wedged on top of the wheel fell to the ground with a smash.

"Oops," Frankie said as Cameron put his box down and yanked the bike free, nearly falling over as the wheels rolled toward him with surprising speed.

I crouched down to pick up the fallen box and its contents. Before I could shove the box back into place, my eye caught a small journal that had probably fallen out. It was the size of a miniature pocketbook, a decimated pencil stuffed into the center with an elastic piece holding the whole thing together. I slipped the elastic off the edge of the book and the pages flew open. The writing was cramped cursive and I had to squeeze my eyes together to decipher any of the words.

Dear diary, it began, and immediately I knew that this wasn't something I should be reading. But the cramped handwriting reminded me so much of Mona, practically shrill if words could speak, that my gut told me it was hers. And while I had no intention of talking directly to Mona, I wondered if it would give me any insight into her. I mean, who wouldn't be curious about the mother who gave them up? Plus, I was pretty nosy. The part of me that knew it was wrong to read someone's diary was quickly snuffed out by the part of me that felt entitled to answers, anything really, that would make my parents' decision make sense.

"You ready?" Frankie called from outside the garage. Cam stood beside me with his skateboard beneath his feet and both of his hands on the bike's handlebars.

"Find anything good?" he asked.

"Nope," I said, stuffing the diary in the same pocket as Gaby's credit card. "I'm ready," I called back to Frankie, making my way back through the obstacle course that was their garage.

Chapter Ten

The ride to the skate park took less than fifteen minutes. Crowds of people were swarming around the trendy Alexandria street by the water. Boats lined the dock, and a row of shops and restaurants led to the park. It would be a nice place for a run early in the morning before it got too hot and mosquito-ridden. I made a mental note to add it to the list of routes I was hoping to start. If I was going to live here, I needed to make it work for me.

"This is actually really cute," I said.

"You sound surprised." Cameron laughed.

"Well, when I think 'home of the Confederacy,' *cute* doesn't really come to mind."

Cameron rolled his eyes. "That's Richmond, which is actually pretty decent now, good food. And Alexandria is like Little DC. You'd have to drive forty minutes west to get the political party ick. Especially Old Town—it's one of the coolest spots we've got." Cameron pointed to a small shop next to an ice-cream parlor. "That's my folks' place."

"The bakery?"

"The one and only," he answered. "A Cupcake a Day. Best bakery this side of the Potomac. In my completely unbiased opinion."

Crowded tables sat along on the sidewalk of mom-and-pop restaurants, covered in cardboard containers filled with tacos, French fries drenched in what looked like lines of barbecue sauce, and Gaby's lauded lobster rolls.

"Feel like we're at a Vans convention," I said as we made it to the actual park. Almost every pair of feet had on Vans or Converses, like this one skate park wiped out the entire shoe catalog. I had never felt so much like a basic bitch in my entire life. I snapped a photo and added it to my story. Olivia hearted it almost immediately.

LivinLaLivia: they just like you fr

Skysth3limit: damn that was fast. stalk much?

LivinLaLivia: and do.

"So what first?" I asked Frankie, putting my feet on the ground to balance the bike. Apparently the stories were true, you didn't forget how to ride a bike. "You gonna use that thing?" I gestured to the skateboard he was clutching to his chest like a life raft.

His cheeks brightened as he sucked on his top lip. He replied with a jittery "Yes" that was barely audible.

"No need to be nervous, little man," Cameron said, nudging Frankie in the shoulder to urge him closer to the large bowl at the center of the park. "I'll be right beside you the whole time."

"And I'll be right here," I said, trying to be encouraging. "On this bench." I pointed to the only bench with no one already sitting on it and plopped down as Frankie followed Cam toward the group of boys sitting along the edge of the bowl. Cameron fist-bumped all of them individually, Frankie following his lead with a big, albeit nervous, smile.

I leaned the bike on the side of the bench and

pulled my feet up, digging the small notebook out of my pocket. The edges were worn with age and the pages smelled like old pencil lead. I flipped back to the page saved by the pencil.

Dear diary,

The wind picked up as I read, sending goose bumps up my arms.

I think I'm going to tell my parents. That might seem like a horrible idea to you, but keeping it a secret is starting to do something to me, starting to make me lose pieces of myself.

I pulled the page closer to my face to make out the rest of the smudged handwriting.

T thinks I should wait until I have more evidence on how they may respond, but he just doesn't understand. His parents would never judge him for being like me.

"Like what?" I said out loud, reading the words a few times. Clearly Mona was hiding something from her parents, something she was afraid to tell them. That was the one thing I always appreciated about Dad. I could tell him anything without fear. I knew how lucky I was to have that kind of support system. Half of my friends in our LGBT affinity group had to hide their true selves from their folks, and even small stuff like Olivia wanting to go to art school instead of becoming a lawyer or doctor was swept under the rug at her house. Maybe that was why it had been so easy for Mona to maintain her double life, the one she had here and the one with me and Dad that she pretended never existed—she was used to hiding.

"I'm sorry?"

I nearly jumped out of my skin as a voice beside me disrupted my thoughts. A girl was seated beside me, her feet balanced on the curb in front of us.

"Shit, where'd you come from?" I asked, placing my hand over my chest. I picked the notebook up from the ground. It had landed face up. The girl eyed it with a bemused expression.

She laughed. "Damn, way to make a girl feel invisible. You are sitting on *my* bench."

"Your bench?"

"Yes, since I staked my claim on it." She held out a small cardboard box filled with cupcakes. "Want one? Normally I wouldn't share, but us journaling manifesters have to stick together."

"I don't journal," I said quickly. She eyed the notebook in my hands. "Oh, well, it's a long story."

"Okay." She shrugged before setting the box of cupcakes down between us. The logo of Cameron's parents' bakery was on the top.

"Oh, I know that place."

"Yeah? I've been waiting for them to open all summer."

"Were they closed?" I asked. No one had mentioned anything about that. I hoped they weren't struggling or anything. But I had seen their house, the best-maintained in the cul-de-sac. If they were struggling, that wouldn't be the case, right?

"No, just opened, I think."

Okay, well, that was confusing. I felt like we were ships in the night, having two conversations that seemed to narrowly slide past each other.

"Um, sure," I responded, reaching into the box for a cupcake. No serious baker ever said no to the opportunity to taste-test. I picked out a vanilla one with what looked like chocolate-and-vanilla swirl icing.

"Bomb, right?" the girl asked as she took her own bite of one that looked like red velvet. "I think I've been there every day since they opened."

"Pretty *bomb*, I guess," I said, imitating her way-old lingo, except that it was an accurate description. The cupcake was beyond delicious, with a melt-in-your-mouth consistency that let me know they knew what they were doing. The perfect cupcake made from scratch was deceptively hard to pull off. And the whipped frosting had the perfect balance of pillowy softness without being too sweet. I folded the now empty cupcake wrapper into a tiny triangle, balancing the notebook on my knee. I looked up just in time to see Frankie eat it going down the bowl, his helmet knocking against the ground.

I jumped up at the same time that Cameron slid down the side of the bowl to help him up. Frankie laughed and gave him a thumbs-up. I felt my chest tighten and then release. Not me already being concerned about what happened to this kid.

"You don't have to worry about him," the girl

said. She smoothed her hand over her high ponytail made of micro knotless braids. "The boarders are total airheads but they're good dudes. And I swear they're made out of titanium steel. My best friend wiped out once, literally so much blood. Walked away with just two stitches and the tiniest scar on his chin. I thought he was going to be one of those people in a coma for sixteen years."

I blew air out of my mouth and dropped back down beside her, picking the notebook up from the ground. I stashed it back in my pocket. Now that I had company, it seemed especially awkward to be reading Mona's diary.

"You know Cameron?" I asked her, draping my arm over the back of the bench.

She squinted as she took in Cameron still hyping Frankie up after his fall. "Not really, but he seems okay," the girl said. "Seems like cool people. Anyway, verdict on the cupcakes?"

"Heaven," I moaned, licking extra frosting from the corner of my mouth.

"I knew I liked you. Good taste is hard to come by. I wish I could make anything half that good, mmmm."

"You bake at all?" I asked her.

"Absolutely not," she answered, choosing a

chocolate cupcake with chocolate frosting that looked as if it had been rolled in Cocoa Pebbles. "I cannot cook, or bake, or whatever skill is needed to make edible goodness. That gene definitely skipped a generation. My mom's a great cook. Meanwhile I'd rather die than be stuck in somebody's kitchen."

"Can't relate," I laughed. I, on the other hand, loved being stuck in somebody's kitchen.

"You cook?" she asked.

"I can cook a little bit, the basics, but I bake mostly."

"You any good?"

"I do okay." I shrugged, trying to be humble. We all knew I got busy in the kitchen.

"Well, feel free to bring some snackage next time. All these cupcakes are going to send me to the poorhouse."

I laughed again, surprised at how genuine it sounded, before I was hit with a wave of guilt. Was I supposed to be happy so soon after Dad's death? It felt uncomfortable for life to return to business as usual so quickly. When you loved someone as much as I loved Dad, didn't you owe them some level of never being okay again?

"So, I haven't seen you around here before."

The girl closed the now empty box and crushed it beneath her feet. She kept it underfoot, presumably to stop the wind from shooting it across the concrete.

"No, just moved here."

"Sweet." She nodded. "Let me guess, your dad got a new job and packed up your entire family to make a new life in good old DC-adjacent? Let me guess, military contractor?"

"Not even close. Are you projecting?" I asked. As I thought about my response, I started collecting the cupcake's ingredients in my head, letting my palate sort through the flavor explosion still coating my tongue.

"Maybe a little," she finally responded. "Except it was my mom."

"Gag," I blurted before I could stop myself. "Shit, sorry."

"No, I think that's the appropriate response." The girl lifted herself from the bench to pull her shorts out from where they'd gathered between her thighs. "She can be pretty gag."

"Mine's not great either," I said. She shot me a questioning look. "Long story."

"You seem to have a lot of those."

"You have no idea." She watched me again and

then decided to let it go with a shrug. "So which Neanderthal is yours?" I asked her, looking out into the sea of kids, letting the sound of wheels rolling over sidewalk cracks ring in my ears.

"None of them. I usually come with my best friend, but he must be in jail or at church or something."

"Those are very different things," I said.

"Are they really?" She smirked.

"Touché." I nodded. "But that means you're just . . . sitting in a park . . . watching children." I glanced at her out of the corner of my eye. "Very *SVU* of you."

"Okay, relax, *Law & Order*, I'm not trying to snatch a kid."

"Mmm, I think that's what a kid snatcher would say." To further my point, I scooted down the bench away from her. "Gotta make sure I'm not in the shot when they put you on the Most Wanted List. I'm not trying to be a fuzzy anonymous witness in a true-crime documentary."

"What's true crime?" she asked, reaching up to redo her ponytail.

"Yeah, so you definitely live in a basement with barred windows. I'm officially concerned." The only thing bigger than true crime right now was pickleball. No way anyone who didn't live under a rock didn't know what it was.

"I'm serious." She poked me with her elbow. "Is it like that *Cops* show?"

"Well, seeing as you've described all the programming on CBS, I'm gonna say no. It's, like, books and stuff about real crimes that happened. You know, true, um, crime. They, like, investigate and lay out all the facts. Unsolved stuff a lot of times, or just something crazy with a really good story."

"Ah, well, that explains it. I hate reading."

I clutched my hand to my chest. "You take that back!"

The girl put her hands up in surrender. "I'm sorry," she laughed. "In our house, if you're reading a book it better be the Bible or *Chicken Soup*, which is like *The Bible for Dummies*."

"Oof," I responded. Dad believed religion was only what could be found at the end of a guitar. Music was his God. "I'm Skylar, by the way. Most people call me Sky, though. Probably shouldn't piss on your Jesus without introducing myself first. You know, so you know who to smite at church and stuff."

"Clare. And no worries, I'm not vibing with

Jesus too much these days." She waved her hand in an awkward hello.

"Yeah, I'm not vibing with him too much these days either."

Mona's car was already in the driveway when I wheeled her bike back into the garage. Great, another afternoon of awkward nonconversations.

"Skylar?" Mona called from the kitchen the second we opened the front door. Frankie looked at me wide-eyed like I was in trouble. I appreciated that he joined me in my apparent death walk to the kitchen as some sort of moral support.

"Hi," she said. "Sit." She gestured to one of the many empty chairs. "Frankie, can you give us a moment?"

Without any hesitation, Frankie sent me an apologetic look before disappearing back down the hall and up the stairs. I sat awkwardly, holding my hands in my lap. Mona's diary was burning a hole in my pocket. If she knew I'd taken it, and even worse, had read it, I wasn't sure how to explain that violation of her privacy. Did I like her? No. Did I still abide by the human social contract? Yes.

"So, I know I owe you . . . a lot."

I snorted. "I'll say."

She didn't take the bait. I had to admit, if she was in therapy, that person was worth their weight in gold.

"And," she continued, "those conversations will happen in due time."

"Time?" I scoffed. "You think you should take even more time to tell me what the hell you all were thinking?"

"Language aside, I agree with you. But I don't think it would be a productive conversation at this stage of our relationship." She wasn't necessarily wrong, but it annoyed me that she was being so reasonable about it. If the circumstances hadn't required me to hate her, I might have actually liked her. I could see how Dad had fallen for her—she seemed levelheaded, a trait he always craved in the people around him. But that made me even madder—that she had probably broken his heart and made him agree to this fucked-up arrangement.

"So you called me in here to talk about how we won't be talking? Cool." I pressed my hands against the table to stand up, but she raised her hand to stop me.

"I called you in here because I should know how you're dealing with your father's death."

Your father's death, like he was a stranger and not her ex-husband and the father of her child, the same child she'd left him to raise alone.

"I'm not *dealing*," I told her.

She nodded like she understood. "That's okay. But I think you should talk to someone about it, and since I know you're not going to talk to me, I think we should get you a grief counselor."

"Like a shrink?" I asked, aghast.

"Like a grief counselor. Someone you will hopefully feel comfortable confiding in."

It wasn't that I was against therapy per se, I just had never considered myself to be someone who needed it. I wasn't crazy or depressed, I didn't have compulsions or anything I thought a therapist would help with.

"I have someone who came highly recommended. I can make you an appointment if you want."

I eyed her suspiciously. What was her play here? Was the grief counselor in her pocket and would they spill the beans on everything I said? Was she trying to butter me up by appearing to be helpful and considerate?

"Skylar, this isn't a trick. I want you to be okay, even if you don't believe that. How about I make the appointment and you can decide if you want to go?"

"Fine," I said, already pretty certain I wasn't going. I didn't need counseling. I needed my dad back. I needed to go home. And I needed to go back to when I thought my mother was dead. Life had been so much better before all those things changed.

Three days later, I was sitting on the front porch steps, a business card clutched between my fingers.

Diana Portman, LCSW. Specializing in family therapy, anger management, grief, anxiety, and depression. Cameron was in his driveway, rinsing off the Bronco, wet T-shirt clinging to his chest. I had to admit that I had spent at least a few minutes of my pondering watching him.

"Like what you see?" he called across the yard, throwing his head back in a dramatic *Baywatch* fashion.

"You wish," I laughed, surprised once again at the ease with which the laugh came out. I looked down at the card. Mona had scheduled my appointment for an hour from now. I still hadn't decided whether I was going and she, keeping to her word, hadn't pressed the issue. She had left the business card with the date and time of my appointment on my pillow and hadn't said another word about it. "I need a favor." I got up from the steps and made my way toward him.

"Count me in," he responded.

"You don't even know what the favor is."

Cameron shrugged. "Hey, if you need someone to help you bury a body, I'm your guy."

"That's a dangerous precedent."

"What can I say, I like to live life on the edge." He nudged me with his elbow and I stumbled dramatically to the side. "Ha ha, very funny."

"I need you to drive me somewhere. I'd take the bike," I offered, nodding at the garage. "But I don't actually know where I'm going and trying to GPS while staying upright seems like a bad idea."

"For sure, for sure," he laughed. "Let me just make sure Tay doesn't need the car, but shouldn't be a problem. Give me five minutes."

He waved as he ran through his front door.

The sound of a piano floated out the door before it snapped shut again. It took less than the five minutes for Cameron to come back, halfway through pulling a new, dry T-shirt over his head. I looked away from his bare chest like it was something scandalous, catching him smirking from the corner of my eye.

The car ride was silent after I plugged Diana Portman's address into my phone, connecting to Cam's GPS via CarPlay. Well, as quiet as it could be with the chattiest person I had ever met. Cam talked about different restaurants and landmarks that we passed, giving his expert opinion on the best mom-and-pop ice-cream shops and antique stores. Apparently his mom was a devout collector of useless junk, his words, not mine.

"So, where we headed?" he finally asked when we were just a few minutes away.

I pointed to the GPS. "There."

"Okay, what or who are we headed to?"

I sighed deeply. "Mona wants me to see a grief counselor. So that's where we're going."

"Right on."

I turned my head to him. "You're excited I have to go to grief therapy?"

"I'm excited you *get* to go to grief therapy," he said.

"Elaborate."

"Well, I've never grieved an actual death, but pretty much everyone could benefit from therapy in some way. Most of us spend our lives biting our tongue and ignoring our problems and therapists don't let you get away with either. Especially in the Black community, I mean, that generational trauma has to be addressed at some point, right?"

"I guess," I agreed, not finding any real holes in his argument. Therapy *was* especially taboo in the Black community. Truth was, therapy should probably just be a part of reparations if you took into account all the trauma involved in being Black in America.

"Plus, you're going to a good one," he said, pulling up to the curb and putting the Bronco in park.

"How do you know?" I asked.

"Because this is my therapist." He laughed. "Diana, right?"

"Yeah. Wait, *you* are in therapy?"

"I am," he confessed.

"Why? You're, like, obnoxiously chipper."

He laughed harder now. "Imagine what I was like before therapy. For real, though, Diana is great. She's no bullshit, though, so take heed. And make sure you have some tissues."

"Why?"

"Because she's going to make you cry." He reached across my lap to release my door. I breathed in the smell of confectioners' sugar, soap, and sweat.

"Great," I said, climbing out of the car.

"Have fun, sunshine," he said as I slammed the door with a roll of my eyes. Something in my brain sparked around him, the warmth with which he approached life so similar to my dad's that it almost took my breath away. So while I wanted to be completely annoyed with his insistence on making me smile, I couldn't get all the way there.

He waited until I was inside the building before pulling away.

The lobby had the air-conditioning on max and I wrapped my arms around myself as I made my way to the elevator. Suite 600, so I pressed 6. Thankfully, the elevator didn't have that god-awful music and I relished the quiet of the short ride up. The doors opened directly into the office, with the receptionist giving me a warm smile as I approached.

"Good afternoon, do you have an appointment?" she asked.

"Uh, yeah. Skylar Morrison," I replied.

She clicked a few buttons on her computer before nodding. "Got you right here. You can have a seat and we'll call you back in just a few moments."

My butt had barely touched the seat before a Black woman, hair loc'd into a high bun, came toward me.

"Skylar?" she asked.

"Yes, ma'am." You can take the girl out of Texas, as they say.

"Diana Portman," she said, holding out her hand. "You can call me Diana."

"Oh, hi," I said, grabbing her hand. "Skylar, but you obviously already know that."

She gave me a smile warmer than a ninety-degree day in August. "You ready to come on back?"

"Yeah, I guess." I followed her through a short hallway into an open office. A large executive desk faced one wall, with a large couch and armchair on the other side of the room.

"Have a seat," she instructed as she grabbed a legal pad off her desk.

I chose a seat on the couch, since that was usually where I saw people sit in movies, all stretched out and comfortable. I was definitely not comfortable, so I stayed upright. Plus, it would've been super weird to just lie on this lady's couch.

"So, Skylar, this first meeting is just an introduction so you can get to know me and I can get to know you. Together, we can decide if I may be able to help you."

"Okay," I said.

"So first, why don't you tell me why you're here?"

I shrugged. "Mona made me an appointment."

She smiled knowingly; she was used to evasive responses.

"And who is Mona?"

"My...I live with her now."

"Now?" she asked. I could tell this lady was going to annoy me—she was too observant.

"I just moved here, from Austin."

"Mmm. And why did you move?"

I couldn't tell if she already knew the answers and wanted me to confirm them for her, or if Mona had truly not told her anything about me when she made the appointment.

"My dad died," I told her.

"I'm sorry to hear that. Were you close?"

"He was my best friend. It was just us for a really long time so I guess you could say the world kind of ended."

"Except you're still here."

I shrugged.

"So your dad died and you had to move to Virginia, with Mona, I presume. And what's your relationship to her?"

"She's my mom, I guess."

"You guess?" It was like she wanted me to draw out every answer, like I was a pen she was taking apart to see how it worked.

"She's my birth mother. I thought she was dead until my dad died."

Her eyes widened, like finally I'd said something juicy she hadn't heard before.

"You thought she was . . . dead?"

"That's what they told me."

"Who told you that?"

"Mona and my dad. Except"—I suddenly realized—"I guess it was just my dad." Mona obviously couldn't tell me she was dead, which meant it had been Dad's lie the whole time. Did she put him up to it, or did he come up with it himself? And if so, why?

"So your dad told you that your mother was dead, and when he died, you found out that wasn't true? Well, I think that's a lot for anyone to handle, especially someone of your age."

I nodded, fighting back the tears welling in my eyes. I wasn't sure why her acknowledging how young I was made me so emotional, but it was true. I *was* too young to be dealing with this much shit. Everyone kept telling me how strong I was being, but I didn't want to be strong. I wanted to be a teenager.

"I think I can help you, if you want me to."

"Well, I'm here."

"And that's a great first step." She nodded. "Let me ask you something, are you angry?"

"About what?"

"About anything." She shrugged.

"Yeah," I answered.

"What are you angry about?" she asked.

"What am I *not* angry about?" I laughed, but it was shrill, more fatigue than humor. Being mad and sad all the time was exhausting.

"I'm sure it feels like there's a lot on your plate right now. Are you angry about the move?"

"Yeah, I mean, it's going to be my senior year and I have to start out in a whole new place without my best friend. It's not fair."

She nodded, made a note, and then looked up at me again. "Are you angry with your father?"

"Wouldn't you be?"

"I would," she agreed. Then she nodded, made a note, and looked at me again. Rinse and repeat.

She paused and cleared her throat before continuing. "Are you angry that your dad died?"

I hadn't thought about anger when it came to Dad. Sure, I was mad that he'd lied, but could I be angry that he was dead? And who would I be angry at besides the obvious one to blame, the guy who got behind the wheel after a few too many? Could I be angry at the concept itself, the idea that Dad wasn't here anymore?

"Yeah," I said finally.

"In what ways?"

"I'm angry that he lied to me and died before I could ask him why." Diana nodded. "I'm mad that he didn't trust me with the truth. I'm mad that baking isn't as fun without swatting him away from the batter. I'm mad that I don't get his Jeep he promised me because it got totaled and it would've been something I had left of him. I'm mad that he left me here alone. I'm mad about all of it."

"That's good, that you can get all of that out. It's all very heavy."

"I'm mad that I didn't give him one last hug the night he died. He asked and I wouldn't do it and I don't know why and now I can never give him a hug again." The tears were free-flowing now, like someone had run into a fire hydrant and it had exploded.

"Thank you for sharing that, Skylar. Guilt is a very real phase of the grieving process. And so is anger. Everything you're feeling, it's normal and expected. You don't have to apologize for it. You don't have to feel shame for it. But you do have to process it."

I could barely hear her. I was crying harder than I had ever cried in my life and I was scared that now that I had started, I was never going to be able to stop. I was only minimally aware of her as she got up from her chair, retrieved a box of tissues, and sat it next to me on the couch. No matter how many of them I used, it felt like the tears were just as present as ever.

"I'm very proud of you, Skylar."

"Sky," I hiccuped. "Everyone... calls me Sky."

The air was swampy as I made my way back outside. Sobs still wracked my body as I tried to catch my breath. A loud car honk nearly startled me down the stairs.

"Yo!"

Cameron was leaning across the passenger seat of his Bronco, which seemed to have materialized out of nowhere.

"How long have you been there?" I asked, placing my hand over my chest to quiet my heart, which was beating at warp speed.

"Just got here," he said, pushing open the passenger door. He settled back into his seat and turned down the radio as I clicked my seat belt into place.

"You never left, did you?" I asked with a smile that was fighting its way through the tears.

"Nah. Didn't want you having to Uber home. And I wanted some pizza."

"What's wanting pizza got to do with me?" I asked, rolling my window down to let in the breeze.

Vintage cars like Cameron's O. J. Simpson–esque Bronco were cool until you threw your shoulder out trying to get some fresh air.

"Well, you can't eat pizza alone. It's like drinking alone. If you're doing it, you may have a problem."

"Don't let me stop you, then." I felt his glance graze along my cheek like fingertips. "Can I help you?"

"She made you cry, didn't she?" he asked.

I waved my hand around my face generally. I hadn't looked at myself in a mirror, but I already knew my eyes were red and puffy and my cheeks looked bloated, as that was what always happened when I cried. Not that I had ever cried quite this hard.

"Yeah, she's good at that."

"What do you see her for?" I asked.

He smirked to himself and then put the car in drive. "You do really look like Mona sometimes. Mostly when you're glaring at me."

"Are you changing the subject?"

"Absolutely." He nodded. "You can't ask why someone goes to therapy; it's like asking a middle-aged woman her age."

"You know why I went to therapy."

"And I'd never tell a soul. Driver-passenger confidentiality."

I rolled my eyes and threw one of my used tissues at him. I made sure it was the snottiest one.

"Ew!" he screeched, somehow managing to control the car as he ducked. "You're disgusting." He made a right into traffic, expertly navigating the merge lane.

I had only taken a few driving lessons with Dad and never on the highway. Just another thing we'd never get to do. I bit down on my tongue to keep the waterworks from starting up again.

"So I hear you met my sister. She nearly talked my ear off about your cake."

I nodded. "She offered me a job at your folks' place."

"Well, that won't do."

"What? Why?" I hadn't decided whether I was going to apply, but now that I knew he seemed to not want me to, I was offended.

"Not that I wouldn't love working with you. You just can't work at the shop and be in the competition, and I saw your eyes light up with competitive spirit when you heard about Paris."

"It *is* Paris," I said.

"Oh, I get it, for sure. Though if you really don't care, then yeah, definitely come work with us."

"You just can't get enough of me, can you?" I joked.

"I actually wake up every morning hoping you'll give me the time of day. Plus, you'd get to spend time with me too."

He exited the highway and drove less than two blocks before turning into a barren parking lot. An assortment of run-down stores lined the strip, with a bright neon pizza sign nudged into the corner spot. It was the only place with cars parked outside it.

"Joy," I mused aloud.

"You don't actually hate me, right? That's just your schtick?"

Part of me felt bad. I hadn't treated him great and he'd done me a huge favor by driving me out here. And picking us up from the airport. And letting Frankie shadow him at the park. In fact, he had actually been kind of great since the moment we met. "Sorry," I muttered. "Guess it's hard to feel positive about anything right now."

"I get it. Well, actually, I don't really get it but I can imagine." He hopped out of the car and ran to my side, then held the door open for me.

Chivalry was indeed not dead. I skirted past him into the small pizza parlor. Four peeling tables sat around the room, with plastic chairs that looked like they'd barely be able to hold our weights. Only one of the tables was empty.

"Trust me, whatever you can imagine, multiply it by, like, a thousand." I had classmates in Austin who had lost parents, and I always thought I could imagine what it would be like to lose Dad until I actually lost him. Nothing came close to how empty I felt knowing that I wouldn't see his smiling face and disaster pancakes in the morning, or hear his assigned ringtone go off on my phone when I was late getting home from Olivia's house. I could not shake the disbelief that I was never going to see him again.

Cameron and I ordered two slices each at the counter and settled in at the empty table. Him, pepperoni. Me, classic cheese. You could size a pizza place up in one bite based on their cheese pizza.

"So," he said as we waited for our food, "you really hate Mona, huh? She really that bad?"

"It's not about how bad she is or isn't. It's that having to live with her after she clearly wanted nothing to do with me my entire life isn't fair.

And it's not like she can act like she had some change of heart or something. If my dad was still alive, I'd still not know she existed. Trust me, she doesn't want me here any more than I want to be here."

"Did she say that?"

"Of course she didn't say that. She's not, like, evil. Or maybe she is. I don't know. But I can feel it. It's not like she's trying to get to know me."

"Would you even let her if she did try?"

"Absolutely not."

"Then maybe she's just trying to give you your space, until you're ready."

I rolled my eyes in response. I was tired of everyone defending Mona as some ultrareasonable person when she had done the least reasonable thing imaginable and stood ten toes down on it for sixteen years.

He threw his hands up in defeat before getting up to grab our order off the counter, balancing two plates on his forearms and carrying two in his hands, the telltale sign of someone with waitstaff experience. He then proceeded to wolf down both of his slices in thirty seconds flat.

I had never seen anyone down two slices of anything so quickly. As I ate at a much more leisurely pace, I endured a history lesson on the shop and the owner, Lewis, who had opened it at the same time Cameron's parents opened their bakery seventeen years ago. When I was finished, Cameron reached over, paused for permission, and snagged my crust from my plate. The guy was a human garbage disposal.

"I don't know how someone who loves to bake doesn't appreciate the absolute perfection that is Remy's pizza crust. Buttery, not too doughy. Perfection."

I scrunched up my nose. "I just don't vibe with crust. Now, DiGiorno croissant crust? Say less."

"You did not just compare Remy's to DiGiorno. Sacrilegious."

I shrugged. "What can I say? They've mastered pizza crust. I could probably top them, though, if I tried."

"You should put your money where your mouth is. What's it going to be? Become a tax-paying member of society or catch that first-class flight to France?"

"Still deciding." I shrugged.

"Well, either way, you have a judge in your pocket," he said with a wink. "All it takes is one planted hair to lose a round, so use me."

"You're the absolute worst," I laughed. "Why are you soooooo obsessed with me?"

"Let's just say I like having you around, Morrison. You keep me on my toes. Can't say I've ever had anyone show such pure unadulterated annoyance toward me so quickly before."

"There's plenty more where that came from, just wait," I told him.

"Oh, I plan to," he said with a smile.

Chapter Eleven

The bakery was a bustle of sound as I sat in a corner booth, a half-eaten orange scone on the table in front of me.

"Job experience?" I looked up to see Taylor standing in front of me, a white apron wrapped tight around her waist. She sat down and balanced a clipboard on the edge of the table, making this interview feel a lot more official than I had initially been led to believe. "Sorry for the wait. Yeast emergency."

"Um, no problem," I answered. "And no, no job experience." Not for lack of trying. Dad didn't believe in teenagers with jobs, thought it was drilling capitalism into us before we'd be eternal servants to it anyway.

"That's okay," Taylor said. "Cameron and I had never worked before this job either."

"Don't your parents own the place?" I asked. My eyebrow tilted upward of its own accord.

"Yeah, but the Forresters are hardcore anti–nepo baby. We were on probation for a year and I swear they tried to ride us into the ground. I had to stop doing my nails and everything, just coated with flour and fondant at any given time."

Taylor went on: "We used to live on Braddock, but the rent got outrageous, so when my mom inherited this place from her mom fifteen years ago, we moved to Old Town. But before my mom could even touch this place, my grandma made her go to a legit pastry chef school and everything. Apprenticeships, all of that. And when my mom met my dad, my grandma made him her bitch boy for years. Basically, ran my parents ragged trying to prove themselves. Anyway, that's just the long way of saying not having any experience is totally okay and, in a way, tradition."

I adjusted myself in my seat. Taylor was the only person I'd ever met who could rival Olivia in run-on sentences, but I found myself liking her more the longer she spoke. She didn't seem to care what anyone thought and seemed to say things as soon as they occurred to her. Which was kind of refreshing. Everyone had been tip-toeing around me since Dad died, scared that if they said the wrong thing I'd spiral. But the joke was on them, because I was always spiraling. Nothing anyone said was going to change that.

"I do have baking experience," I offered. For some reason, I really wanted this job. It would give me a wisp of independence. And less time around the house meant less time dodging Mona and her way-too-observant and calculating glances, like she was trying to solve me.

"Oh, I know," Taylor said. "Your lava cake is living rent-free in my head. Like, that ho moved her boxes in and already unpacked. It's so serious."

"Thank you." I found myself blushing, but I still wanted to set reasonable expectations. "But I've never done anything professionally, just hobby baking mostly."

"Don't sell yourself short." Taylor threw the clipboard on the table between us and stood, taking a deep breath. "But the truth of the matter is I've been advised not to hire you under penalty of death."

"Wh-what?" I sputtered. "Then why put me through this interview?"

"Because I wanted to get to know the girl that's got my brother's nose wide open," she said, shrugging. "You can't be in the baking competition if you're an employee here. That's, like, the only rule, remember?"

"This again. Who said I was joining the competition?"

"I did."

I turned to find Cameron ducking out from the kitchen with a shit-eating grin on his face.

"I know you're Miss Antiestablishment, but I think you could rock the competition, and we have one spot left for the first round."

"I already told you I don't want to be in the competition."

"Yes, but sometimes I think I have a gift of knowing people better than they know themselves. And you're just looking for a distraction. This is the perfect one."

I glanced at Taylor, who was giving me a huge smile that bared all her perfectly straight teeth. She nodded at me encouragingly.

"All you have to do is fill out a form," Cameron explained.

Taylor seemed to produce the form out of thin air as she thrust it in front of my face.

"Do you know how to make bread? Because that's round one." She slammed a pen on the table in front of me.

"I thought the first round was cookies?" I looked at Cameron conspiratorially. He responded with a shrug.

"Our parents decided that was too easy. Major bakers—like yourself, of course—need a real challenge."

I gave the heaviest sigh I thought my chest was capable of. "You're not going to let me say no, are you?"

"Absolutely not," the twins said in unison.

I picked up the pen and started filling out the form. It explained that the first round, which started in a week, would have ten contestants; the second round, a month afterward, would have six; and the final round would be in mid-August.

The idea of making bread kind of freaked me out. According to the contest rules, I could do any bread I wanted, which was already an overwhelm of options. Out of all the things I did know how to bake, I'd never tried to master bread. I had basically protest-avoided the Great Sourdough Starter Movement of 2020, and I'd never seen the point. Unlike with other homemade baked goods that were vastly better than store-bought, when it came to bread it was so easy to buy exactly what you wanted from the store. If you've tried one good loaf of rye, you've tried them all.

"I don't know shit about bread."

"That's okay, we'll teach you. Well, Taylor will teach you, I'm mostly the taste-tester." Cameron looked to Taylor. "Right?"

"I guess that's fine. The only *rule* is no employees. Our parents never said anything about friends. Besides, we're not even the judges."

"I thought you were an honorary judge," I said to Cameron smugly.

"Oh yeah, by that I meant I do secondary judging when I eat all the food after the real judges, who are actual professionals, make their decisions."

"You really do just insert yourself into things, huh?"

"Not all things," he said with a wink.

"If I could block a person in real life, you would so be gone," I said with an outward groan. These two were going to be my thirteenth reason.

Cameron held his arm out toward the kitchen. "How do you feel about focaccia?"

Six hours later, I fell into the bed the second I got home. If Taylor ever decided to leave the desserts business, she most absolutely had a career as a drill sergeant in the bag. I had never been directed to do so many things in such a short time. My feet ached with a pain I'd never thought possible. Worse than any race I'd ever run, even the long-distance conditioning ones that Coach made us do. I kicked off my sneakers (definitely the wrong choice this morning) and all the blood rushed from my feet to my head, making my shins tingle.

I opened the nightstand drawer to dig out my phone charger. Mona's journal was stashed in its far corner. I had meant to return it to the box, but I hadn't made it back to the garage. At least that was what I told myself.

I pulled it out and flipped to the last page I had read, smoothing my fingers over the crinkled pages.

Let's just say, nothing has gone to plan. And now I have to go. I really thought my parents would be better than this, that I wouldn't be kicked out of my own home because I never want to be with a man. Like who I choose to love negates every ounce of care my parents ever had for me. I don't know how to believe in their God, one who they think teaches them to hate this way. I don't really know what to do now. T offered to let me crash at his place until I figure it out, but I know he'd be risking a lot with his own parents—as cool as they are, they're going to want to be honest with my parents that I'm staying there and boy, will that cause a rift. We found a shelter, Hawley House, in the city that apparently takes homeless youth that are old enough to not have to go into the system. That might be my only option now.

I reached behind the nightstand to plug in my phone and impatiently waited for it to turn on. It felt like it took a hundred years before the white apple flashed and the lock screen appeared. I typed *Hawley House* into the Google search bar.

I expected to find something dilapidated,

since so much time had gone by since this journal entry. But instead the house reminded me of the one in the original *Casper* movie, except it was painted forest green and had a Pride flag in the front window. According to the Google Street View, an image saved a year ago, it was far from defunct. The address was only thirty-four minutes away by car and nearly an hour on bicycle. I pulled up the step-by-step directions and screenshotted them.

A soft knock sounded on the other side of the door.

"Yes?" I said, quickly shutting the notebook and stuffing it back in the drawer before the door swung open slowly.

Mona stuck her head into the room. Deep circles persisted under her eyes like she'd had a long day at work after little sleep. I didn't blame her; I hadn't been getting much sleep myself.

"You have a second?"

"Um, sure." I shuffled uncomfortably on the bed, hoping Mona wasn't planning to be here long or have much to say. I eyed the drawer like it was a grenade with a missing pin, hoping she wouldn't have any reason to open it and find her diary.

"I just wanted to check on how you're settling in. I know it's a big change."

"I'm fine." I was keeping my responses short and to the point. While I had somewhat adjusted to having to live here, and even sometimes enjoyed it, I wasn't ready to form a relationship with her just yet.

"Okay. Well, I talked to Naomi and she's having your things shipped by the end of the week, so they should be here soon. She said your dad's stuff was going into storage in Austin and we can get it anytime you want. For your things, I figure we can store them in the garage for now and unpack as you feel comfortable. The garage will take a little tidying first, is all."

I shrugged in response. I knew I'd have to get all my things and unpack, but it made the move from Austin feel too final. I really was never going home. I wasn't going to do senior year with Olivia and the track team and even Simone. I wasn't going to go to UT Austin with my precious in-state residency. It felt like everything I had ever dreamed for myself was blowing up and I had no control over any of it.

Mona nodded in answer to my shrug and

clasped her hands in front of her. "I understand this is all really hard on you."

"You understand?"

"Yes, I understand."

"Did you understand when I was the only one without a mother at Donuts with Mom Day at school, or when I had to get ready for my eighth-grade dance by myself? Maybe when Dad brought up YouTube videos to try and help me put in a tampon? Or what about the years I spent questioning why I liked boys and girls and whoever when I had a queer mom right there who could have explained a thing or two?"

It was the most words I'd said to her consecutively and each one burned on its way out of my mouth like I was spitting fire. I hoped she felt scathed, but more than anything, I hoped she heard me. I hoped she felt the full weight of her decision. It wasn't just dishonest, it was cruel.

Mona stiffened but her face remained blank. She was good at hiding her feelings—she never let an emotion show itself that she didn't want anyone to see.

After a pause, she took a deep breath and finally spoke. "Well, I don't want to argue, so I guess I'll go."

She paused at the door before seeming to convince herself not to say whatever was on her mind.

"Have a good night, Skylar." And then she was gone, closing the door tight behind her.

Chapter Twelve

I stared at the dot leading to Hawley House on my phone's GPS as I teetered on my bike at the red light. I'd already been pedaling for half an hour and had quickly learned that track conditioning had absolutely nothing on riding a bike for an hour. My thighs were burning and sweat was settling into the collar of my T-shirt.

I put my head down and kept pedaling, like we were at mile twenty-three and I had to kick it to the finish line. I followed the directions in my AirPods until I finally heard Siri tell me I'd reached my destination.

I stopped and took in the green building across the street, a rainbow flag taped to the inside of a front window, a transgender Pride flag taped to the other. A sign leaning against the stone steps leading up to the door read WHERE ALL ARE WELCOME.

I was moving to cross the street, one foot on the asphalt, when a loud honk sounded from my left. A Nissan Altima zipped past me as I leapt back onto the sidewalk, nearly tripping over my bike.

"Everyone in this town is always in such a hurry," I muttered under my breath.

"Isn't it the worst?"

I yelped at the sudden intrusion. Clare, the girl from the skate park, broke into a giggle that sounded like marbles in a flower vase.

"Sorry," she laughed, clearing her throat to cut off her laughter like a root ripped from the dirt. "You really are jumpy, aren't you. What are you doing here?"

I pressed my hand to my forehead, coming down from first being nearly run over and then being startled by Clare's sudden presence. "Jesus, Clare. Warn somebody."

"I said sorry." Clare rolled her eyes with mirth, her irises narrowing like a cat's in sunlight. She shook her head as she waited for a red light and then led me past the stopped cars toward the shelter's front steps. "Again, what are you doing here? Did you know I lived here?"

"You live here?" I asked, wondering what she was doing living at a homeless shelter for teens. But I didn't have the nerve to ask—it was the kind of information that had to be volunteered.

"For now," she said, not elaborating.

"Oh, okay. Well, this is purely coincidence," I told her. "I read about this place and wanted to check it out."

"Read about it where?" Her eyebrows quirked up toward her hairline.

"Oh, it was just in a book I found around the house." I didn't know if she'd judge me for reading Mona's journal so I kept that under lock and key.

"Sure." She shrugged, leading me up to the front door. She barely leaned on it before it swung open.

"Y'all don't lock doors around here?" I questioned, following her inside the gaping foyer. An oak staircase faced the door, with shoes and backpacks lined up near the bottom. The place smelled like lavender. Despite its purpose being rather somber, something about the house felt happy, warm, even though it was quiet enough to hear a pin drop.

"Not during the day," Clare answered. I followed her through the house and into the kitchen. "Ma likes to make sure anyone who needs this place can find it without too much trouble. It kind of leaves us open to getting sprung upon, I guess, but better to make sure we're a resource than run scared of our mission. At least that's how Ma sees it."

"Your mom runs this place?" I asked as Clare pulled ingredients from the refrigerator.

"No." Clare laughed. "As much as I wish. Ma is like"—she considered her next words for a moment—"a house mother, I guess. Like an RA but old. For a lot of us, she's the only mother we've got, though. Calling her Ma is how we show our respect."

"Cool." I leaned my elbows on the large kitchen island, all the cabinetry the same shade of green as the building, but faded in most places so that you could see the wood peeking out from beneath the paint.

"Do people tend to head out during the day?" I asked, noticing how quiet it was. Based on the number of shoes by the staircase, this place should be full of raucous teenagers, but it was giving library.

"Usually. Most everyone has a job so we can contribute to groceries and stuff. Ma gets a stipend from the government, but it only covers a few of us on a good day."

"How many of you are there?" I took the eggs Clare nudged in my direction as she rifled through the fridge.

"It fluctuates every day. Some people go back home, some find their own spot. I think right now there are ten of us, but hey, that could change by dinnertime."

"And we're making?" I found myself asking a lot of questions. I'd heard of places like this but had never been to one. I was always lucky that Dad hadn't batted an eye when I told him I was bi. I couldn't imagine having to leave home because of the person I loved. For a moment, I wondered what it was like for Mona. She hadn't mentioned any other family and I hadn't seen any hints that she was in touch with anyone outside of the people who lived in their house. Dad certainly never mentioned any grandparents on my mother's side, and for reasons that had never been explained to me, Dad hadn't spoken to his parents for at least the entirety of my life.

"I don't know yet." Clare struggled to peel the silver wrapping from a can of whipped frosting. "Ma's birthday dinner is tonight and I was voluntold to make the cake, but like I told you before, ya girl does not cook, bake, grow my own vegetables. None of that. I microwave and I toaster oven."

"Have you tried an air fryer?"

"What's an air fryer?" she asked.

"Girl..." I didn't really know how to respond to that. Who didn't know what an air fryer was in the year 2026?

"Mi-cro-wave," she enunciated. "That's all I do and that's all I'm gonna do."

"You don't cook, you don't clean, I hear that."

"No, I do clean, though. It's relaxing. Taking something dirty and making it shiny and new? That's my shit."

"Then if you put us together we'd be the perfect housewife, because I throw down in the kitchen but I'll die before I mop."

"You're tripping. I could get high off some fresh Fabuloso. Would put it in my bathwater if it wouldn't fry my skin clean off."

"Okay," I laughed, watching in amusement as she put an assortment of ingredients on the counter that would be truly horrendous if combined. "Did you look up any ideas?" I asked. "There's an app where you can add in all the ingredients you have on hand and it'll come up with a recipe. It's a part of ChatGPT but I think we can be forgiven for some water use because this looks like an emergency."

"You just said a lot of words I'm not even sure are real. Chat-what?"

"Yeah, I hate it too. Awful for the environment. Maybe we should just brainstorm." I glanced over the array, combining ingredients in my head to try and come up with something that would be delicious and not terribly onerous to make.

"Oh!" I shrieked when it came to me. "You have everything you need for strawberry shortcake." I pulled the sugar, eggs, salt, flour, baking powder, milk, vanilla extract, and strawberries. "Do you have heavy whipping cream and shortening?"

"Uh…" Her eyebrows scrunched together. She had no idea what I had just asked for.

"Pantry?"

She pointed to an almost hidden door in the cabinetry. The place was surprisingly well stocked, but there was no shortening. And a deep dive into the fridge revealed no heavy whipping cream either. I could still make a good cake without them, but they really were the fastest way to get a good icing. While searching, Clare had opened a bag of chocolate chips and grabbed a handful.

"I can try the corner store," she offered with a full mouth.

"That would be great."

Clare nodded and then gathered up her wallet and JanSport backpack.

"If I'm not back in twenty minutes, call the police."

"Fat chance," I said. We exchanged a knowing glance, both aware that the only time you called the police was if someone was already dead, before getting the hell out of Dodge so you didn't end up joining them.

While Clare was gone, I started mixing the dry ingredients into a bowl, hoping she wouldn't take too long. There wasn't much I could do without the shortening. Sponge cake was simple, but it took a perfect alchemy of ingredients or it tasted like a dish sponge and felt like one too. Luckily, Clare was back in half the time promised, but with way more than I sent her out for.

"Okay, so I got the stuff. And I also got us snackage for while the cake stuff is percolating."

She dumped everything onto the countertop and out rolled every type of Utz chip ever made.

"The cashier has a thing for me, so most of this was basically free on the mere promise that I would one day consider going out with him. Poor baby. I don't swing anywhere near his way," she said. "But he's cute, objectively. Maybe for you?"

"No, thank you." Cameron immediately came to mind and it must have shown all over my face.

"Oh, you got someone already?"

"I do not." I tried to drop my head low enough to hide the smile I knew was spreading.

"Look at you! Tell me all about them."

"It's literally no one. And didn't you say this cake needed to be finished ASAP?" I grabbed the rest of the ingredients, focusing on combining them, mixing in the dry ingredients as I poured in the milk.

"Mmm, changing the subject, my girl is in L-O-V-E," she sang.

"You're so obnoxious." I grabbed two cake pans from a lower cabinet.

She laughed and watched as I worked through the recipe in my head, one I had made dozens of times.

"You're good at this," Clare said as she crunched on the cheesy Utz Chex–type mix.

"Baking is about precision," I told her as I poured the batter into the pans. "Precision and patience." Both things that I wished applied to more in life. I'd had too many surprises lately.

"Two things I was not blessed with."

"Me either. But I had pretty bad ADHD as a kid, or I guess I still have pretty bad ADHD and it's just managed well. But my dad wanted to get me into something that I could focus my mind on. He'd heard that baking was good for that sort of thing, and the second he introduced me to it, I was in. Granted, he couldn't even bake a cake from a box so how he led me to this, I have no idea. But I was—*am* good at it. I guess we're attracted to the things that make us feel like we have something to offer. Something we can control."

I used a rubber spatula to scrape the rest of

the batter into the pans before sliding them into the preheated oven behind her.

"And that's how you make strawberry shortcake. Or at least the cake part." Cutting the strawberries was probably my least-favorite part because it could be so tedious. But it always resulted in the prettiest and easiest cake one could work on.

"Ta-da," Clare sang, handing me the bag of chips. It was already nearly empty.

"Ta-da," I laughed, taking a deep breath to lessen the pressure that seemed to hover over my heart. Since making the lava cake, I hadn't really even *wanted* to bake much, which was part of the reason I had been so hesitant about the competition. I'd shared so much of my baking with Dad, I wasn't sure I could love it the same without him.

"And happy birthday, Ma."

Chapter Thirteen

"Do you know the stages of grief?" Diana asked me.

"There are stages?" I asked, surprised. It all just seemed like one big clusterfuck of Suck. "How many?"

"Five," Diana answered.

"Oh, well, no." I sat up now, having actually become the kind of patient who *did* lie down on the obnoxiously comfortable futon couch. I bet she would even let me really sleep on it if I wanted to.

"First is denial, have you felt that?" she asked.

"Like denying Dad is dead? I don't know. I mean, sometimes I sit and I think it can't possibly be true. That any second my phone is going to ring and it's going to be him and he'll tell me he needed a breather or something and I'll be so happy he's alive that I won't even be mad at him."

"That's interesting," she said.

"I hate when you call something interesting." Every time she said it, Diana wanted to dig deeper. And digging deeper always made me cry. We hadn't had a session yet that didn't leave me in tears.

"I'm sorry, I know." She smiled. "But I do find it interesting that you said you wouldn't be mad at him for letting you think he was gone if he were actually alive because you'd be too happy he was, indeed, alive."

"Did I say that?"

"You did." She nodded. "Do you think that's ironic?"

"What's ironic?"

"That finding out your dad was alive after thinking he was dead would be such a relief you would forget all about the lie. How would you apply that to your situation with Mona?"

"They're not the same thing," I said.

Her head tilted to the side. "They're not?"

"Of course not," I insisted.

"How so?"

"Well, I actually knew and loved my dad. I would obviously rather have him back no matter the circumstances."

"But you would have preferred Mona to, in some sense, stay dead."

"Yes."

"Oh?"

"I mean, no, I wouldn't want someone to be dead who isn't dead. You know what I mean."

"I've got to admit, Sky, I'm really not sure that I do."

"If my dad died, it wouldn't be because he wanted to leave me. In fact, the only thing I feel pretty certain about is that my dad did not want to leave me. He would have hated dying, I'm sure he *did* hate dying. But Mona 'died' so that she could leave me. Those are different things."

"So I'm going to rephrase and you tell me if I've got it right. You would be relieved that your dad was really alive because you know he wanted to be with you. But you wouldn't be, or aren't, relieved that Mona is really alive because you know—or rather, I'll use the word *think*—she didn't want to be with you."

"Yes."

"Okay, so what if you also know that Mona

wants to be with you? Do you feel the relief then?"

"No."

"No?"

"No, because she doesn't."

"Have you asked her?"

"Asked her what?"

"Why she left? Why she maintained this lie for so long? Anything?"

"No."

Diana leaned back in her chair triumphantly. "Well then, I think we just figured out your homework."

"You want me to ask Mona why she left?"

"I want you to talk to her. I don't care what it's about. You can ask her what her favorite breakfast cereal is if it'll get a conversation started. I think these questions will answer themselves, once you two get the ball rolling."

"And if the truth is she really didn't want me?"

"Then you can say 'I told you so,' " she said. "But I have a hunch that's not the case."

As usual, Cameron was waiting at the curb when I got out of my session. Once I had climbed in,

I slammed the door in frustration, crossing my arms as I leaned back into my seat.

"Ah, what wound has Diana reopened today?"

"Is she always like that?" I asked him as he pulled into traffic.

"Cut right to the white meat, huh?"

"Yes. I hate it."

"That's why they pay her the big bucks."

"Is she expensive?" I wondered.

"Very." He snorted. "You got some expensive-ass trauma, sunshine."

"Apparently, so do you. You never did tell me why you're seeing her too."

He tapped his hand against the steering wheel, clenching his lips together.

"You're really never going to tell me?" Part of me was a little offended and another part was concerned. How bad could it be that he really couldn't tell me why he was in therapy?

"Let's just say I kind of lost someone, not really, but only kind of."

"Like a friend? Did you get dumped?"

"Excuse you, I have never been dumped."

"I find that extremely hard to believe."

"Ah, see," he said. "Why crush on someone who will crush back when I can have zesty disdain?"

It didn't surprise me that he had a crush on me—he had made it pretty damn obvious—but it did surprise me that he would be so forthcoming about it.

"This is when you say, 'Cameron, I'm so madly in love with you too,' and give me a big kiss on the cheek."

"Tell me, when you plotted this conversation out with your Barbie dolls, did they tell you that you're a deeply unserious person?"

"Only Skipper."

"I hate you."

"You love me."

I rolled my eyes but turned sideways and looked out the window so he couldn't clock the smile spreading across my face like honey.

Chapter Fourteen

The baking competition hadn't started yet, but the room already smelled like dough. Cam and Taylor's parents had rented a large warehouse in Springfield that was just a twenty-minute bike ride from their house. The room was massive, with individual baking stations spread throughout and a judges' table at the front. Along the back sat a large section of chairs on risers for spectators, which was already starting to fill in. A local television crew huddled in a corner. This thing was going to be way bigger than I'd thought. I smoothed my hands over my braids, suddenly self-conscious that I was going to be on camera.

"You made it!" Taylor squealed as she gave me a tight hug. She smelled like jasmine and snickerdoodle cookies. She shared Cameron's high cheekbones and catlike eyes, which made her face look beautiful in an interesting way. Where Cameron was muscle, she was soft.

"Told you I would," I responded. "I didn't realize this was being televised."

"Oh, don't worry about it. It's basically a local PBS no one watches except for, like, the people at the nursing home who have no choice in television stations. But I can't wait for you to meet our parents, officially."

"Yeah, I thought I would have met them by now. They haven't stopped by the bakery while I've been there and they don't seem to ever be home."

"Small business owners," she said with an eye roll. "They're pretty busy. Getting new sponsors, vending at some conference or festival. Consummate entrepreneurs, you know."

"They're where the money resides. I get it." I was used to having a parent who seemed all over the place, constantly hustling to make the dream happen and support us at the same time. Dad was always headed some place or other, except he brought me along with him as often as he could, unless I had school or track.

"Well, today should be pretty straightforward. We start in about"—she looked at the Apple Watch on her wrist—"fifteen minutes. You'll be assigned a station, which will remain yours as long as you're in the competition, so you can stash anything you'll need. We have provided all the basics, courtesy of Williams Sonoma and A Cupcake a Day, so top of the line. Hopefully that's good enough for our *GBBO* enthusiasts. The first round, as you know, is bread. You can make any bread you'd like, it just has to be perfect. Four people get eliminated this round, so if you can make your bread something special or one that's especially hard to do"—she winked at me, knowing we'd practiced all week on some of the toughest breads to make—"that'll go pretty far in the points."

"Got it. Make special bread."

I glanced around the room, looking for a familiar face.

"Cameron will be here soon." Taylor gave me a knowing look that made me grateful for my dark complexion so she couldn't see my cheeks heat up.

"Aren't they going to tell us all this in the introduction or something?" I tried to remember how these cooking shows often went on TV. It seemed like in every episode they were explaining the premise and reward as if someone had jumped into episode 11 with no idea what was going on.

"Yeah," Taylor said, shrugging, "but now you can ignore them and size up your competition. Get settled at a station that you think you'll be happy with for the next month. I suggest something near the back left corner if you're camera-shy. I have a feeling you'll be sticking around for a while." With that, she patted me on the shoulder before scurrying off to greet another contestant.

"Nervous?" a voice asked behind me.

I let out a deep breath, recognizing the voice immediately. I decided not to acknowledge the calming effect it had on my tense shoulders, which lowered in relief.

Cameron was smiling at me when I turned around, his hands hidden behind his back.

"I got you something," he told me with a conspiratorial half smile that only raised one side of his face. A dimple appeared, and I felt the urge to put the tip of my finger into it, but I didn't, because that would be *totally* weird.

"Little old me?" I joked.

He brought his hands from behind his back to reveal an apron with small daffodils embroidered all over it. "I don't know why, but it immediately made me think of you."

"That's actually really sweet, Cam." I took the apron from him, running my fingers over the embroidery.

"They seem happy, right?" he asked.

"They do seem happy. Do I seem happy to you? Is that why you call me *sunshine*?"

"I don't know. You make me happy, though." He bowed his head to hide his smile.

I cleared my throat, suddenly feeling way too warm in this room. I had joked a little too close to the sun. "I'm going to get some fresh air before we start, but I really do appreciate this."

I gave him an awkward hug before rushing out the double back doors. As per usual, the air was thick with humidity. I took a deep breath that felt like swallowing quicksand, heat sticking heavy to my tongue.

A shrill bell, the five-minute warning, sounded

from inside. I made my way back in and slipped around the edges of the room to avoid other contestants rushing to their stations. There was only one free, far in the back left of the room as Taylor had suggested. Someone had already put my duffel bag on the work surface, and I was immediately thankful. I looked over at the spectators and Cam and Taylor waved at me enthusiastically. I hadn't told Gaby or Mona that I was doing this, so it didn't surprise me not to see them. But an emptiness filled me up at not seeing the pair of eyes I'd always searched for whenever I had a big moment—track meet, awards ceremony, now baking competition. I knew Dad would have been here in the front row if he could have been. I wasn't sure if I'd ever really believed in the power of prayer, and that relationship felt especially tenuous now, but I still whispered a short message to Dad asking that he be with me through this in any way he could. Baking always made me feel closer to him.

Microphone feedback filled the cavernous space and echoed around the walls. Someone who looked like she could have spit Cam and Taylor out stood at the front of the room before the judges' table, behind which were now seated three individuals who looked both serious and sweet, like Sour Patch Kids.

"Welcome, everyone," she said. Her voice was soft, reminding me of baby powder. "Many of you may know me, but for those who don't, I'm Veronica Forrester, the co-owner of A Cupcake a Day, which I run with my husband, as well as our two children, Cameron and Taylor." Taylor stood and gave a flourish of a wave, while Cam simply nodded in acknowledgment. A man who looked like the blueprint for Cam's and Taylor's faces, standing in a corner of the room as far from the cameras as one could get, gave a shy smile. Veronica Forrester went on: "We're so honored that you have signed up to be a part of this year's competition, the prize of which is a two-month residency at a Parisian pastry school."

A round of applause went around the room.

"The first round is bread. You will all show us your absolute best skills in both baking and design. All of your judges have seen bread before, so make sure you're giving us something special. You will have three hours to complete this round." She pointed to a countdown clock on the back wall. "Starting promptly at twelve o'clock. By three o'clock, you should have your bread ready and staged for judging. Anyone without a bread staged on time will be immediately eliminated. And with that, time starts"—she glanced at her watch—"now." The timer started ticking down.

I knew that focaccia, if I did it right, would be the best choice, but making focaccia in three hours was risky. A perfect dough would take days to proof, and I only had an hour or two. But it was the recipe I'd perfected over the past week with Taylor and it should come out okay, even if the dough didn't get as airy as I would like. I was suddenly incredibly thankful for her, as we'd tested proofing in all types of conditions and different time periods. She'd probably had an inside scoop on how much time the contestants would be given and had prepared me for that. I wasn't totally sure if that would be considered cheating, but right now, I didn't care. I was not going to look a gift horse in the mouth.

I began mixing my ingredients for the dough. I worked as fast as I could because I needed to give the dough as much time to proof as possible. Many of the other contestants mingled as they waited. As I was the youngest by a pretty big margin of years, no one really came to talk to me, though an older woman with a strong Jamaican accent, from what I could hear across the room, would catch my eye every so often and send me a warm smile. Even Cameron and Taylor remained in their seats, probably so it didn't look like there was any favoritism by the Forrester children, even though neither they nor their parents were judges.

The crowd started to trickle out as the exciting start to the competion died down. I considered leaving, too, to call Olivia while I waited on the dough, but I was nervous someone would try to sabotage me while I was gone. I was getting some pretty serious glares from some of the other competitors, and even though cameras were set up around the room, I was also too risk averse to be trusting. I slid down to the floor and sat criss-cross applesauce in front of my proofer, scrolling through TikTok as I waited.

"You sure are young to bake with so much confidence."

I looked up to find the older woman standing beside me. Before I could respond, she had already stooped low to the floor to sit.

"How old *are* you?" she asked.

"Um, sixteen," I answered. I wasn't quite

sure how to continue the conversation, since I couldn't ask her how old she was. I wasn't sure at what age that became inappropriate, but I was sure that she had passed it.

"Goodness, my youngest granddaughter is sixteen. The time sure does fly." She nodded to herself like she was acknowledging the memories she'd just summoned. "I'm Angela."

"Skylar," I offered.

"You been baking a long time?"

"Kind of. Six or seven years."

"I'm sure that's a lot longer for you than it is for me." She laughed. "But good on you. I wish I'd chased my dream when I was your age."

"What was your dream?" I asked her.

She laughed again. "What *wasn't* my dream? I wanted to be an astronaut and a college professor and a circus performer and a snake charmer. Always had my head in the clouds, my mother would say."

"Did you do any of them?"

"Oh no, sweetie." She reached for my hand and patted it. "I got married, had some kids, chased new dreams, I guess. Got every single one off to college and then some."

"Do you regret it? Not becoming an astronaut?"

"Nope," she said. "Sometimes people think all parents do is sacrifice, sacrifice, sacrifice, but really, I felt like I got a new life with my children. Whatever I was before, I became something far greater. Had a pride in them unmatched by any pride I ever had in anything on my own. Hell, I'm sure your parents are quite proud of you for doing this today."

I hadn't cried in days, and I had started to think that maybe I was over that part of the grieving process. But her words conjured tears immediately, and they filled my eyes as I tried to blink them away.

"Oh, honey," the woman said. "Come here." She grabbed my hands and pulled me to my feet and then into a hug. "What's the matter?"

"My parents don't know I'm here," I said into her shoulder, unsure if she could even hear me.

"That's okay," she said. "That's okay."

I pulled away and pressed the heels of my hands into my eyes, trying to suppress any new tears, especially since my dough was probably done proofing. I needed to get moving and I was sure this lady did too. I was surprised she'd already spent so much of the allotted time with me.

She cupped my face in her palms. "It's something deeper in there."

"My dad just died," I told her. "I used to bake mostly just for him."

"Well, I'm sure he's still proud of you, and he's here all in this room, all in your hands and your heart. Looking down, mouth watering." That finally drew a smile because his mouth definitely would be watering; it smelled amazing in here. "So you make him something good, okay?"

I took a deep breath to steady myself. "Okay." I nodded.

"Good girl," she said before patting my cheeks and hurrying back to her station. I leaned my hands against my countertop and took three breaths before pulling my dough from the proofer. I glanced up to see Cameron give me a questioning thumbs-up. I gave him a thumbs-up in return and got back to work.

I poured olive oil into the bottom of a pan, dropped the dough in, and waited another hour for the dough to flatten naturally. I glanced at the clock; less than forty-five minutes to get this done. A sweat broke out along my neck and forehead. Other than practicing with Taylor, when the stakes had been making bread faster than

Cam could eat it, I'd never been timed while baking before and I definitely didn't like it. There was no chance to second-guess myself or double-check that I was doing something right. But the fact that other contestants already had their bread in their ovens was making me nervous.

Once I was done dimpling and placing my rosemary in a wreath shape on the dough, I immediately put it into my preheated oven. It should only take twenty minutes, which would give me plenty of time, but my chest was starting to hurt with worry.

"Come on, little focaccia, you can do it," I told the bread encouragingly. Like a watched pot never boiling, watched bread never rises, but I couldn't take my eyes off it. My nose was practically pressed to the glass.

With twenty minutes left, all across the room, bread was coming out of the oven. The room smelled like heaven, but I felt like I was in hell as I watched everyone plate their bread. I shot a worried glance over to Cameron and Taylor, who gave me identical thumbs-ups. Apparently they didn't think I was screwing this up, but I could feel in my bones that I was. *Farewell, trip to Paris. Farewell, pride.*

Finally my timer went off and I was happy with what I could see through the tinted glass, so I took my bread out of the oven and set it on a cooling rack. It could be a little better browned, but I was okay with it. My butter knife made a satisfying scraping sound as I ran it along the top of the bread. With three minutes left, I transferred the bread from the cooling rack to a nice rectangular porcelain plate and placed a couple of sprigs of rosemary on top. The wreath design was a little wonky but still kind of beautiful.

The clock let out an obnoxious buzzing sound when time was up. Everyone had managed to get their bread plated. I held a breath in my chest until I felt like my lungs were going to explode. In fact, I didn't think I breathed the entire time the judges were making their way around the room, cutting into the fresh bread and taking bites. I couldn't hear their commentary and tried to read the tea leaves of their expressions, the tilt of their smiles, whether their eyes seemed satisfied or disappointed.

I almost blacked out when it was my turn to be judged. Taylor leaned forward, trying to hear, but I doubted it was any use. The sound of the overhead fans cooling off the room filled up all the empty space.

One of the judges knocked her knuckles against the top of my bread to check the crust. When they cut into it, it looked like I'd hoped it would, airy and light, though I didn't know how dense it would feel when they bit into it. I was pretty confident it wasn't overproofed, since I'd barely had time to proof it at all, but I was nervous it could be underproofed. And if it was underproofed, it would be too dense and the flavor wouldn't be there.

The older male judge nodded as he took a bite and let out a small sound that I convinced myself was one of disgust. The woman's face was unreadable as she made a note in her notepad. The younger male gave me a small smile before setting the rest of his slice down on the plate. Yep, I was done for.

As I was the last one to be judged, in order of the workstations, the judges returned to their table when they were done with my focaccia. It took them twenty minutes to deliberate before they lined everyone up at the front of the room. My head was practically buzzing.

The woman spoke first. "Thank you all so much for the effort you put into today's challenge. We can honestly say that every single one of you put your best foot forward. We are so incredibly impressed with your clear talent. Which makes this the hardest part of our job as judges, because all of you truly deserve to be here and participate in this year's competition."

The older man went next. "Because there are only three rounds in the competition, we unfortunately have to make some big cuts at this stage, so four of you will be leaving us this afternoon. Please do not take elimination to mean you lack talent. Again, as Joanne said, we are very impressed, and I wish I could eat all of your delicious breads all over again."

"With that said," put in the younger man, who seemed to be the most about his business despite being the youngest and the only one who gave me a smile when judging, "we will now announce who will be leaving the competition." He gave each of us a look before he flipped the page on his notebook and began reading off a list. "The contestants we will be saying goodbye to are"—he paused and looked directly into the camera that zoomed in on his face—"Tyra

Cunningham, Kelsey Benjamin, Gregory Lipner, and Meredith Cho."

There was a collective release of breath by the six remaining contestants.

I made it.

I survived the first round. I looked down the row and exchanged a smile with Angela, who pressed a hand to her heart and bowed her head to me. I spotted Cameron in the crowd, giving me one of his biggest smiles and clapping like he'd just found out he'd won the lottery. He took Taylor by the shoulders and shook her like a snow globe.

"Congratulations to everyone who has advanced to the second round," the woman said after the eliminated contestants said their goodbyes. The room felt a hundred times emptier now that they were gone. "Until next time, get lots of rest and we'll see you in one month."

The judges departed, leaving the rest of the contestants to clean up their stations. This was my least-favorite part of baking: cleaning up. But it was a ritualistic part of the process, and sometimes, like now, I relished the time it allowed me to quiet my mind.

"And she made it." Cameron stood in front

of me with his hands around his mouth like an announcer.

"Probably only thanks to you and Taylor."

"And I will take that. Though I suck at bread so it was really Taylor."

"You were a great taste-tester. Any hints on the next round?" I asked him as he ripped off a piece of my bread.

"Now, sunshine, are you trying to pick my brain for an unfair advantage?" He closed his eyes as he chewed. "This is some good focaccia."

"Thank you," I laughed. "And no. I'm going to win this thing fair and square."

"Oh, so now you want to win?"

"Well, I didn't come here to lose."

"Okay, Jimmy Wayne."

"Who?"

He groaned. "Early-aughts country music was wasted on the youth."

"You are the youth in question," I reminded him.

"Yeah, but I'm wise beyond my years."

I untied my daffodil apron and hung it on the stove handle of my station so the folks doing setup and breakdown would know which one was mine and I wouldn't have to lug my KitchenAid back and forth. I was surprised at how permanent leaving my mixer and new apron felt, like I was putting my stamp on this place. Not just this room, but Virginia in general. Like I was starting to put down roots that I'd never imagined planting.

"Let's get some pizza, kid," Cam said, tossing his arm over my shoulder.

"Do you eat anything but carbs?" I asked, letting him pull me toward him.

"Absolutely not," he laughed. "Absolutely not."

Chapter Fifteen

A stack of boxes was taking over the living room when I got home and collapsed onto the couch. Normally I avoided the common spaces for fear of running into Mona, but the house seemed pretty quiet. Baking didn't typically wear me out so much and it was only a few hours, but this was the tensest I'd ever been. Although my muscles were delighted at finally sitting down for a minute, too much energy was pent up in my body. All I wanted to do was run. But first I had to talk myself into getting my muscles off the couch and up the stairs. I didn't know how I was going to do the next round of the competition in a few weeks—my limbs felt like they'd be Jell-O forever.

It took some time to dig out my sneakers, a pair of socks, and some shorts. I didn't think too much about where I would be running and just dropped a pin for the house so that I could eventually find my way back. Then I took off, letting the ache in my legs carry me forward. The best thing about running alone was that it was just me against myself. The only person I had to beat was the one inside my head. I didn't know if I was running away from something or toward something. I didn't notice I was crying until I realized the moisture I was licking off my lips wasn't sweat. It felt good, though, to let everything go. Finally I could focus on the pain in my body and not just in my heart.

By the time I got back to the house, the sun was already starting to set, making the house feel much cooler and less like the inside of a washing machine. The oversized boxes were still taking up most of the living room. I leaned toward one to find my name listed on the address panel. My boxes from home. I wished I'd been there for the packing so I could have snuck some of Dad's stuff in before it got loaded into storage.

I ripped into the first box to find Dad's records lined up. Naomi was thorough, which meant if she'd included these, she had done it intentionally. I could have given her a hug right then and there. She knew how much these would mean to me, and even from so far away, it was nice to be known. I dragged box after box from the stack and kept ripping them open until I found the one with his record player, knowing Naomi wouldn't have sent his records with no way to listen to them. Pushing the couch away from the wall, I found an unused outlet. I unwrapped the record player's cord and plugged it in. Then I shuffled through the records until I found my favorite one—Whitney Houston.

I set the record player on the floor, put the vinyl on the turntable, and carefully dropped the needle. Whitney filled the room, and the song immediately made my bones vibrate with the kind of calm one can only find at the other end of her voice. The soreness rippling through my body suddenly seemed fuzzy and so far away, like listening to someone speak from the bottom of a pool. I lay down on the floor, placing my head right against the side of the record player so that I could feel the music's vibrations through my skull. I used to lay my head right next to

Dad's, letting his humming along lull me to sleep. I missed him more than I ever had, in that moment as I listened to his music alone. A tear slid down the side of my face and settled into the carpet.

Grief was a hard and unrelenting thing, ever present but ebbing and flowing. Some days felt impossible and others I hardly thought about Dad at all. Those were the ones that filled me with the most guilt, as I imagined those days turning into weeks and then months until he was pushed far enough back to not matter so much. It scared me. But then, just when I thought I'd started to move on, it hit me again like a ton of bricks that he was gone forever. That our last text would always be our last text. That I wouldn't wake up in the morning to a ton of TikToks he'd found during a sleepless night. That he'd sent too many silly videos and I had stopped responding, and now I wished more than anything that I had just taken a moment to open and laugh at every one so he knew how much I loved him. I thought that was the hardest thing—did he know how much I loved him? Did he know how hard it would be to lose him?

"Skylar?" Mona stood over me, bringing her face into my line of vision.

I blinked back the rest of my tears, sniffing so I could swallow them.

"Are you okay?" Mona asked.

"I'm fine," I told her, sitting up.

"Okay," Mona said uncomfortably. We still hadn't learned how to just be around each other, though part of that was because I didn't give us much time in the same room together. "Your stuff got here," she said, pointing out the obvious.

"I'll unpack it as fast as I can so you can get your living room back," I told her. I hugged my knees to my chest as tightly as I could. Whitney filled the quiet space between us.

"Oh, don't worry about it," Mona said with a wave of her hand. "There's no rush."

She reached into one of the boxes and pulled out a record with a smile. Three 6 Mafia. "I remember the day he got this at the record store. We were, gosh, sixteen maybe? Right before my parents kicked me out of the house."

This perked my entire body up. "Your parents kicked you out of the house?" I remembered her mentioning something like that in her journal, but I never imagined that it was a full-on expulsion from her home. She must have ended up living at Hawley House after all.

Mona blew air through her nose. "Yeah, practically my seventeenth-birthday present. They found out I was gay and let's just say it didn't go over well."

I swallowed, once again grateful for having been raised by a guy like Dad. "What did you do?"

Mona cleared her throat. "I married your father."

"As, like, a solution?" Was this the part of the story that no one had bothered to tell me yet? Why would she marry Dad when she already knew she was a lesbian?

"We weren't really thinking it all the way through. I was scared to be on my own and your dad had a compulsion for getting me out of bad situations. And we thought if we got married, we would have more control over the situation. They let married folks do a lot of things they don't necessarily let dependent kids do. I don't know, we weren't being very smart. But the day we got this record was the first time we talked about maybe telling my parents I was gay. My folks were pretty religious, did everything by the

Good Book. It took me years to unlearn their version of Christianity."

"So it was a God thing?"

"For them it was. I think they thought they were setting a good example by forcing me into being a God-fearing woman. They wanted me to have all the things they didn't, and they couldn't see a prosperous future for me if I was gay."

"I bet you hated them."

"I did for a while. I don't anymore. Lots of therapy, thank goodness. I certainly struggle to forgive them for the years of self-hatred they instilled in me. I think I married your father partly to get away but also because I thought it maybe could work. Maybe I could ignore who I really was and build a family with a good man, maybe then they would accept me."

We were getting into dangerous territory. At some point we would have to talk about why she left, but I wasn't ready for that conversation now. Maybe like Mona was with her parents, I wasn't ready to forgive her and Dad yet either. Maybe I never would be.

"I'm going to take these upstairs," I told Mona, gesturing to the box in front of us still filled with records.

"Oh yeah, okay." Mona gave me a small smile. One of her front teeth was chipped, but it gave her smile character.

I hauled the box up the stairs, still listening to Whitney as the record played downstairs until the needle was moved off the vinyl. I dumped the records out on my bed, looking over Dad's collection. Music was to Dad what oxygen was to lush forests—so requisite as to be life-giving. The records were pristine, and I knew it was not because Naomi had dusted them when she packed them. While they could get a little dusty if he didn't listen to some for a while, the cases were all in excellent condition, a tough task for a collection of over two hundred records kept meticulously in alphabetical order no matter how many times they had been played. To Dad, it was all about respect. Respect the music, in any way it came. Because music was the only thing in the world that gave you everything and took nothing in return. I held my breath and counted to ten as grief built in my chest.

I re-sorted the records into alphabetical order, stacking them up in the closet. I would have to get milk crates or something for them, but this would do for now.

My phone vibrated in the thigh pocket of my leggings. I nearly let myself fall into the bed with it before I realized I hadn't showered yet and I was covered in flour and sweat. So I lay on the floor instead, thinking about how much time I had spent today on the floor.

A FaceTime request popped up on my screen and I answered before I checked to see who it was, assuming it was Olivia. She was the only person who ever FaceTimed me. But instead, Cameron's face filled the screen. I saw my own reflection in the irises of his brown eyes and it did not look pretty. *Haggard* was probably the best word.

"Hey," he said, smiling into the camera. "You busy?"

"I mean, I am planning to take the longest nap in history," I told him.

"I think that's called a coma." He laughed.

"What do you want, Cam?"

"I was wondering if you wanted to hang out."

"We were just together. Aren't you sick of me yet?"

"Never."

"Who all's going? You, me, and Taylor?" I asked.

"No, just you and me."

It was starting to sound suspiciously like a date. Was I ready for that?

It was a bad idea to have feelings for Cameron. For one, we were next-door neighbors and if shit went left, it would make living here even more awkward and Taylor would be sure to give me hell. For two, I was definitely not emotionally ready to date someone, my trust issues were crazy, and, again, I was a little afraid of his sister. So I guess I had five reasons, really, why it was a bad idea. But then there was the fact that it was Cameron, and despite trying to fight it, there was something about him that made me want to know him better. Like the way he was smiling at me now, and how it reached his eyes and practically made them glow the most beautiful brown ever found in nature. Crayola should bottle it and sell it in a carton with nothing but that shade of brown.

"Sure," I found myself saying.

"Great, I'll pick you up in ten minutes."

"Wait, you want to go right now?"

"When did you expect?"

"Well, I don't know, next weekend or something."

"Do you have something to do between now and next weekend that will make it hard to see each other?"

"You know I don't." I never had anything going on. He knew that.

"Cool, so ten minutes?"

"What are we going to do?"

"Do you want me to ruin the surprise?"

"Fine," I grumbled. "I'll see you in ten minutes." I hung up and looked down at my outfit. I was still wearing my workout clothes, which were under a layer of perspiration and cake ingredients.

I hopped into the walk-in for the quickest and most efficient shower known to man, clocking four minutes to wash and rinse my entire body. It would have to do for now. None of my nice clothes were easily accessible, probably in the myriad of boxes downstairs. But Cameron had seen me every day—he knew I lived in joggers and tank tops. I pulled on my nicest Nike pair and a Lululemon top. It was the best I could do, and maybe this would set good expectations. If I tried too hard, he might actually get some ideas, and my goal tonight should be to dissuade him from chasing after my emotionally unavailable ass.

“Welp,” I told myself in the bathroom mirror, “here goes nothing.”

A knock sounded on the front door and I listened as Mona exchanged pleasantries and updates with Cam like old friends. She seemed surprised when I jogged down the stairs, but I at least waved goodbye as I shoved Cameron out the door.

“The fact that you’re friends with my… Mona… is weird,” I told him as we made our way to his car.

“The fact that you’re my Mona’s daughter is weirder. I mean, I’ve known the Morrisons my entire life. It’s like they adopted a new dog or something with you.”

“Did you just compare me to a shelter animal?”

“You are kind of a stray.”

“Fair. So where we going?”

“Are you ready for the culinary experience of your life?”

I raised an eyebrow at him. “You told me you don’t cook. Did Remy’s get a Michelin star in the past week that I don’t know about?”

“Funny.” But instead he shoved his thumb at the back seat, pointing out a picnic basket and a bottle of sparkling grape juice. “I may not be the best chef in my family, but I can throw down when it comes to finger sandwiches and charcuterie."

"Wow, fancy."

"Shut it," he laughed before pulling away from the curb.

After about fifteen minutes of driving, we made it to an overlook with the best view of the city and the river that divided Washington, DC, from Virginia. The Washington Monument glowed brightly in the distance and the sky was clear enough to cover us in a blanket of stars.

"Not too shabby, huh?"

"Not too shabby at all."

He removed the picnic basket from the back seat and placed it on the hood of his car.

"May I?" He held out his hand to boost me up and followed me, slamming down onto the hood like he didn't care about leaving a dent.

"For you, my lady," he said, pouring sparkling juice into a plastic champagne flute before handing it to me.

I snorted. "You're ridiculous."

"You like it."

I blushed because he was not wrong. "Maybe. So are you ever going to tell me anything about yourself?"

"What?" he gasped, sputtering sparkling juice all over himself. "Are you being serious?"

"You're not exactly forthcoming."

"That's rich! Have you met yourself?"

"Hey now, you actually know way more about me than I'm comfortable with. This is a maybe-date and you already know my dad died, my mother abandoned me, and, like, all of my hobbies. It's like I had a complete Bumble profile and all you had were some blurry photos."

"And you swiped right anyway."

"I'm serious," I said, nudging him. "Tell me something. Anything."

He sighed deeply. "I'm not trying to be elusive, I promise. It's just that I feel like so much of my story is tied to someone else's and I can't really talk about it with you right now."

"Why not?" I asked.

"Because it isn't my story to tell? But then that feels shitty, too, because I'm my own person and it makes it seem like my problems are the result of another person, and they're not."

"I'm barely keeping up here, my guy."

He smoothed his hand over his face in exasperation. "Let's just say I went through a phase of a lot of learning and unlearning on my part. And I know that sounds cryptic, but it's all I can give you, at least for now."

"Okay, well, tell me something you can share without breaking whatever Unbreakable Vow it seems you made."

"Hmm." He tapped his chin with his pointer finger. "I don't actually eat a lot of sweet things."

"You work in a bakery," I said. "Your main food group is bread."

"Yeah, well, I usually have to pre-bolus beforehand."

"Pre-bolus?"

He lifted the sleeve of his T-shirt, revealing a small device attached to the back of his upper arm.

"What is it?" I asked, touching it with my fingertips.

"Continuous glucose monitor. I'm diabetic," he said before I could even ask the question.

"No you're not," I said. "No, sorry, I don't mean that in an invalidating way, more in an

I-can't-believe-it way. You eat like a garbage truck."

"There are actually a lot of tricks to keeping your blood sugar in line. Plus, I take insulin. It's manageable. I can't, you know, go binge-eating at a Golden Corral, but I do okay."

"Wow," I said in almost a whisper. "So these finger sandwiches and charcuterie?"

"I will be tearing up the charcuterie but the sandwiches are mostly all you."

"Got it," I said with a nod. I watched as he lowered his T-shirt sleeve, surprised that I had never noticed the monitor before. Had I really been so wrapped up in my own shit that I wasn't noticing the things around me?

We continued to talk for the rest of the night. He never broached the subject of Mona, and for that I was eternally grateful. I still didn't know what to make of her, or if my feelings about her even made sense anymore. This evening's conversation over Dad's records made me feel like there was at least one side of her I *might* be interested in getting to know. But I still couldn't shake my anger over why she and Dad had lied, and how they would've continuing doing so if Dad hadn't been in that accident.

There was so much I wanted to know and so much I didn't. But for now, I leaned against the front windshield, letting the evening heat settle into my bones, listening to the sound of Cameron's voice as he told me another story.

Chapter Sixteen

"Wow, you look like shit," Clare said as I leaned against the park bench I'd started to claim as ours.

"Gee, thank you," I muttered. I lowered my sunglasses over my eyes. I hadn't gotten a wink of sleep thinking about Cameron after he dropped me off last night. So now the bags under my eyes practically had their own zip code. "Allergies." I rubbed my nose for extra effect.

"In June?" Clare asked, scooting closer beside me.

"There's pollen in June, Clare."

"Sure," Clare said with a whistle and a laugh. "Want to talk about it?"

"Not really," I answered. I took my phone out

to snap a photo of Frankie, who had just picked up a new trick from Cameron. Pride beamed out of him like sunrays. I was starting to love Frankie way too much. I wished there were better circumstances for me to become a sister because it was a role I could really get behind if it didn't have so much baggage attached to it now.

"Well, want to get a tattoo?" Clare asked, her tone earnest.

"I don't think any reputable tattoo parlor is going to give two teenagers tattoos without a parent or something." But I straightened up in my seat. Getting a tattoo was something reckless and unexpected. I'd spent my life being predictable when unpredictability was just two steps behind me. Maybe I should lean into it. Dad would think it was pretty rock-and-roll. And it wasn't like I had anyone to scold me about it. Dad was gone. And Mona didn't get an opinion.

"We don't need a tattoo parlor." Clare opened her backpack. A cute but small bag, barely big enough for a cell phone, sat on top of a stack of notebooks. Inside were plastic bags filled with what looked like a deconstructed sewing kit.

"Is this when you kill me?" I asked. "Death by embroidery?"

Clare rolled her eyes so dramatically that her braids fell into her face. "It's stick-and-poke," she explained.

"I have no idea what that means, but it sounds painful."

"It's not." She stood up from the bench and yanked me up by the elbow. She pulled me back toward the line of shops leading to the skate park and then into the entrance to a dark alley. It smelled like trash, and my nose scrunched up with disgust.

"So this *is* when you kill me." I moved to leave the alley but Clare held me in place, jerking me down to the ground to kneel alongside her. My good sis was way stronger than she looked, and it did start to scare me a little that I was alone in this dark alley with her and a bunch of needles.

"Stop being dramatic." Clare took the Ziploc baggies from her purse. One contained a sewing needle, dental floss, and a short pencil that looked like the stubby ones you get at the library or doctor's office. Another was filled with small containers that resembled paint-by-number paints. The last was filled with individually wrapped antiseptic wipes and a miniature Vaseline jar.

"Whoa, you *are* the tattoo parlor," I said, reaching for one of the bags. Clare slapped my hand away.

"No touchie," she chided as she carefully removed an antiseptic wipe. "It's all sterilized. Give me your hand."

"Oh hell no," I laughed. "I'm not trying to catch gangrene or whatever is on the end of that needle." I didn't know a lot about easily transmissible diseases, but getting my skin stabbed a hundred times in a back alley felt like a Netflix documentary waiting to happen.

"Gangrene is not transmitted through tattoos; you get it, like, when you're in a war and lose a limb or something. In, like, the Korean War, not now. And I promise your hand won't fall off. I've done this loads of times. The worst you'll get is tetanus."

"Gee," I mumbled. "Good thing I didn't panic."

"But I told you, it's all sterilized. I clean my needle with antiseptic and alcohol, so you'll be fine, trust me. I'm doing a heart like this one." She showed me the inside of her palm, just below her thumb, where a stark black outline of a heart sat. It was still a little red, indicating that it was almost as fresh as the one she was about to give me.

She wiped my hand and then meticulously wiped her own with two separate prepackaged cloths. I looked away when she reached for the needle. I couldn't even get my vaccination shots without feeling queasy, so whatever Clare was doing with that needle, I didn't want to see it.

Clare hummed as she worked and I nearly bit her when I felt the first prick. I squeezed my eyes shut as she went, the feeling of being stabbed by a baby knife burning in a somewhat sweet way, a pain that as soon as it was over, I almost wanted to reach for again. In less than ten minutes, Clare was finished and I understood how someone could get addicted to getting tattoos.

When I looked at my hand, it was bright red where Clare had worked and a black outline of a heart sat raised on my skin like a giant welt. Clare took a long tongue depressor and swiped Vaseline over it before taping plastic wrap around my hand like a botched surgery. Then she popped the plastic gloves I hadn't even seen her put on off her fingers one by one, flipping each glove inside out before stuffing it in a nearby trash bin.

"Now we match," Clare said, holding her

hand up to mine, even though my tattoo was now covered. "Make sure you take that off when you get home so it can breathe."

"How do you know so much about this? Are back-alley tattoos your side hustle?"

Clare stared at me a long time before breathing heavily out of her nose. "Okay, so I kind of lied when I said I've done this loads of times." She held up her hand. "This was the first time and that was last night."

"Oh my God!" I squealed, waving my freshly tattooed hand around. "I'm going to get rabies! Oh my God."

"Oh jeez, calm down," Clare said, reaching for my shoulders and holding me in place. "I've watched my housemate, Rita, do it a ton of times. Like, actually a ton. And if I can do it on myself and make it look halfway decent, don't you think I can nail it on you? You saw it!"

"You can't see rabies with the naked eye until I start foaming at the mouth." I didn't know if that was true but now I really was starting to panic. I couldn't believe I'd just let Clare stick a sewing needle into my hand. Where was my instinct for self-preservation? Because it definitely was not in the room with us.

Clare rolled her eyes again, like I was the one acting irrationally. "You get shots for that. You'll live."

The only reason I didn't kill Clare in this alley where no one would see me commit the crime was because the heart did look kind of cute, at least what I could remember of it before Clare had taped over it. And it made me feel like a bit of a badass having a tattoo, like the rock-and-roll girl Dad always believed me to be but I rarely saw in myself.

"Fine," I muttered. "But if I wake up in the morning and my hand is halfway across the room, rotting from within, just know I'm going to sing like a canary."

"Deal," Clare laughed. "Now let's go get some cupcakes."

The house had the familiar scent of sugar and vanilla when I got back, the front door slamming behind me. Frankie ran past me up the stairs, already late for a Fortnite session with his skate bros, as he called them. I was proud of how much he had come out of his shell so far this summer.

I traipsed into the kitchen to find Mona

standing before the island with a confused expression. Her face was covered with more confectioners' sugar than her working surface. I would've preferred to avoid speaking to her much, but I couldn't quite leave behind a baking disaster in the making.

"Are you okay?" I asked, barely audibly, in the hope that maybe she wouldn't hear me and I could still consider my obligations to the pastry world fulfilled.

"I knew how to make this at one point, but I'm just blanking," Mona responded. Her eyebrows knitted together in concentration. "The cakes keep coming out tasting like raw cookie dough."

I noticed the sliced strawberries on the counter, and the mess of ruined shortcakes dumped into the sink for the garbage disposal to handle.

"Strawberry shortcake?" I shrugged off the coincidence that I'd just made these a couple of weeks ago myself. It was summer, and strawberries were the prime fruit to use in desserts this time of year. Plus, shortcake was pretty easy to make. Well, most of the time.

"Do you . . ." I started, nearly wanting to bite my own tongue out. But I just couldn't leave a cake emergency untended to. It would be like a firefighter walking out of a burning building to take a smoke break. “Do you need help?”

Despite Mona’s deep brown cheeks, I could see a blush spreading across her face. “If you don’t mind. I know you’re the cake queen around here.” She tried to laugh, but it sounded more like she was choking on her own spit. At least she was as uncomfortable around me as I was around her.

“Uh, yeah, sure.” I stepped behind her and washed my hands in the clean side of the sink, cringing at the mutilated cakes on the other side. They didn’t have to go down like that.

Mona moved to the side but not entirely away. It seemed she was intent on contributing, though I would rather have just done this for her by myself. Alone. I hoped Mona didn’t think this was mother-daughter time but understood it for exactly what it was—a near professional stepping in so no more eggs had to suffer the same fate as their brothers-in-arms.

I walked her through the beginning steps of making the sponge cake, but eventually whatever muscle memory Mona did have took over and she was completing the next steps before I even had to tell her what they were.

"I used to make these as a teenager, but I haven't made them since..." Mona stopped talking abruptly and refocused on the task at hand.

"Before what?" I couldn't believe I was egging on a conversation with her, but my curiosity got the best of me.

"Well, your dad used to love them." Mona spoke quietly, like her voice would disrupt the weird balance we'd achieved out of necessity. "I made it once with a friend, and when your dad had a slice he just about became obsessed. Asked for one damn near every weekend after that. And it was the only thing I could make, so I usually obliged."

"He did love strawberry shortcakes." I smiled, remembering how he would ask for one every year on his birthday. I could practically make them in my sleep because of it.

"Oh, I bet he ran you ragged making them." Mona laughed. Her laugh was soft and unpracticed, like hands that hadn't been used very often.

"He did," I said, chuckling and grimacing. I never thought I'd be talking to my mother about my father, especially not in the past tense.

"Sorry, I know it's hard to talk about him."

Mona's cheeks were a shade just south of maroon again. She moved to the other side of the island and began slicing the strawberries with so much vigor that she barely flinched when the knife cut through the tip of her thumb.

"Goddammit," she cursed.

She ran her thumb under the faucet, shaking her head in what seemed like disbelief. At what, I wasn't sure. Thumbs were always the casualty of baking war.

I grabbed one of the hand towels hanging on the oven and wrapped it around Mona's still-bleeding thumb.

"Thank you," Mona muttered. Her gaze caught on my bandaged hand. "What happened?"

I could lie, but you only lie to your parents when you're worried what they might think. I couldn't have cared less what Mona thought about me. Hell, maybe if she thought I was rebellious she'd send me packing. But to where, I didn't know.

"I got a tattoo," I admitted. I didn't tell her it was a back-alley stick-and-poke. That might be too much for anyone, and I didn't want her thinking I was a complete idiot. I did have Dad's raising-a-daughter-by-himself reputation to protect.

"You did *what*? By whom?"

"By a friend."

"And does this friend know that you're not eighteen?"

"Are you going to have them locked up or something? Do you really think that's the worst thing anyone has ever done to me?" I raised my eyebrows at her.

"I think if you're going to get a tattoo you should go somewhere reputable. Did you go somewhere reputable? Not that I did, when I got one."

My face warmed in anger. Mona wasn't upset about the tattoo or even me, she was upset by the principle of the thing. That no respectable tattoo parlor should give a tattoo to a kid without a parent present.

"Why do you even care?"

"I care because I don't want anything to happen to you."

I couldn't help but snort.

"I'm serious, Skylar. My friends and I used to give each other terrible tattoos when we were kids. I was nearly hospitalized once. Just don't be stupid about these things."

"I'm not stupid."

"I didn't say you were," Mona sighed. "Look, I really don't want to fight with you. Can we at least try to be cordial?"

"Sure," I responded. "I'm happy to go back to pretending like you don't exist. I've had a lot of practice."

Mona's chin quivered for just a moment before she stilled her expression into nothing once again. Her eyes scanned my face like she was looking for something in my features, but she simply let out a steady breath and nodded like she was trying to convince herself of something.

But I didn't care if my words were a bit harsh. She deserved every last one of them. I turned to leave the kitchen, but before I did, I spun back around and scribbled the rest of the baking instructions on the back of one of Gaby's bridal magazines, sliding it across the island at her before storming out. No more shortcake and whipped topping needed to die today.

Chapter Seventeen

While Frankie skateboarded with Cameron, Clare and I had taken to riding our nearly identical bikes down a path that trailed from Alexandria through Arlington and back, the same route I had taken to running in the mornings now that I had finally settled on a routine. Wake up, run, shower, breakfast cereal with Frankie, skate park, Cameron, bed. Sometimes baking practice, sometimes just more Cameron time. I had yet to eat a single dinner at the house and no one had pressed the issue. How Cameron was getting out of family dinners, though, I had no idea.

Clare and I paced each other as we pedaled.

A long Twizzler hung between her teeth as she talked out of the side of her mouth.

"So why'd she leave?" she asked, removing her hand from the handlebar to quickly rip the Twizzler out of her mouth, biting a chunk off the end.

"Your guess is as good as mine. She married my dad to get out of her home life, but she never said why it didn't work. I mean, beyond the obvious, that she was a lesbian married to a man."

"Right." Clare's voice trailed off as she thought. "It's not a totally crazy idea."

"What isn't?"

"Marrying your best friend when your parents abandon you. I mean, I've never thought about it before, but it would solve a lot of problems."

"You're kidding, right?"

"For instance, my best friend is my favorite person in the world. Aren't you supposed to marry your favorite person in the world? In a safe environment, something I've never had before. I know he'd take care of me, and my parents would finally get off my back."

"Clare, you like girls."

"Maybe you can ignore all that when you're just trying to be safe. I don't know, it seems harsh to judge her when she was clearly just trying to survive."

"Am I in the Twilight Zone or something?" I put my feet to the ground to stop my bike. Clare stopped beside me. She turned toward me with a look I definitely didn't like. "Tell me you're not actually thinking this could be a solution to your problem?" I said. "I thought things were working out at Hawley House."

"They are." Clare shrugged. "But Hawley House is, like, a transitioning place. No one stays there long before figuring their shit out. And I don't want to live in a shelter forever."

"You'll be eighteen in just a couple of months. Soon you can go do anything you want."

"With what money and what security? I can't just wish my problems away when I turn eighteen. And maybe that's what Mona was thinking too."

"Okay, let's just assume I give leeway on doing what I think is the dumbest thing ever, bound for failure. How do you explain *faking her own death* and lying to me about it my entire life?"

"Well, if we're being technical, she never lied to you. She never communicated with you in order to lie. Technically your dad lied to you," Clare argued, echoing my last session with Diana.

I felt anger rise up in me like I was an active volcano. "Are you seriously trying to blame my dead dad?"

"Of course not. I'm just saying sometimes when we're out of options we make decisions that don't make sense to anyone else. If my best friend said yes, I would marry him in a heartbeat. And maybe it wouldn't work, but maybe it would. Maybe we would have an open marriage and do whatever we actually wanted with the guarantee that we would have someone and some place to go home to. I mean, isn't that what we all want, after all?"

"God, I feel like we were figuring out my problems and all I've done is give you the worst idea ever. Please don't marry him. If anything, my life should prove that it would only end in disaster."

Clare gave me a wink before pushing off the ground once more. "No worries, he would never say yes."

"The fact that that is the only thing holding you back is so beyond scary." I pedaled behind her with a shake of my head, worried that I really had seeded an idea that was destined to fail.

But as much as I resisted the idea of what Mona had done—and maybe Clare was thinking about doing now, thanks to me—I somewhat understood the desire for control. It was like everyone knew what was going on in my life except for me. Mona and my dad always knew the truth, and they just kept it from me. God, or whatever, took my dad away before he could give me any answers. And I was just here, having things happen to me.

"I wish life was more predictable," I told Clare as we pedaled. "Or I was stronger, tougher, like an . . . an orca."

"Orcas are crazy motherfuckers. No impulse control, you feel me? Just attacking shit for no reason."

"Don't you kind of want to feel that way, though? Like you have teeth, like you won't just take things lying down?"

"Whew, girl, all the time."

"Do you think you'd ever go home?" I asked her.

"I don't know if they would even take me back. I wouldn't want to live somewhere I can't be authentically myself. But I miss them for sure.

I know it sounds crazy, but I love my parents, and I have to believe they love me too. They're just confused, too invested in what their church says about the Bible, rather than what the Bible shows them. I believe in it, you know. God and Jesus and his goodness. I know he doesn't teach what the church teaches."

"But how?" I asked, genuinely interested. "I mean, the Bible might say that the ultimate goal is loving your neighbor and being kind and stuff, but all these people follow it and all they do is hate. At some point, isn't it less about the theology of it all and more about the people you choose to align yourself with?"

"I align myself with Jesus. That's where my fellowship happens, in my relationship with him. He led me here, and it's not perfect, but I've found a good life here. Not to say I didn't used to wish I could pray the gay away. But I feel like when I had the most reasons to hate him, that's when he was there. Like that poem."

"What poem?"

"You know," Clare said, "the one in, like, every Black grandmother's home. 'Footprints,' or something. 'When there is only one set of footprints, that's when I carried you.' "

"I just don't know if I can believe in any of that," I responded.

"And I'm not going to try to convince you." Clare laughed. "We all find our way the best way we know how."

Gaby was on her knees in the living room, pieces of scrap paper and vellum surrounding her on the carpet. I tried to sneak past her to the kitchen—I needed to make a mousse, something creamy and delicious that would make me feel better about my conversation with Clare and how easy it was for her to still hold attachment to people who had betrayed her.

"Oh, Skylar," Gaby called just as I nearly made it past her unseen. "Sky, come in here, would you?" I did a double-take at the use of *Sky*, at its familiarity.

I considered going quietly up the stairs, but Gaby already knew I was there. Unlike Mona, Gaby was hard to say no to. I sighed and went into the living room. I sat beside her on the carpet, avoiding the stacks of card stock, envelopes, and ribbon that littered the floor in stacks.

"It's a mess, I know," Gaby said, giving me a

smile that only inhabited one side of her mouth. A stress line was burrowed into her forehead. "I've been trying to put these invitations together for weeks now. Less than two months out, can you believe I'm still working on this?"

"Um" was all I had to offer. I didn't know anything about weddings or when things were supposed to happen. My nearest proximity to anything bridal was the *Say Yes to the Dress* episodes I binge-watched whenever I couldn't sleep, and the nights Dad would play for receptions, but I wasn't the kind of person who'd dreamed about every detail like some of my friends.

"I know, it's tragic. Joke's on me for wanting to do something elaborate instead of choosing a Minted package like your mo—Mona suggested." Gaby caught the slip of her tongue. So far, everyone had been pretty good about not referring to Mona as my mother. I felt like it took more than just pushing a kid out of your vag to be considered a mother, like there were qualifications and disqualifications for the title and Mona hadn't met any of the prerequisites. "Are you feeling arts-and-craftsy?"

I wanted to say no, again, but the truth was that I did love arts and crafts, anything creative that I could get my hands on, really. That was why I'd loved helping at Dad's shows. Just moving an amp with my very own hands could change the whole experience for the crowd.

"I could be," I told her, because I didn't want to sound too eager. I needed to be here under duress, not to spend quality time with her. Gaby was like a gateway drug to Mona, and I wasn't trying to get high.

"Perfect," Gaby said, her smile almost big enough to fill up the room. "Okay, so what you're going to do is take one of these invitations and one each of a detail card and an RSVP card. People can RSVP online, too, but our planner is all about tradition."

"Aren't you the planner?" I asked, amused.

"Shhh," Gaby said, placing a well-manicured finger over her lips. "Once you have everything stacked together like so"—she demonstrated by putting the invitation on top and the two smaller cards beneath—"you're going to take this vellum sleeve and wrap it around. Then you're going to cut off exactly nine inches of ribbon and tie it like this."

I watched her in awe as she put the disparate parts of the invitation together. It was so meticulous and precise, like baking. Maybe we weren't so different after all.

"Here's the tricky part—you have to get a small piece of tape underneath your knot because we're going to go back and put wax seals over them."

"Isn't this a little much?" I asked, and Gaby stilled, like it was not the first time she'd heard that question and she was just about sick of it.

"It's not rocket science, Skylar. It just takes some patience. I want the invitations to be beautiful, you know. I want people to open up their envelopes with beautiful calligraphy and ooh and aah."

To me, it seemed like she was doing a lot of things for other people's perceptions rather than her own happiness, but who was I to judge?

"Okay, got it?" Gaby asked, and I nodded.

Gaby took over cutting exactly nine-inch scraps of ribbon as I stacked the invitations, RSVP cards, and detail cards into separate piles and wrapped them in vellum. The ribbon portion made me the most nervous, so I saved it for last. We entered a relaxed silence as we worked, until the quiet got so loud that I had to stop and track where Gaby was in her process, the snipping of the scissors long quieted. I found her staring at me.

"Am I doing it wrong?" I asked, nervous that somehow I'd ruined stacking papers on top of each other.

"No, I was just thinking, sorry." Gaby shrugged. "I was just thinking that this is quite nice."

"Oh." I felt my cheeks warm.

"Do you think it's nice? Actually, no, sorry, you don't have to answer that."

"Uh, okay." But it was quite nice, until she pointed out how quite nice it was.

"It's just, I'm a talker and I'm used to Frankie keeping me pretty much updated but you're a tough nut to crack, Skylar. Not that I don't understand why, I mean, I'm sure this was a huge adjustment, and finding out the truth after all these years . . ."

"Did you know?" I asked, suddenly certain that Gaby's answer would change my perception of her forever. "Did you know she had a daughter?"

This time it was Gaby's cheeks that turned a solid shade of maroon. "She told me she had a past life she wasn't proud of, and that she had a child in that past life. To be honest, I never asked as many questions as I should have. I figured she would tell me when she was ready, and over time we just kind of settled into our life."

"You never thought it was weird that she wanted to adopt Frankie when she already had one kid she wanted no part in raising?" I could feel my voice getting louder, like a lever was wedged beneath my rib cage and it was ratcheting up my anger. "You never thought it odd you'd never met me?"

"Like I said." Gaby broke eye contact now. "We settled into our life, as spouses, as parents. I think a small part of me was always terrified of upsetting that balance. I'm not proud of it. I'm not proud of letting her run away from her problems."

"Right, me, the problem."

"No." Gaby shook her head. "We've talked about it a lot since you got here. I mean, you're a great kid and it is shameful that neither of us had any part in raising you. Your dad did a great job. They were best friends and kids when they decided to have you, and I think they made childish decisions that they didn't know how to back out of once they were made, like life was quicksand and they couldn't figure out how to get out of it without pulling each other down. Your father wanted as little upheaval as possible in your life; he wanted her to stay away if she couldn't be there one hundred percent."

"So you're blaming my dad for Mona treating me like garbage on the side of the street?" I found myself standing, as if my body was on autopilot.

"No, Skylar, of course not. Your dad was an angel as far as I'm concerned. And he wanted to tell you the truth. They talked about it. Just a couple of days before, they talked about it. But..." Gaby paused. "Maybe this is a conversation you should have with your mo—Mona. I shouldn't have said anything, really. I just look at you and wish I had been there to watch you grow up, and I wish badly that you would let us in now."

Gaby's eyes pleaded with me, but I stepped carefully out of the circle of invitations she'd put together. "I'm pretty tired, actually. It was a long day at the skate park."

"Right," Gaby responded, gulping loudly enough for me to hear it from the foyer. "Of course, you should get some rest before bed." Neither of us acknowledged the irony there.

I stomped up the stairs and into my bedroom.

I threw my jacket on the bed but it didn't make me feel any better.

I would not cry over people who didn't want me.

I would not cry over people who didn't want me.

It was hours before I registered that Mona must have been who I'd overheard Dad talking to, pleading with, really. That same week that he died. So he wanted to tell me, which meant she wanted to keep lying to me. I knew Dad wouldn't have kept this from me if he'd had any choice. Mona was every bit the monster I thought she was, and I was ashamed I'd almost let her and Gaby break through.

Chapter Eighteen

The second round of competition was getting uncomfortably close and I still wasn't sure if we had practiced every test it *could* be. Not knowing definitely stressed me out, but I wasn't nearly as stressed as Taylor sounded on the phone that morning when she begged me to come help with a cupcake emergency.

Frankie bounced on his toes beside me, excited to be spending the day eating cupcake discards and practicing his performance of being Cameron's shadow.

Jazz music poured out of the Forresters' front door when she opened it, a too-wide smile taking over her face, so much so that it was nearly comical.

"You're right on time!" she squealed as she stood perched in the doorway.

"Uh," I muttered, my hand still half raised, "hi."

"Frankie, good to see you again," Taylor said. "Cameron said you guys are going to tear it up in the backyard." Taylor turned to me in explanation. "Our dad emptied the pool out so Cam could use it as a skate pipe, you believe that? The height of summer and I can't even have my beloved pool until July."

I laughed. "Yeah, I think you need a new brother. Frankie would never sacrifice the pool."

"Never ever." Frankie nodded, though from the bounce in his toes I could tell he was champing at the bit to get to the backyard.

"Get out of here." I shoved him lightly and he took off through the house.

"So, you mentioned cupcakes?" I asked, slipping my sneakers off at the door. Taylor was wearing her baking Crocs, but I didn't feel right wearing shoes in other folks' homes.

"Yes." Taylor clapped her hands. "We got a last-minute birthday party order and I thought I'd have time in the kitchens to work on it today but lo and behold, my ovens have forsaken me. So now we have to use our kitchen to get it done."

"Is that even legal?" I asked. "I mean, is this a commercial kitchen?"

"It is not," Taylor answered. "But our mom got a special license for the day or something? You can only get one, like, every six months, so hopefully nothing else goes wrong because we're hella booked all summer. But I have no idea how it works. I just know it's chaos."

"You could tell them you can't do it."

"I could, but being there for people in their hour of need is kind of what the bakery is all about. It's how it's remained standing through every economic downturn you can imagine. People trust us. And I can't break that trust. Besides, I love any excuse to bake."

Once we got into the kitchen, I could barely keep my jaw from hanging loose on its hinges. If this was a ruddy kitchen setup, I'd hate to think what it would take for Taylor to consider it world-class. The appliances gleamed like they had been wiped down to a spit shine, and everything I looked at was state-of-the-art. I washed my hands in the sink and tied an apron around my waist. I filled the apron pockets with the essentials—extra piping tips, a small hand whisk, and a wooden spoon. Taylor did the same—the baker's arsenal.

We got to work immediately, the only noise being whisking and stirring and our quiet breaths and the scrape of skateboard wheels against concrete sounding from the backyard. Every once in a while it got so quiet, I could almost hear the flour doing its thing with the wet ingredients. Before long, we were placing pans of cupcakes in the double oven and starting on the next batch. I could barely feel my shoulders ache as I made the repetitive movements that went into a large order, and thanked the gods above that we had not one but two KitchenAid mixers.

The accordion back doors slid open and a blast of wind rattled everything on the kitchen island.

"Watch it!" Taylor scolded as she grabbed parchment paper mere millimeters from hitting the floor. "We're working here."

Cameron gave me a nod, Frankie close at his heels, as he opened the oversized refrigerator and pulled out a pitcher of lemonade. An actual pitcher, not the Minute Maid carton I was used to. These people were fancy as hell.

"You read my mind," Taylor said, smacking

her hands together. Excess flour cascaded to the floor. "It's break time."

"Have you given Skylar the grand tour?" Cameron asked, his cheeks slightly puckered from the lemonade. "Frankie said our house is like the inside of Stark Tower."

Frankie smiled and nodded. "Go see the basement," he said, once again bouncing on his toes. I nearly took the glass of lemonade out of his hands. This kid had had way too much sugar already. "It has AI that sounds just like Ultron."

"I thought Ultron was the bad guy," I asked, eyebrows lifting.

"It's not AI AI," Taylor assured me as she led me through the house. "It's like an Alexa on very mild steroids that Cameron coded."

"Cameron codes?" I asked, taking a sip from my glass. My lips puckered involuntarily. I could see why Cameron got got—it was tart as hell.

"Oh yeah, ever since we were kids. He found he was decent at it after learning that in a family full of bakers, he would only ever be really good at inspiring sugar-free recipes. But he turned out to be really talented. Going to be some big-deal engineer who creates the next Twitter or something one day, just with less racism and more security."

"Well, can he hurry up?" I asked. "Twitter's on its last leg as we speak."

"You ain't never lied," Taylor laughed.

I was surprised that Cameron was so into something he'd never mentioned. I already knew he had a hard time talking about himself, most of his stories seeming to involve the world around him, with him as a spectator. It was odd for someone who was pretty gregarious to be so closed off.

I glanced at the photographs lining the walls. Cameron, their parents, and another teen boy were framed throughout the house. Taylor was only in a couple, all of which seemed pretty recent.

"You can ask," Taylor said, stopping to lean against the staircase banister.

"I would, but I'm honestly not sure what my question would be," I confessed. My thoughts itched my brain but I just couldn't seem to scratch the right spot.

"Well, I'm just your friendly neighborhood trans girl," Taylor explained. "We finally figured it out when I was fourteen, even though I kind of always knew, you know. Right spirit, wrong body, my dad calls it." God, did I know anyone who wasn't just extraordinarily queer? The thought almost made me giggle.

"Why keep the old photos up?" I asked as I followed Taylor up the stairs.

Taylor shrugged. "I guess it felt weird to erase years of my life like they didn't happen. And I don't hate that body or that person, it just wasn't really me. I don't feel bad looking at myself like that. But I feel a whole hell of a lot better looking at myself like this."

Taylor gestured toward the photographs that went up the stairs, staggered to cover nearly every square inch of wall space. Taylor and Cameron in school sports, Taylor hugging Cameron at what looked like the awards podium at a robotics competition—based on the sash crossing Cameron's chest and the team behind him holding up a battered yet functional wheeled machine that looked like an incredibly rudimentary version of R2-D2.

"Cool," I replied.

"Cool." Taylor nodded. "Anyway, Cameron's room." She pointed to her left. "My room." She pointed to her right. "And my parents' room down the hall. Nothing special. Now let's go meet Cam's AI baby."

Chapter Nineteen

Mona's journal sat open on my lap, detailing her first few months of living at Hawley House. It seemed her relationship with her parents had deteriorated rapidly, and now they weren't even mentioned in the pages anymore. Their absence was almost as loud as the words that did make it onto the page. Teddy, my dad, became even more prominent.

Tomorrow I turn 18. Sometimes I'm shocked that I made it this far. So many times I thought I would be dead by now, but we made it. I'm trying to convince myself that I don't care if I hear from my parents tomorrow, but only because I don't know how I'll feel when I don't hear from them. And I know I won't. Mom is too proud and Dad is too docile. I miss him the most and I like to think that if he had his way, we'd be curled up on the couch right now, doing Sunday's crossword puzzle with his favorite blue ink pen.

Teddy and I are going to get our marriage license in the morning. And then we have sixty days to change our minds. That's insane, I know. But Teddy gives me freedom I've never had before, and sometimes I think I could be a good wife, even if I know we could never make each other truly happy. I don't know how to repay Teddy for the sacrifices he's making to give me my life back.

I closed the book in exasperation. It was such a foolish idea, one that anyone could have predicted wouldn't work. And it didn't. In fact, it failed spectacularly. This couldn't be what Clare had in mind. If so, I had to warn her about how it would turn out. Mona was a cautionary tale, and I wouldn't let a good friend fall into the same trap.

I climbed off the bed and slipped on my slides

at the door, my stark white socks standing out against the black shoes. Clare was usually at the skate park this time of day, though I still couldn't tell who she came with. I'd never seen her talk to anyone but me. I assumed she went with the mysterious best friend and he just hung out with a different crowd than Cameron and Frankie.

The bike ride to the park was quick despite having to traverse crowds of people taking advantage of the warm, but not muggy, day. As expected, Clare was on our bench, a box of cupcakes on her lap as she stared at a group of boys practicing ollies by the ramps.

"Hey," I said as I leaned the bike against the back of the bench and circled around to sit beside her.

Clare handed me the box of cupcakes without a word and I grabbed my usual chocolate on vanilla. Cramps were starting to build at the bottom of my belly and I was in desperate need of something sweet before the period monster came out in full force.

"Thanks," I told her as I took a monstrous bite.

" 'Tis what I'm here for." Clare closed the box and placed it between us. "Where's your brother?"

"Frankie? He's not my brother."

"Then where's your boyfriend?"

I nearly choked on a bite of cupcake. "My what?"

"You know, tall, dark, and handsome who's always staring at you like you invented sunlight?"

"Cameron? Absolutely not my boyfriend."

"But you did know who I was referring to as tall, dark, handsome, and obsessed with you." Clare gave me a knowing smirk and I rolled my eyes in response.

"I have eyeballs. Cam is objectively attractive. I've revealed nothing."

"Sure," Clare sang with a laugh. "I'll let you think I believe that."

A moment of silence passed between us before I laughed. "He is pretty hot, isn't he?"

Clare laughed even harder now, placing one hand over her stomach. "I only like girls and even I can admit that."

"Speaking of girls, how's that whole plan of child marriage going with your friend? Is he here, by the way?"

Clare ignored the question and shoved my shoulder. "It's not *child* marriage."

"You're literally seventeen."

"I won't be when we're married."

"Oh God, you said *when*. So you're telling me you've decided."

Clare let out a deep sigh. "For centuries people have gotten married for purely logistical reasons."

"Not in the twenty-first century. Maybe in the seventeenth century."

"Why do you hate this idea so much?"

"Because it's a terrible one. Look, I've been reading…something," I started, not wanting to admit that I'd been reading another person's diary. Surely that was frowned upon in any civilized society. "And all signs point to this being a terrible idea."

"Not as terrible as living on my own and trying to support myself. At least now I'll have help."

"Maybe he can help you as a totally platonic roommate."

"We get more benefits as a married couple. Even more if we have a kid."

"Please don't tell me you're planning on having a kid."

"I think I'd be a good mom."

I stared at her now in disbelief. "This is going off the rails fast."

"I'm not planning on having a kid, but I wouldn't hate having one, I don't think. Maybe I could correct some generational trauma."

"I don't think people should have kids in order to heal themselves. Maybe the healing should come first. Get a therapist, not a husband. Or maybe even a puppy."

"Black people don't go to therapy," Clare remarked with a grimace.

"Oh boy, lots to unpack there."

"Look, I know it's not the best idea in the world, but I have someone who wants to commit to building a life with me, and it may not be the perfect life or the one I envisioned for myself, but it's a safe one. You couldn't possibly understand what it's like to be this afraid of the future."

"You don't think I'm afraid? The only person I know for sure ever gave a shit about me is gone, only for me to find out that he lied to me my entire life. I have no idea who to trust or if I even can trust anyone ever again."

"It's not the same thing."

"It's not the same, no, but we all have something that we're afraid of. And we don't have to make terrible choice upon terrible choice, because there's always an option."

"You sound naïve."

"I just think you're giving up, and I've seen plans like this go left."

"Yeah, when?"

I took a deep breath. "Remember—Mona married my dad because her parents put her out too. And it didn't work out. Look at my life."

"I'm not Mona."

"I think you're following a pattern that has been proven not to work."

"Haven't you ever wanted to just not be what you are? Not even for a second? I mean, maybe that's taboo to say, but there are times I think life would just be a whole hell of a lot easier if I was into boys. But I'm not. So I have to be in hell."

"Is it really that bad?" I asked. "The shelter seems great."

"It is great," Clare said, "for a shelter. But that isn't my family. Those aren't my parents or my cousins. They're all strangers. And we're all there because our people didn't want us. And so it may be great to have movie night every day of the week and always have homework help, but it's pretty fucking shitty to know we're all there out of necessity, out of self-preservation so we don't have to live on the streets."

Clare took a deep breath, her shoulders nearly hitting her ears as she breathed in and out. "Do you know that homeless queer youth are one of the biggest demographics of the homeless community? Kids. Like you and me. On the streets because their families are too closed-minded to give them a welcoming home. Sometimes that's the hardest part, knowing that all of my favorite people in the world don't have families that care about them. It's almost harder than being alone myself, the secondhand fear you feel for your friends. We can't stay at Hawley forever. And then what?

"So maybe I'm a bad person because I think: Marry my best guy friend, pop out a kid. Maybe my mother would take me back, maybe they'd accept me. Maybe I wouldn't have to worry about what will happen to me if Hawley loses funding or I get too old and age out. I'll be taken care of. It just sucks that I have to lose so much of myself for those things to happen."

I didn't know what to say to her that would make any of this better. I didn't know what I would want said to me if I didn't have anywhere to go but into the arms of someone I could never love. Mona might be the world's most unaware mother, but maybe she wasn't the world's cruelest. She took me in when I literally had nowhere else to go. Maybe that was the law, but I was sure she could have fought it if she'd really wanted to, refused to pick up the phone. And she accepted me for who I was, even accepting my silence in order to keep the peace.

"I just want to be able to go home and not feel like I'm my parents' worst nightmare," Clare continued. She took a long pause, twisting the end of one of her braids around her finger. "I tried it once."

"Tried what?" I asked.

"It."

I stared at her in befuddlement. "It?"

"You know, It It. S-E-X."

I burst out laughing, the sound releasing like a popped balloon. "Clare, you don't have to whisper. We're sexually liberated these days. And we're in an open-air park. No one is listening in."

"With my best friend, I tried it."

"Clare..."

"No, I know. It was totally stupid and dumb unenjoyable. Like, no lie, I sent a prayer up for all my heterosexual sisters because there's no way that's enjoyable for, like, anybody. I felt like I was being drilled like a pothole, mined for gold, something unpleasant."

I laughed again. My interest in boys had always been aesthetic at most, as in I could appreciate a pretty face on just about anyone, but sex seemed universally unappealing. With anyone, really.

"Why'd you do it?"

"Like I said, I'm not proud of it, but I went through that whole pray-the-gay-away phase. I thought, hey, maybe you're knocking it before you've tried it. Well, I've tried it and dick is decidedly not for me. But sex is only a small part of marriage, and he's a really great guy. I think we could make it work."

"Isn't sex, like, the leading cause of divorce or something?" I asked.

"I think that's money."

"Oh." I nodded, despite how bad an idea I thought it was to marry someone you could never be attracted to just to be free. All she'd be doing was swapping one prison for another.

I reached for Clare's hand and pulled it into my lap.

"It's going to be okay," I told her. "Everything is going to be okay."

But I wasn't sure whether I was trying to convince Clare or myself.

Clare gave my hand a squeeze before gently pulling hers away. I got up from the bench and stretched before grabbing my bike. "You should know I care about you and I'm willing to help you with whatever you need. Just don't do something stupid because you feel alone. You're not alone. And you deserve to live a life that excites you. Both of you."

Clare gulped audibly before I pushed off and started back to the house.

Once there, I dumped the bike on the front lawn, noticing that the wind was always much tamer at home than at the park. I wondered if the bowl had something to do with it, like it was some kind of vortex or wind chamber.

Gaby and Mona were sitting at the kitchen table with an A Cupcake a Day sample box.

"What's going on?" I asked as I made my way to the sink and poured myself a glass of water.

"We're taste-testing cakes and icing so we can let Taylor know what we'll be ordering for the wedding," Gaby said.

Mona gave me a quick glance before looking

away. The two of us were still treating eye contact like one of us was Medusa—avoid at all costs. But I loved talking cake.

"What's the favorite so far?"

"Lemon cake with strawberry compote," Gaby said, taking another bite and closing her eyes as she chewed.

"I like the carrot cake," Mona said.

"We're not doing carrot cake for our wedding," Gaby responded. "Too risky. Carrot cake is too polarizing."

"It's cake. People can either eat it or not."

Gaby turned her head to look at me, drawing me in with a glance like we were on the same side. "She doesn't get it," Gaby said, though I regrettably had to agree with Mona. A good carrot cake could be a great option. But I wasn't about to side with Mona. So I just shrugged and took another sip of water.

"Want to try some?" Gaby asked, pushing the box toward me. Six small squares of cake with bites taken out of them sat in the box.

"I'm okay. We had lots of sweets at the bakery today."

"Why were you at the bakery? I swear, it's like you work there or something. You don't work there, do you?" Gaby asked. "Because we should probably talk about you having a job, if so."

"No, we were just practicing."

"Practicing for what?" Gaby asked.

I realized that I had never told them about the competition. Gaby and Mona stared back at me in confusion. "Oh, I, um, entered that baking competition Taylor was talking about."

"Oh!" Gaby perked up, forgetting entirely about the cake in front of her. "When does it start? We'd love to come support."

"Oh, it actually started a while ago. I made it past the first round."

Gaby's shoulders lowered. "Oh." I could tell she was disappointed that I hadn't told them. "Well, maybe we'll stop by for the second round." She hit her palms against the marble countertop before hopping off her stool. "I'm going to go check on one of my clients. She was having a meltdown about the design for her office and I need to convince her that mahogany is not modern enough for her all-white aesthetic."

I placed my glass in the empty sink. Mona cleared her throat behind me.

"You know, she really wants to be a part of your life," Mona said. "You should let her."

"Are you trying to give me life advice?"

"I'm trying to make this situation as comfortable as I can for all of us. Gaby doesn't deserve the blame for what happened."

"So you lied to her too?"

"I told her about you, if that's what you're asking."

"So she *is* to blame too. She didn't make you do the right thing."

"So much time had gone by that it was hard to know what the right thing even was anymore. Your father and I just wanted you to have as little upheaval as possible."

"Well, y'all did a *great* job."

"Okay, well, I don't think this is going to be a productive conversation so I'm not going to push. But when you're ready, I'm happy to talk about it with you."

Mona left the kitchen and I waited until I could no longer hear her footsteps to go upstairs to my room. Mona's journal was still open on the bed. I slammed it shut and shoved it back into the nightstand.

Chapter Twenty

The audience for the second round of the competition was sparser than it was for the first challenge, but there were still more pairs of eyes on me than was comfortable.

I pulled my daffodil apron from my oven handlebar where I had left it and tied it around my waist. I smoothed my fingers over the embroidery with a smile. Cameron caught my eye and gave me a thumbs-up. I scanned the equipment and ingredients in front of me, trying to parse out what the challenge would be. Based on the ingredients, my best guess was pastry, but that still meant it could be anything. That was the one thing about pastries. If you were stuck on a desert island with just a certain number of ingredients, you could make dozens of different things.

Mrs. Forrester took the mic and cast a glance over the room. Every contestant stiffened to pay attention and the audience went silent.

"Thank you so much for joining us again this morning." She smiled brightly and I was surprised at how much more she looked like her twins. "Today is pastry day and we're so excited to watch all of our contestants complete the day's technical challenge. I know there's been a lot of chatter about what the technical challenge may be." She drummed her fingertips together conspiratorially and I shuffled from foot to foot in anticipation.

An assistant wheeled out a cart carrying a covered dish. With a flourish, Mrs. Forrester uncovered the dish to reveal the chosen pastry. I strained my neck until I could see the small mille-feuille in the center of a ceramic plate. An involuntary and panicked gasp spilled from my lips. It wasn't one of the recipes we had practiced, and it required perfect execution of puff pastry and zabaglione, which I'd never made before. I found Taylor in the crowd and she shrugged, having also had no idea. At least I was in luck that we had practiced puff pastry, but mine never came out as light or as flaky as I wanted.

"The mille-feuille, as I'm sure you're all aware, originated in France and is a popular dessert in Europe that combines some of the most delicate components of pastry cuisine. You are all challenged to make one perfect pastry and present it to the judges in just three hours, so not a lot of room for mistakes or redoing anything if you mess up. At the end of this stage, three more contestants will be eliminated, and the final three will come back in a month to face off in our final challenge."

The assistant came back to roll the cart away, and Mrs. Forrester smoothed her dress over her hips, the microphone letting out feedback as it rubbed against the fabric. "And with that, your time begins"—she pointed at the clock, which ticked off one second—"now."

There were more ingredients than I needed to pull this off, and I started to wonder if some of them were red herrings. I separated those out first, leaving me with the ingredients I actually needed. They'd provided a premade puff pastry, but I also had the ingredients to make a puff pastry from scratch. It was risky, because a dough from scratch should normally stay in the refrigerator for two of the three hours we'd been allotted, so I'd have only the remaining hour to prepare it before chilling and construct it after. But on the other hand, I didn't know who made the prepared puff pastry or whether it would be good enough to get me through to the final round.

"Fuck it," I muttered to myself as I began to combine ingredients for my own dough. Hopefully it would be better than taking the quick route.

I went through all the steps a hundred times in my head as I worked, until the dough was ready to be smoothed out. I placed it in the freezer on a timer for ten minutes, hoping it didn't get too cold or too stiff. Maybe less time at a colder temperature would do what longer time in the fridge would do, like cooking food in a Crock-Pot on high versus low.

I started preparing the cream while I waited. I'd never made it before, so I stuck to making something similar to éclair cream. That wasn't completely right, but it was the only thing I knew how to do that would be close. When the timer went off, I rushed to take my puff pastry from the freezer, only to find it hadn't stiffened up or chilled. I followed the freezer cord to its outlet, where the plug lay on the floor. It was either an accident or deliberate sabotage, but either way, it was a disaster. I fought the tears of frustration making their way up and out.

"Honey?" A hand pressed into my shoulder. Angela.

I turned around slowly, shaking as I showed her my pastry dough.

"Oh dear," she said, touching it to confirm it was still warm. She glanced back at her own station and then gave me a determined look. "I think you grabbed mine by mistake."

"Wha—" I began, but she had already rushed to grab the perfectly malleable pastry from her station. She ran back much faster than I expected from someone her age. The lady was spry.

"I can't," I told her, dodging the pastry she was trying to shove into my hands. "That's your hard work."

"Honey," she said, "I've been around a long time. It's your time now."

"No," I repeated, hiccuping.

"Is something wrong?" Mrs. Forrester approached us, a look of concern on her face.

"This young lady grabbed my pastry and I'm just trying to switch them back," Angela explained.

"No," I tried to interject, but Angela dug her finger into the soft tissue of my inner elbow.

"Well, you both have to submit *your* work for judging. You'll be disqualified if you use someone else's pastry," Mrs. Forrester explained.

Angela stepped closer to me, close enough to whisper in my ear. "Better one of us stay than both of us go, hmm?"

She once again attempted to take my dough away, and this time I let her. She led me back to my station and placed her dough in front of me.

"You knock 'em dead," she said before taking my pastry back to her station. There was nothing she could do with it. I felt awful for letting her trade, but if she was going to insist, then I had to make it count. I had to make the best millefeuille the judges had ever tasted. For Angela. So that she might not have gotten the win, but would most definitely hear the praise. I hoped that was enough.

The clock wound down as I worked. I listened to the sound of food processors (bad idea) and whisks. The audience chatter became background noise until, with twenty minutes to go, everything felt way too loud. Sweat was pouring down my forehead and neck and my T-shirt was starting to stick to my back. I used a clean cookie sheet to fan myself while I waited for Angela's pastry to cool down—if I put the cream on the too-hot pastry, it would melt immediately and not hold its form. I glanced up every few minutes to see how Angela was faring. She seemed to still be working; she hadn't given up yet because of my pitiful dough.

I assembled the mille-feuille with two minutes to spare and placed it on my presenting plate. Unlike in the first stage of the competition, one contestant didn't finish in time and was immediately eliminated. Despite there being fewer of us, it felt like the judges took even longer to taste-test and make their notes this time.

The judges were even more stone-faced as they tried my mille-feuille. The younger man who'd smiled at me last time avoided eye contact, and the woman didn't even nod as she wrote in her notepad. The deliberation took twice as long. I could barely listen as they read off the finalists. I didn't even realize they'd said my name until Cameron yelled across the room.

"Go, Skylar!" he whooped, pumping his hands in the air.

I had made it. Angela had not. As she was escorted out with the other eliminated competitors, she squeezed my hand and gave me a quick kiss on the cheek. "And I'd do it again," she said with a smile.

The audience clapped and cheered, and other than me, there were just two other contestants standing at their stations. Even though it had been Angela's choice, making it through this round didn't feel particularly good. Not only had I cheated, I had taken down a good baker and an even better person in the process.

Taylor crashed into me for a giant bear hug.

"You did it!" she squealed. "Good job not going with the prepared puff pastry. One of the people who got eliminated didn't make their own. I knew it was a mistake. I was so relieved when you picked your handmade one to serve."

"I almost didn't," I muttered. Nerves were still making me shiver.

One of the other contestants still left in the final three glared at me over Taylor's shoulder, and I wasn't sure if it was because they were offended a teenager was still in the competition or because Taylor was the Forresters' kid and we were clearly friendly. Maybe they thought I was getting special treatment.

"We should get out of here," I told Taylor,

leading her out of the double doors as Cameron ran to catch up with us. My whole body being tensed for so long had left me exhausted and all I wanted to do was lie down in my bed and sleep until the next, and last, round.

"Wait," Taylor said, twisting out of my grip. "I have to talk to my mom about Mona and Gaby's cake. I have to start on the tiers in a couple of days, and I think they gave her their final flavor picks this morning."

"So," Cameron said as Taylor bounced back into the room. "Nice puff pastry."

He knew, and my eyes watered instantly.

"Oh no, don't cry," he said, pulling me to his side as we walked to the Bronco. "I'm pretty sure I'm the only one who even noticed."

"She sacrificed herself. It isn't fair."

"Okay, well, this isn't *The Hunger Games*, it's just baking. Angela will be okay, she mostly does these things for fun."

"I didn't deserve it."

"You never think you deserve good things. But you do. And speaking of good things, are you ready for another Cameron-planned outing?"

"Now?" I asked with a groan, the thought of my bed getting further and further away.

"Tonight," he replied. "Don't worry, I know you could probably use a nap. It was a physically and emotionally taxing day. Taylor says serious baking makes her feel like she just ran a marathon in a pair of Ugg boots."

"That's weirdly exactly how it feels."

A shadow moved behind him and a familiar face came just barely into view.

"Clare?" I called out, but got no response.

Cameron looked over his shoulder. "Who's Clare?"

I blinked, wondering if I had really seen her at all. A shiver ran down my arms as an unnatural gust of wind seemed to whip through the parking lot before all the trees stilled once more.

"Sky," Cameron said, shaking my shoulder slightly. "Who's Clare?"

I shook my head to loosen the fog. "Uh, nobody. Well, not nobody, my friend from the skate park. I thought I saw her."

Cameron nodded and faced me again. "So, what's your favorite Christopher Nolan film?"

"Am I supposed to have a favorite?"

He rolled his eyes. "I'll pick, then. I swear, you and my sister are so uncultured. Nolan is a cinematic genius and icon."

"Aw, sounds like you have a crush."

"Oh, I would totally marry the guy. But only if Cillian Murphy was part of the package deal."

"I can agree with you there."

"Okay, I'm ready," Taylor said, rejoining us. "Let's blow this Popsicle stand. I have carrot cake to prepare."

Cameron's car idled in front of the house as I zipped up my hoodie. Despite how warm and swampy it got during the day, all the way up to five p.m., the late nights in Alexandria were surprisingly cool.

Cameron turned the music up after I closed the door so as not to disturb the neighborhood. His speakers blasted a girl band who screamed into the microphone with enough rage to leave goose bumps up my arms. The kind of music Dad would love. Cameron reminded me of Dad in a lot of ways. Calm, reliable, persistent.

Cameron pulled into the Remy's parking lot.

"Ah, we've come full circle," I said. "I do love a callback."

"I'll be right back." He threw the car into park and jumped out, jogging to the small restaurant.

In what felt like mere seconds, he ran back out, two pizza boxes in his hand.

He drove us to a local park and parked at the far corner of the lot. The music stopped abruptly when I swung my door open, the only sound that of wind in the treetops.

I carried the pizza boxes in both hands as Cameron carried a mysterious third box. He placed the box on the top platform of a jungle gym and climbed up. I followed his lead, putting the pizzas beside the other box and then vaulting up the rickety structure, clearly built for people much smaller than us. We were both tall, lanky, and clearly over this thing's weight limit, which was only probably a solid thirty pounds.

Cameron sat cross-legged and opened the box. Inside were a small projector, a sheet, and what looked like stone paperweights. He removed the sheet and draped it over the slide side of the jungle gym, placing the paperweights on the structural beams to keep it in place. He then pulled out a blanket from the very bottom of the box and spread it beneath them. Finally, he took the projector out of the box and set it up at our feet, just far enough away from the sheet to project full-screen.

"I hope you like *The Dark Knight Rises* because that's all I downloaded," he said as he pressed play on the small machine.

"I love *The Dark Knight Rises*. Bane is so... man in finance, trust fund, six-five, blue eyes."

"He quite literally is not," Cameron laughed. "I think that would be Bruce Wayne."

"Yeah, I'm not letting Bruce Wayne into my pants. Selina Kyle, though, her we can discuss."

He settled against the back of the jungle gym and used his phone to control the projector's volume and brightness.

"This is kind of baller," I said as we dug into the pizza, just as good as the first time. Remy's got another point for consistency.

"Thank you," Cameron said. "Sometimes I just need to get out of the house, and it may be an empty park but I always feel safe here. So, still trying to get out of Virginia?"

I shrugged. "I don't know, it's kind of grown on me." I nudged him with my elbow.

"It's not so bad. I mean, I know some messed-up shit happened with you and you're still working all that stuff out, but there are good people here."

"Sometimes I feel guilty, when for just a

moment it's like I forget that my dad is dead and I'm just living life."

"I think that's what you have to do. You never ever forget them. But life goes on and you can't be miserable for the rest of it."

"What do you know about loss?" I asked him, in a tone that was surprisingly less irritated than it normally was when it came to talking about this stuff.

He shrugged as if he wasn't going to answer, and then he took a deep breath in resolute acceptance.

"I wouldn't say I *lost* someone, per se. But, you know, one day I had a twin I was inseparable from and then the next, I had . . . someone else. And that's not, like, a woe-is-me thing, because Taylor is my person and I'm happy she felt safe enough to be her true self, but I can't say it wasn't hard. It sounds shitty and I'm pretty sure it *is* pretty shitty to feel like my brother died or something. Especially when people like you actually had someone die and I just had someone become who they really were the whole time. But there are times I miss being *the boys*." He looked at me out of the corner of his eye. "You think I'm trash now."

"No," I responded. "I think you're honest and I think it's okay to not really have the language for how you're feeling. You can be happy and sad about the same thing, I think. I hope."

"You ever feel happy and sad about the same thing?"

"Well, I obviously feel sad about my dad and moving. But then, times like this with you, with Taylor, hell, sometimes even with Gaby or Frankie, I feel like... well, not happy *now*, but like all of this could make me happy one day."

"So therapy," he laughed.

"So therapy," I agreed.

I nodded and took another bite as the movie played.

"What would you do if your parents lied to you about something major?" I asked. "Something life-altering."

"I really don't know. I mean, I like to think I know my parents pretty well, and if they were lying to me about something, it would be because they thought it was for the best. I have to believe they wouldn't be doing it to try and hurt me. And sometimes we're just bad at knowing what the right thing for other people is because we don't bother to ask, or don't feel like we can ask."

"I guess I just get so stuck wondering what good reason they could possibly have had to make me think my mother was dead? And I can't ask him."

"You can ask Mona. I know you don't want to foster any type of relationship with her, and I get it, but like I said, there are good people here and I consider her one of them. She isn't the type of person to hurt people on purpose. Maybe they were just really misguided on what they thought the right thing to do was. She didn't have the easiest childhood."

"Oh, you know about her parents kicking her out?"

"I didn't know that, but she never talks about her family and there's something about her that's always a little bit sad. I think she's had to make a lot of sacrifices that I will never understand or have to make."

"So you would forgive her?" I asked.

"I don't know if I would or not. But I think it's worth a conversation. I mean, like it or not, you're stuck with her. Might as well make it copacetic."

"God, I hate when you make sense."

"It's a gift."

"Shut up," I laughed.

He put his arm around my shoulders and pulled me in to him before lying back, leaning his head against the jungle gym.

"This is nice," he mumbled into my ear.

"Yeah." I smiled, nudging my head farther into his neck. "It is."

Chapter Twenty-One

I was woken up by a knock on my bedroom door.

"Yeah?" I called, sitting up and tossing the comforter off.

"Hey," Gaby said, poking her head into the room. "Can I come in?"

"Uh, sure." I pulled my bonnet off my head, letting my braids fall down my back from the makeshift bun I had them twisted into.

Gaby entered the room carrying an opaque black dress bag, which she laid across the bed.

"I don't know if you plan on going to the wedding?" She looked at me expectantly. The wedding was just a couple of weeks away now. I could hardly believe I'd been here nearly the entire summer. School would be starting soon. Mona had registered me at my new high school, where I wouldn't be sharing homeroom with Olivia or hanging out with my track team. I wasn't even sure I wanted to sign up for track here. I wasn't trying to replace the things I loved in Austin.

"I'm really not sure," I told her.

"Mrs. Forrester, Veronica, stopped by to talk about the cake last night while you were out and mentioned that the final round of the baking competition is that morning."

"Yeah."

"Well, in case you end up having time to come, we would love to have you there." Gaby looked at the dress bag like it was going to leap off the bed.

"Okay, well, I'll try to make it."

"Great." Her eyes gleamed as she wrung her hands in front of her. "Look, I know things are weird around here and I could've done more over the years to make your mo—Mona face her past, but it always felt like something we couldn't really talk about. That's not your fault, it's mine. But I do want this to feel like a home to you because we all really enjoy having you here. I regret that we don't have more years of memories, but I'm hoping you can let us make them now. Starting with the wedding."

Gaby leaned forward and unzipped the dress bag, pulling out a maroon lace gown that hit her at the ankle as she held it up to herself. It would probably stop at my knees.

"Mona and I picked maroon for our wedding color even though it's a summer wedding, and while we weren't going to have a bridal party, we both thought we'd really like you to be a part of it—if you wanted. I mean, I know that's a big commitment and you may not feel comfortable doing so, but we wanted you to have a dress just in case you decide to come."

She laid the dress back down on the bed on top of the dress bag.

"Um, thank you," I told her. There was no way in hell I'd be wearing that dress or participating in the wedding, that was way premature, but it was a nice thought. "For wanting to include me. I know it's a big day for you two."

"It really is." She sat on the edge of the bed now, her shoulders slumping forward. "We've waited such a long time it almost doesn't feel real."

"When Frankie's dad died, did you ever think you'd be getting married again?" I asked.

"No," Gaby laughed. "I had pretty much sworn off marriage at that point. But then I met Mona. Talk about a plan not working out. I had always kind of suspected that I was, you know, not straight, but it was something I made myself ignore. I didn't think it would be something I would ever be brave enough to pursue. Mona gave me a lot of space to figure it out. But I knew I loved her. I envy you, you know."

"Me?" I snorted. "For what?"

"You know exactly who you are and you're not afraid of it. I'm sure a lot of that has to do with your father. Mona told me how great he was."

"He was the best." My voice cracked. "All of my friends were actually pretty jealous." I laughed now at the memory. "I had arguably the coolest dad around."

"I'm sure." Gaby laughed too. "My parents have turned out to be pretty accepting, but I can't imagine how different my life would have been if I had felt comfortable showing them that side of me. Sex and relationships weren't really something that was discussed in my home growing up. It never even occurred to me until I was well into adulthood that life didn't have to look like man plus wife plus kids."

"It seems like you've figured it out."

"Yeah." Gaby nodded. "Well, I don't want to keep you, I know it's still pretty early in the morning. I hope I didn't wake you up."

She had, actually, but I decided not to tell her that. "No, I was up, just scrolling my phone," I lied.

"Oh, good." Gaby stood up from the bed and paused at the door. "Thanks for, I don't know, chatting, I guess. You know I'm here if you ever just want to talk, right?"

"Yeah," I said, because I was starting to know that. Gaby was a nice person, and despite how angry I still was at Mona, I was glad they'd found each other. Everyone deserved to be loved.

Gaby left and closed the door behind her. I grabbed my phone and scrolled down my recent call log.

"This better be good," Olivia mumbled into the phone. Through the FaceTime video, I could just make out her chin and one elbow. She must have still been in bed. Couldn't blame her, since it was even earlier in the morning there than it was here.

"Can't I just miss your face?"

"Of course you miss my face. It's stunning. How's Virginia?"

"Not so bad, I guess."

Olivia sat up suddenly and I could finally see her whole face. A falsie hung on for dear life and mascara was smudged beneath her eyes.

"Wow, late night?"

"It was salsa night at the cantina." The family of Olivia's situationship, Anthony, owned a local cantina that hosted a salsa night once a month. It was one of our usual haunts every third Thursday.

"You look rougher than salsa night at the cantina," I told her with a chuckle as she tried to blink away the false lash before finally ripping it off.

"Well, then Roger—you remember Roger, right? Anthony's soccer buddy? He had a kick-back at his house—parents out of town, you know the deal—and we stayed there until two a.m. Let me tell you, I suck at flip cup and I paid dearly for it."

A weird feeling filled my belly. We used to do everything together. If there was a party, we were a package deal. Now Olivia was going to parties without me and I was going on dates with people

Olivia didn't set me up with and hadn't even met. Our lives, which were once so entangled, were starting to diverge.

"Wow, you're having so much fun without me."

"Don't be like that, Ms. Baking Master. Yeah, I've seen your Insta stories. You and that smokeshow of a boyfriend."

"Cameron is NOT my boyfriend."

"Well, he certainly keeps his camera on you like he's recording you for posterity."

"I mean, we've gone on dates, but we're not anything official."

Olivia squealed into the phone. "Love how you conveniently haven't told me anything about this. God, when's the last time you were dating a guy?"

"Like, two people before Simone. It's been a while."

"Well, you know they say it's like riding a bike," she said. I hadn't told her about my new bike-riding pastime, but the irony made me laugh harder than I had in months.

"What?" she asked, confused. "I mean, I know I'm hilarious but I wasn't even trying with that one."

"No, nothing, inside joke, I guess."

"Wow, you talk about me and you've got inside jokes I'm not on the inside of?"

"It's kind of an inside joke with myself, so no one's in on it."

"I used to be in on those too." She pouted her bottom lip dramatically.

"Well, thank God for FaceTime so at least I can see your beautiful smudged face."

Olivia flicked me off and stuck her tongue out. "I'm declining your call next time. We can't all wake up beautiful, beautiful."

"I do have a gift."

"All right, well, I should be in the studio. I have to get my portfolio ready for applications and I still need Mrs. Nielsen to review it." Mrs. Nielsen was our art teacher and she was pretty much Olivia's biggest fan and mentor. Olivia was applying to art schools for college, but with her talent and Mrs. Nielsen's letter of recommendation, I didn't see her having a problem getting into any school she applied to. Unlike me, who had absolutely no idea where I wanted to go now that UT Austin was probably off the table.

"Talk to you later, hater," Olivia sang before hanging up the call.

Chapter Twenty-Two

"Do you want to go?"

Diana looked at me expectantly. Her pen was already poised in her hand, ready to take notes on what she would psychoanalyze me on later.

"I don't know." I shrugged. "I mean, it is kind of a big deal. A generation ago, Mona and Gaby could never have gotten married, lived in the Virginia suburbs, raised a child together, none of it. So in an I-have-respect-for-the-historical-significance kind of way, I do want to be there. Especially now—who knows how long people like us will be able to do this?"

"But?"

"But," I repeated. "Going feels like cosigning that I support this life she's chosen."

"One that excluded you."

"Right."

"One that led to a lot of lies."

"Yes."

"Have you had a chance to talk to Mona yet about her reasons, what she may have been going through at the time?"

"No, and I know it was my homework or whatever, but I really don't plan on it. I don't *care* what the reasons were. It was fucked up, and I think it's okay to feel that way."

"Of course," Diana said. "You're free to feel however about it—there's no right or wrong when it comes to that."

"Then why does it feel like you're judging me?"

"Skylar, I'm your therapist. I'm not judging you. But I do want to push you. You just said yourself that a generation ago, this life would not, could not, exist for her. How do you think you would think and behave if that were the case for you?"

"I don't know," I said. "I'd probably be pretty scared."

"Mm." Diana nodded. "I think I would be too. Do you think you make sound, reasonable decisions when you're scared?"

"I've never really been scared, I guess."

"Why not?"

"I guess I've never wanted anything that I wasn't supported in pursuing."

"Mm." Diana grunted again. "If I may say so, that seems very fortunate. Certainly not universal." She raised her eyebrow and gave me a knowing look.

"I hate when you have a good point," I told her. "Like, legitimately, it pisses me off." I almost laughed, but I really did hate it.

Diana raised her hands as if surrendering. "I'm just here to help you shape your thoughts, not place them in your head."

"Why can't you be here to just validate me instead?"

This time she did laugh out loud. "I don't think insurance companies would cover it, to be honest. But my homework for you remains the same. Talk. About anything, about everything. Put the car in gear."

I rolled my eyes and leaned back on the sofa. "Ugh."

For the first time, I couldn't sleep but I didn't want to bake anything. The competition was almost over and I was pretty sure I wasn't going to win—the contestants left were crazy good and a lot older. Sometimes it felt like more their time than mine. I would have so many chances to live the dream they were fighting for now. But even more so, Paris meant leaving again, and I was just starting to really get into the hang of being *here*. And then of course, Diana's directive spun around my head like a top. I didn't *want* to talk to Mona, but it was the only way to get answers. I would never know why Dad engaged in this whole thing, but I could at least get her side of it. Maybe. One day.

I lay in bed in the dark, counting the stars I could see through the window blinds before I finally turned on the nightstand lamp. My phone read 12:10 a.m. I opened the drawer and pulled out Mona's journal. I hadn't read it in days.

I flipped to the last page I'd been on, squinting to make out Mona's cramped handwriting. An audible gasp escaped me as I took in the words.

> *I'm pregnant. I haven't told Teddy yet. I'm still a bit in disbelief and I guess I thought writing it down here would help me believe it but it still feels like it's happening*

to someone else. We only did it one time, more out of curiosity than anything else. But I guess that's all it took—we were stupid and not very careful. I don't know what I'm going to do about it. Part of me thinks I should handle it, not say anything to Teddy, and go on about our lives. But part of me wants to keep it, maybe give it the kind of life and loving family that I never had. If I do that, though, I think we have to get married. I know that's what Teddy will want to do. Unlike me, he's not the kind of person who runs from his problems. I hope it's a boy, not that I think boys are better, I just think girls require a certain kind of love that I never learned how to give. I'm worried I will put my expectations on a girl like my mother did to me. The truth is, it's hard to be a young Black girl in this world, and I'm terrified of messing it up, making her inherit the same type of claustrophobic trauma that I have.

I slammed the book shut with a gulp and tossed it across the bed. I'd always known Dad was young and had me in his teens—nineteen, to be exact—but I'd figured I was conceived after they were married, not before. It seemed like they had already decided to get married, but was *I* what pushed them over the edge?

I got out of bed and headed downstairs. All the lights were off except for the one over the oven, casting the kitchen in a dim blue glow. I poured myself a glass of water and tried to take deep breaths through my nose. Still, it wasn't enough.

I found myself leaving the house without thinking about it. Placing my glass on the corner of the porch and not caring about being barefoot, I started running, going wherever my subconscious took me.

The street leading to the skate park was desolate this late at night and wind blew along the line of shops, lifting my braids from my neck. Thoughts of Mona filled my head until I had to stop. Kicked out of her home, accidentally pregnant. What would I have done in the same circumstances? Would I have made smarter decisions? Probably not.

The skate park was empty except for one person.

Clare was sitting on our bench, her head bowed.

"Clare?" I asked, grateful to now be walking on smooth concrete. She turned her head stiffly and the tears streaming down her face glistened under the moonlight. "Are you okay?" She used her wrists to wipe the tears away and sniffed hard. Her heart tattoo stood out, even in the dark.

I sat on the bench beside her and placed my hand on her shoulder. "What's going on?"

She shook her head silently. Her mouth opened a few times but words didn't come out, like Ariel when Ursula stole her voice. "I'm so stupid," she whispered.

Finally she looked up at me. Her eyes were swollen and her nose was running.

"I made a mistake," she told me, her voice barely audible.

"Oh God, don't tell me you married him." Had I been talking to a wall this whole time? I really thought she would listen to me in the end.

She shook her head again. "No, not that."

She didn't elaborate. Instead, she grabbed my hand off her shoulder and pulled it onto her lap.

"I think I have to go," she said.

"Go where?"

"I don't know. Just away from here. I can't stay at Hawley anymore."

"Why? Because you turned eighteen? Would they really kick you out?"

She cried harder now, her shoulders shaking. I scooted closer and wrapped my arms around her, trying to hold her together as she fell apart. We sat like that for what felt like hours, until I was sure she'd cried every tear she could possibly have had in her body. Then she dry-heaved, leaning over the side of the bench to throw up.

"Oh my God," I screeched, rushing to hold her braids back.

She turned her head slowly and gave me a sad smile. She took a few deep breaths through her mouth, and I could tell she was trying not to throw up again.

"You're a good friend," she told me before she looked off into the distance. Finally she stood up, letting my arms drop away from around her.

"Where are you going?" I asked. The moonlight cast a white aura around her head like a halo.

"I've made a lot of mistakes," she said, "but I'm happy we met."

"Why does it feel like you're saying goodbye?"

Tears slid from the corners of her eyes that she didn't wipe away this time, letting them fall freely. She turned away from me and grabbed her bike from the ground.

"Clare," I said, trying to stop her. "Tell me what's happening. Tell me what you need help with. I can help you."

"No you can't." She gave me another small smile. "It's time to start helping myself." She grabbed my hand as I approached her, lining up the small black ink hearts on our palms.

"Bye, Skylar," she said, squeezing my hand. From her voice, I could tell that this goodbye was real. That it was final. And then she climbed on her bike and pedaled away.

I felt tears running down my cheeks as I watched her ride out of sight. I started walking back home. Spiritually, I didn't have the energy to run. I never got to say goodbye to Dad, but if I had, maybe it would have felt like that. Something made me doubt I would ever see her again.

When I got back to the house, I closed the door quietly behind me and went to the kitchen.

"Skylar?"

Mona was at the kitchen table, sitting in the dark with a mug in her hands. A tea bag hung over the side of the cup. Like it had with Clare, the moon sat just behind her, making her glow in the still room.

"Where were you? Do you know what time it is?"

"I just needed some air. I went for a run." I didn't tell her about Clare or making it all the way to the skate park. She wouldn't like that I went that far this late at night.

"You can't leave the house at this hour without telling someone. It's a safe neighborhood, but anything could happen." She paused and took a sip of her tea. Or at least attempted to.

She stood up and grabbed the electric teakettle off its base. She put two scoops of tea leaves into a small reusable tea bag and poured the hot water over it. She stashed the tin back in the cupboard with a bunch of similar-looking containers.

"You really like tea," I said as she handed me the mug.

"Mmm," she mumbled around a sip. "My mother used to make a hot cup of tea for me before bed every night. I guess it's stuck with me."

Despite what I knew had happened between her and her mother, I was still jealous that she'd actually gotten to make memories with her mom. Everything I remembered about Mona was recent, rotten, and tainted.

We sat in almost comfortable silence as we drank our tea.

"How'd that cake turn out?" I asked her, grasping for something to talk about that wasn't our past.

"Cake? Oh, the shortcake. God, I practically forgot about it. It turned out terribly," she laughed. "I appreciate your help, though." She placed her mug on the table and held her hands out in front of her. "The fault was all mine. These boots just aren't made for walking."

My eyebrows lifted in confusion.

"Sorry, old saying. These hands aren't meant for baking."

"It just takes practice," I assured her. "I got to practice a lot. You know Dad and his sweet tooth."

She laughed, her eyes glancing past my shoulder like she was watching a scene play out behind me. "Yes, I do remember. He could clear out an entire night of our trick-or-treat stash in just under twelve hours."

"Oh, I had to hide mine from him entirely." I shook my head with a chuckle and then fell silent again. Memories of Dad still hurt too much to linger on for long.

"I don't know how you're doing it," she said finally. "I already miss him so much."

"Did you two talk? I mean, once you left?"

"Not very often. Maybe once every few years he would give me an update on how you were doing. It was easier to go kind of no-contact."

"Did he ever try to convince you to come back?"

"He did and he didn't. The reasons I left were hard on both of us. I knew it hurt him to have to be dishonest with you. He really wanted to tell you. Those last few days, we talked about it a lot. It was like he had this compulsion."

"But you said no." Dad had been begging her in the conversation I overheard, and it must have been about this.

"Yes. It just felt like we had committed to it for too long. I knew it would hurt you to know the truth. But God, if I had known. I can't believe I made him go with that on his heart. It was so selfish. The reasons I left don't even exist anymore."

"And what were the reasons? That you left?"

She took a deep breath and then blew it out

slowly. "I made a lot of mistakes when I was nineteen. We had just had you and it was starting to occur to me how much my life was running off the tracks. Your father and I got married because we thought it would be easier to get all the benefits we needed. I mean, we were practically on our own with a newborn baby. We both knew I was gay, but I think there was a huge part of me that still felt like I could stuff that deep down inside myself and be the wife and partner your father needed. I mean, he was doing all these huge favors for me to get me off the street and out of a shelter. He was putting aside his own dreams of having a family, a wife who could love him back, and so I believed that it was only right for me to do the same."

She raised her wrist to her eyes and wiped away the tears gathering in their corners.

"But we were both so incredibly unhappy. And I had a lot of anger in me that I hadn't worked on or even learned how to handle. Angry at my parents, angry at myself, even angry at your dad. I saw myself repeating patterns from my childhood when it came to you and I didn't like it. Your father definitely didn't like it. So one day, just before your first birthday, your father said I needed to start over, have a real shot at the life I wanted, and I couldn't do that if I was halfway out the door."

"So he let you leave."

"He didn't want me popping in and out of your life when it was convenient for me, so he told me that if I left, I had to really leave, that he wouldn't have you growing up wondering whether your mother loved you or not. And I did, I swear I did, and do. I don't think we ever really planned to make you believe I was dead. I just think 'your mom is gone' transformed into something that neither of us could really control. But how else could we make my absence permanent?"

"And it never occurred to either of you that a mother there half the time would have been better than one not there at all?" I couldn't understand how two smart and seemingly empathetic and compassionate people could make such self-serving decisions. When did paths forward enmeshed in avoidance come to an end?

"I don't think anything we did in those years was wise. I abandoned my family, started over on a fresh life, but everything I've accomplished, I've never been proud of any of it. How could I be when it required so much sacrifice from the people I love?"

"And then he died."

"And then he died." Her voice cracked like she still could hardly believe it. "And Naomi called me, she had my number in case of an emergency, and she told me he was gone, and all I felt was a deep regret that I had let you both get so far away from me. I think getting on that plane to go get you was one of the hardest things I've ever done in my life. And I've done some pretty hard things. I just didn't know what to expect of you, I didn't think I deserved any kind of forgiveness for the mess I had caused. But I was also... happy... that I finally got a second chance at being your mother."

The two of us sat quietly for a moment, letting her words sink in.

"I really don't expect you to forgive me or let me into your life," she said. "But I do hope that you come to consider this place home, and know that no matter what, you are safe here."

She yawned now and polished off the rest of her tea.

"I have an early morning," she said, though

she didn't make any move to get up. "And I might be too exhausted now to actually sleep."

"Yeah, me too." I nodded. "Practicing baking all day tomorrow with Taylor."

"I'm happy you've made some friends. I never really had many friends. Mostly your dad, a girl I met one summer. All gone now." Finally she stood up and placed her mug in the empty sink. "How's that competition going?"

"Pretty good," I told her. "I'm in the final round. It's actually, um, the morning of the wedding."

She gave me a sad smile. "Well, I know we'd love for you to be there, but we understand if you can't. Good night, Skylar."

With that, she left me alone in the kitchen to finish my tea. I pressed my forehead onto the table and took a deep breath. It was the longest conversation we'd ever had, and it certainly put things more into perspective. I tried to imagine what I would have done in her situation, how Dad must have felt having to choose me over his lifelong best friend, how I might have felt if she *had* stuck halfway around. Would I have resented her for choosing not to be with me? Would I have hated her for different reasons? Did I even hate her now? It was getting harder to feel like I did.

Maybe part of growing up was learning that adults didn't have all the answers. Maybe we were all just trying our best to survive. And maybe you had to meet people where they were.

Chapter Twenty-Three

Staying up late talking to Mona and then spending the rest of the night thinking about the talk with Mona did me absolutely no favors when it came to spending a day with Drill Sergeant Taylor at the bakery.

"Please," I begged her after six hours of making fruit tart after fruit tart until I got a perfect glaze. "My crops are dying. I didn't even know a baker could get blisters." I held up my hands as proof. They were so red and overworked they looked like I was wearing part of a Cruella de Vil costume. All I needed was the long cigarette.

"Fine," she said with a roll of her eyes. "But if round three is fruit tarts and you can't get a perfect glaze from lack of practice, I don't want to hear a single word about it." She seemed to think for a moment before her face brightened. "But I do have another good idea. Roof tanning."

"Roof a-what now?" I asked.

"You'll see."

She led me up to the roof exit, where we had to climb a precarious ladder to get above the bakery. I was surprised to find a couple of lounge chairs, tied down so as not to blow away, and a cedar chest with blankets and towels.

"What in the world," I laughed.

"We live too far from the beach so Cam and I built our own, but without all the gross sand."

The sun was blasting down on us, and we both pushed our sleeves up as high as they would go and settled down on the chairs.

"This is the life," Taylor mused as she raised her face to the sky. The sun soaked into her skin like each ray was finding a new home.

"Tell me about it." My feet were sore from baking all morning and I fought not to nod off.

But staying awake meant thinking and thinking meant worrying and there was so much to worry about. I hoped that wherever Clare was, she wouldn't make the same mistakes as Mona.

My inability to convince her sat like a rock in my belly.

My phone vibrated in my pocket and I pulled it out to see a FaceTime call from Olivia.

"Perfect timing," I told her as I pressed accept.

"Are you at the beach?" she asked, taking in the lounge chair behind my head.

"Next best thing." I swung the phone around so she could get a clear shot of the view. From here you could just barely make out the Washington Monument in the distance. I wondered why so many cities liked to have phallic centerpieces, but I was no urban planner.

"Nice," she crooned. "Wait, hold up."

She shuffled around the room and the camera fell from her face as she moved through her house. I caught a glimpse of her mom's HomeGoods collection on the walls. She was a Live, Love, Laugh girlie, but we still loved her.

Finally I saw the green grass of Olivia's front yard. She laid out her own towel and dropped onto the grass.

"It's like we're sunbathing together," she said, once again holding the phone up to her face. "See, we can still do best-friend things even from far away."

I smiled brightly at the gesture. Diana and I had worked out that part of my feelings about the move to Virginia included the fear that everyone back home would forget and replace me, like I was an insignificant blip in their lives they would all move on from. And maybe they would. But Olivia wouldn't. And she was really the one who mattered most.

Because despite how much I'd gotten used to living here, and sometimes even enjoyed it, I missed her so much. I missed having someone who understood everything about me without me having to explain myself. I missed having someone who knew how much of a loss it was not to have Dad in the world. Olivia loved my dad—they'd bonded over their shared love of my baking and more than once had ganged up on me to make a batch of blondies or my signature chocolate chip cookies (the secret was a dash of sea salt).

"This is Taylor," I said as I turned the camera toward her.

Taylor waved enthusiastically, squinting into the sun behind my head. "Hi, Olivia, heard a lot about you."

"All lies, I'm sure."

"Only the good stories," I interjected. "Don't want to tell people how bad of an influence you are on me."

Olivia stuck her tongue out and I perched the phone against the brick of the chimney sprouting out of the top of the bakery like an apple stem. We chatted about the competition and how Austin was doing without me. Olivia and her boyfriend were getting more serious than ever.

"I think I'm ready," Olivia told us. Taylor raised her eyebrows.

"Are you sure?" I asked. Olivia had wanted to wait for her one true love, and I just couldn't imagine that Anthony was it. Not that he wasn't a perfectly decent guy, but he was, to put it nicely, not the brightest crayon in the box. He was earnest for sure, but I wouldn't give him good odds on winning *The Circle*.

"I don't know," she said. "I mean, I feel like I really love him."

"Well, if you love him," Taylor provided, giving Olivia a vote in the go-for-it category.

"Have you, you know, done it?" Olivia asked Taylor, already knowing I had.

Taylor scooted closer so that she could see into the camera. "I haven't, but I've never met anyone

I wanted to do it with. If you're feeling some type of way, might as well try and see."

"And if it's awful?" Olivia asked.

"Oh, it's definitely going to be awful," I laughed. Teenage boys had no clue what they were doing, something I'd learned junior year with Will Reese. Nice guy, terrible stamina. Which was surprising for a star hurdler on the track team.

Olivia sucked her teeth and rolled her eyes. "You're so jaded. Maybe Will just didn't know what he was doing."

"Of course he didn't," I said. "None of them do. And that's why I'm bi. Girls are hotter, more sensual, and know what they're doing. Boys are basically just holding me hostage at this point."

"You're bi?" Taylor asked in a tone of surprise.

"Oh God," Olivia said. "Don't get me started. Her last girlfriend was so hot. A total raging bitch, but hot."

"Hey, Simone was not a bitch," I said.

"I can't even believe you just said that with a straight face. How many times did that girl make you cry?"

I cringed inwardly, my lips turning downward. "Fair point."

"Well, I know someone who won't make you cry," Taylor sang. "Olivia, has she told you about Cameron?" And this was the problem with letting my two worlds collide—a girl couldn't have any secrets when the information-sharing now eclipsed me.

"The hottie next door? Oh, she's hinted. Is there more to the story?"

"I don't know, how did your date go the other night?" Taylor asked conspiratorially.

"Date?" Olivia squawked. "No one told me about a date! Give me all the dirty little details."

"First, it was not a date." Both of them stared at me incredulously. "Okay, maybe it was a date. It was really nice, and that's all I'm sharing with you two tattletales."

"You can't tattletale among best friends," Olivia said, to which Taylor quickly agreed.

It took me aback for a second. Olivia had always been my one ride-or-die best friend, but Taylor and I had gotten so close this summer that she was starting to feel like a best friend. It amazed me how quickly I'd found my people here, and how easy it had been to hang on to an old one.

"Definitely bring this one back with you when

you come visit," Olivia said, pointing to Taylor past my head.

The word *visit* made me surprisingly sad. Austin wasn't my home anymore, and I would be nothing more than a temporary guest in the place that raised me. My life had been split into two parts, the Before and the After, and while I was becoming okay with the After, losing the Before still filled me with anxiety. But other than Olivia, what was I still trying to hold on to?

I was in desperate need of a shower when I got home. The melted sugar glaze baked into my pores from tanning on the roof was so uncomfortable it made me want to just peel my skin off my body and soak it clean.

As I waited for the shower to get hot enough to boil me, I sat on the toilet and prepared for a mindless doomscroll. Before turning Dad's phone off, I had linked everything on his Google Drive with mine, which could have been potentially disastrous but had worked out well. I loved the memory compilations my iPhone put together from the shared photos. I clicked open the one from this morning, titled "Putting on a

Show," and downloaded all the photos it used to my phone.

I set my phone on the bathroom counter while the photos downloaded and hopped into the steaming shower. I closed my eyes and let the water soak into my skin. It was the first shower I'd taken in a while that felt relaxing. The rest had been necessary, tiny attempts at restoration. But this one felt like the hard work had been done and I could enjoy it.

When I was done, I toweled off and threw on sweatpants and an old Rolling Stones T-shirt that had belonged to Dad. My foot accidentally kicked Dad's guitar case and it toppled to the floor, snapping open. Dad's guitar sat in red velvet. It was probably already out of tune, but I strummed my fingers over the strings and a sweet melody released into the room. I would never play it for real—I didn't know how and I wasn't that interested in learning—but I wanted to make sure it was taken care of anyway. I used the hem of my T-shirt to wipe down its face and then shut the case again.

Halfway down the stairs, I remembered my phone on the bathroom counter.

The screen flashed with the downloaded

photos. I sat back down on the toilet and barreled through them, dozens from his last show. I wasn't sure anyone had ever seen them except Mr. Google himself. Tears pricked the corners of my eyes.

He looked so alive onstage, I couldn't comprehend that he would be gone mere hours later. But my favorites were the ones of him before the show. His smile was luminous as he threw his head back with laughter. I ran my finger over the screen and could almost feel his warm skin beneath my fingertips. Sobs wracked my body as I came across one of the two of us, his arm slung over my shoulders as he kissed my forehead. I looked totally over it, but a small smile sat at the corner of my mouth. I wished I had leaned more into it, smiled brighter, so that he knew how much I loved being in the crook of his arm.

One picture in particular caught my eye. It was a photo of Dad bending over his guitar case. A small white corner stuck out of the back pocket of the case, clashing against the red of the velvet. I couldn't tell what it was from the small corner, but I was curious.

The guitar case was where I'd left it on the bedroom floor. I snapped it back open and knelt in front of it like I was about to say a prayer. I reached into the pocket and pulled out a folded envelope that felt empty. I untucked the back flap and a picture fell into my lap. It was an old Polaroid, the back inscribed with *our little family 2009*. I flipped the picture over and instantly recognized my dad. Even though he was quite a bit younger, he still had the same glint in his brown eyes, the same crooked smile. His hair was in locs, which I didn't remember. My eyes slowly took in the rest of the picture, and the small photograph immediately fell from my fingers.

"What the fuck?" I gasped as Clare's face stared back at me.

Chapter Twenty-Four

I hurried down the stairs and out the front door. For the first time, I didn't want to run away, but I didn't know exactly what to do or where to go or who to go to. No one would believe me. I mean, I barely believed me. I didn't know how long I paced up and down the front yard, but I was surprised I hadn't worn a path into it by now.

"Yo, you good?"

I looked up to find Cameron approaching me from his own yard. His skateboard dangled loosely from his fingers.

"You look like you just saw a ghost," he said with a smile.

It made me want to throw up. Was she a ghost? No, she was real. I saw her. I touched her. She gave me a tattoo. I flipped my palm up to make sure the heart was still there. The ink had started to spread a bit into my skin but it was clear as day, still slightly red and scabbed as it healed. A ghost couldn't do something like that. Could it?

"You see this, right?" I asked, holding my palm up to him.

"Your janky tattoo, yeah," he laughed. "Who gave you that thing? Didn't know you did some time on the inside."

"I'm..." I said, my voice trailing off. I was what? Confused? Hysterical? I wanted to tell him but he would probably have me committed. Wait, he saw her too.

"The girl from the skate park gave it to me."

"You let a random girl at the skate park give you a tattoo? Low-key badass, high-key insane."

"Do you remember her, the girl at the skate park?" I asked him.

"There are lots of girls at the skate park."

I rolled my eyes impatiently. "The one who used to sit with me on that old bench."

His eyebrows scrunched together as his eyes followed my pacing worriedly.

"She used to get cupcakes from your folks' bakery, like, every day?" I urged him along.

"Sky, you're the only one who uses that bench. The rest of us are, you know, actually skating."

"*No!*" I shrieked. "You saw her. Braids, a little heavyset, always carrying a backpack suspiciously filled with tattoo equipment?" Okay, maybe he didn't know or need to know that part.

"Sky, are you okay?" he asked, concern lacing his voice. "You're kind of scaring me."

He moved to approach me, his arm outstretched. I backed away from him. Was he trying to make me feel crazy or was I actually crazy?

"You saw her," I whispered this time.

He shook his head slowly, his lips parting but no words coming out. He looked at me like one might face down a rabid dog.

I couldn't handle this. So I did the only thing I'd ever known how to do in overwhelming situations. I turned around and ran.

I ran without direction, my only hope to get as far away from everything and everyone as I could. Surely someone was playing a monumentally mean joke on me. Someone photoshopped that picture—that picture of my dad—and left it for me to find. But Cameron's confusion felt genuine; he had no idea who or what I was talking about.

You look like you just saw a ghost.

I ran for what felt like hours, taking random trails along the way. I found myself in the city, just across the river from Alexandria, a trip that usually took me about twenty minutes on my bike. But I was lost and I'd left my phone on the bathroom counter.

"Idiot!" I screeched, catching the attention of passersby who looked at me like I'd lost my marbles. And maybe I had. I was apparently seeing ghosts and I had no idea how to get home.

But then stores started to feel familiar. It was the same store still at the corner across the street. Which meant I wasn't far from Hawley House. Maybe someone there could help me figure out how to get home, or give me cash for a cab. I felt bad asking homeless teenagers for money, but maybe I could get their number and Cash App them back later. Otherwise, I didn't really know what my options were right now. Without a phone, I couldn't call anyone to come get me. Shit, a cab wouldn't help either because I didn't know where I lived. What the hell did people do before phones? Just get lost forever?

I started to cry in frustration as I took now familiar streets to Hawley House, its inviting green brick standing out against the grays around it. The front door was slightly open, just enough to let others know they could come in without knocking, but not open enough to invite just anyone off the street. I pushed the door open farther. Once again, it was dead silent. Ma must run a tight ship.

"Hello?" I called into the cavernous foyer. A TV was on in the living room, but no one was watching it. It was set on one of those soap operas with horrible writing. "Hello?" I tried again.

"Hello?" a voice responded. It sounded familiar, heavily accented, but I couldn't place it. There was too much going through my brain to process input properly.

A woman emerged from somewhere in the back of the house.

"Angela?" I said.

"Can I help you?" she asked, before stopping in her tracks as she took me in. "Well, I'll be," she said with a smile. "How you now?"

"Wh-what are you doing here?"

"I live here, honey. And work here, but these long years it's stopped feeling like a job." She touched one of the walls affectionately. "But may I ask what you are doing here? Are you in trouble? Only reason folks come looking for me."

"Can I?" I gestured to an armchair next to me. I needed to sit down.

"Take your time, sweetie," she said.

"I'm kind of lost," I told her. Very, very lost. Physically, sure. But at this point, mentally and emotionally as well.

She stared at me curiously. "Well, this is a good place for lost people. Where you hoping to go?"

To an asylum, probably.

"Wait, you're Ma?" I asked, my brain short-circuiting but still trying to put the pieces together.

She laughed from deep in her chest. "That's what they call me."

Then she would know Clare. Clare lived here. Maybe she was even here right now.

"Actually, I wonder if you can help me?"

"I'm all ears." She gave a small laugh that sounded like bits of sea glass hitting each other.

"There's a girl that lives here, Clare? I'm worried about her."

"Clare?" the woman repeated like she was trying the unfamiliar name on for size. "We've had a lot of Clares over the years. And you're sure she lives here now?"

"I'm positive... Well, not positive." I wasn't positive about much right now. Either Clare really existed or she didn't. Either I was having a mental breakdown or I wasn't. Only one way to find out.

I stood up just long enough to pull the photo out of my back pocket before collapsing into the chair again.

"She looks like this?"

Angela reached for the photo, her mouth forming into a perfect O of recognition.

"Where you get this?" she asked. She flipped the photo over and read the back, then finally looked back at me. "Clare." And then she smiled to herself before looking somewhere past my shoulder. "Can I show you something?"

She led me through the house, back past the staircase. The walls were lined with photographs and she scanned each one, stopping at one just out of her reach.

"Do you mind?" she asked me, pointing to it. I reached over her head to pull it down gently. It was a group photo that looked old and worn.

She took the frame in both hands and pointed at the person in the very middle.

"Clare Jefferson," she said. I leaned over her shoulder and lo and behold, there was Clare, smiling at the camera. She was standing just behind Angela, her braids pulled back just like she wore them every day at the skate park. She had on the same overalls, the same backpack. This picture had to be over a decade old, but Clare looked exactly the way she did the last time I saw her. "Well, I guess it's Clare Morrison now, she married that sweet boy," the woman said. "Theodore, I think his name was. How do you know her?"

"I . . . I don't know," I said, now more confused than ever. It was clear that Clare and Mona were the same person, but how? It was impossible, but here I was looking at the proof. Cam not seeing her didn't make any sense. He could see the tattoo, and *someone* had to have put it there. Was she invisible to everyone but me? Was she a time traveler?

"She was one of my favorites. Don't tell anyone," Angela said with a finger over her lips. "I'm not supposed to have favorites. But she was a special girl. Tough life. Those parents of hers, they really dimmed her light. That Theodore really did try to save her."

"Theodore," I repeated. "He was my dad."

"Oh," Angela said before her eyes widened. "Oh. Oh my. You're Clare's girl. My God, I knew it. I saw you and I knew there was something special in you, something I remembered. How are they? Clare and Theo—oh, he passed. I'm so sorry, sweetheart."

Tears fell down my cheeks and this time I didn't move to stop them.

"And how's Clare holding up? Oh, she loved that boy. Not in the way that should have gotten them married. But we all knew Clare, and, well, she loved that boy."

"She left me and my dad when I was a baby," I told her, though not with the venom with which

I usually shared such news. "Couldn't keep lying about who she was."

Angela nodded. "I bet. She was always running away. From her family, from herself, from here. Woke up one day with a note that she was gone. Wasn't really one for goodbyes. But you look just like her."

I stared longer at the photo. I didn't see myself in her. But even more than that, I didn't see Mona in her either. Where Clare was filled out, her cheeks still holding on to baby fat, Mona was thin, almost skeletal, her skin stretching across her cheekbones, making them appear high and sharp. Where Clare's braided ponytail fell over her shoulder, Mona's hair was cut close to her scalp. Where Clare's eyes sparkled, Mona's were dull. I didn't see the girl I'd gotten to know this summer. And I wondered how much of Clare she had left in her. How much she'd lost because of her parents, because of me. How much we all had dimmed the light Angela loved so much about her.

"I don't see it," I told her.

"Well, you remind me of her, but not in the ways that probably matter to you."

We went back to the living room and talked a bit more before I asked if I could use her phone. I had one Hail Mary left.

"You don't happen to still have Clare's number, do you?" I asked.

"Well, hmm, let me see." She scrolled through her phone. "Don't think I've deleted a number in twenty years. Ah, here."

She passed me her phone with Clare's number pulled up. It was still a 202 number; hopefully she had never changed it.

I hit call and crossed my fingers as it went through.

"Hello?" Mona answered, the familiar tenor of her voice filling the receiver. I'd never been so happy to hear her.

"Mona, thank God. I'm, uh, lost. Well, not lost. I know where I am, but I don't know how to get home."

She seemed to not hear the latter part of my statement, because her voice filled with panic. "Lost?" she repeated. "Where are you? What number is this?"

"I'm at Hawley House."

There was silence on her end of the phone that seemed to last an eternity.

"You're where?"

"Hawley House," I repeated. "It's in DC."

"Yes, I... I know where it is. How did you... Never mind, we'll talk about it later. I'm on my way."

"Well, actually, if you can just give me your address, I can catch a cab."

"Skylar." She took a deep breath. "I'm on my way." And then she hung up.

Chapter Twenty-Five

Hello?" Mona announced herself the same way I had when she came into Hawley.

Angela and I both stood up from the couch, hot cups of tea clasped in our hands.

"Clare?" Angela responded. Mona visibly bristled at the name before she fully took in Angela.

"Oh my God," she whispered. I swiftly took Angela's cup before Mona collapsed into her arms. "Ma. You're still here."

"They'll have to wheel me out of here one day, but not yet." Angela laughed into Mona's hair.

Mona's eyes found me as I stood behind them, leaning against the entrance to the living room. Despite the difference in appearance, I started to see Clare in her now. The patience she had showed me since we met. The ways in which she'd allowed Gaby and Frankie to be their authentic selves. Clare had welcomed me, and so had Mona, even if I wasn't ready to be welcomed quite yet. When Mona finally smiled during her hug with Angela, that was when Clare really came alive. I didn't know how it happened, and I definitely couldn't explain it. I tried not to dwell on it too much now, but man, was therapy going to be a ride.

"How did you find this place?" Mona asked me as she released Angela from the hug.

I didn't know how to explain Clare to her, or to anyone, really. But there was still part of the truth available to me.

"I read about it," I told her. "In your old journal."

"My old journal?" Her eyebrows pulled together in confusion.

"When I borrowed your old bike, there was a box that fell and your journal slipped out. I know I should have put it back, but, I don't know, I was curious. I didn't know what it was at first. But then I started reading it, and I guess it helped with the questions I wasn't ready to ask you yet. I wanted to understand you and your decisions, but on my own time."

Somehow the journal had brought me closer to her. Maybe even so close that it had conjured up a version of her I could better relate to. It had given me Clare.

"I understand," she said. "But I would like it back when we get home."

I nodded in agreement. It wasn't mine to keep.

"Well, tell me about yourself," Angela said, once again leading us all into the living room. "Tell me everything. Skylar here told me about Theodore. I'm so sorry. I know how much you loved him."

"I just wish I had been there for him more, like he was there for me. Feel like I let him down."

"I'm sure that didn't make him love you any less," Angela assured her.

"It should have."

"It didn't," I offered.

"What do you mean?"

"Well, if he didn't love you, he would've been okay with me hating you for leaving. But he never told me that you chose to leave. He always wanted me to still love the idea of you. You would only do that for someone you love. Dearly." It was only now that I realized he'd given us this chance to one day know each other—with some baggage, but not so much as to be irreconcilable. But that was Dad.

"Maybe," Mona muttered, though she didn't seem convinced.

Angela and Mona spent the next half hour catching up. Mona told her that she'd stopped going by Clare when she left, choosing to use her middle name as another part of her effort to start over.

"Every time I heard the name Clare, it was like a jump scare."

"Sometimes you have to start with a clean slate. Tabula rasa." Angela patted her hand.

"Where'd you learn Latin, Ma?" Mona laughed.

"Hey, I pay attention when you kids study around here. I know more about World War Two than you would believe. I swear that's all they teach you kids about these days. And don't get me started on the Black History Month curriculum."

"It is a shame, isn't it?" Mona laughed. I laughed along with them—there was nothing like being from Texas that showed you Black history was not a priority in most school systems.

Finally Mona stood up, still gripping both of Angela's hands in her own. "Well, we should probably get going. My wife is a bit on edge at the moment."

Angela tilted her head with a questioning look.

"Our wedding is on Saturday."

"Didn't you say she's your wife?"

"It's a long story," Mona explained. "But we never really had a wedding, so now's our chance."

"Well, that's not a long story at all."

Mona smiled and then bent down to give the much smaller Angela a hug. I followed her lead and Angela held me tight.

"Take care of her," she whispered in my ear, giving my hands a squeeze before letting me go.

Once at the door, Mona stopped and turned back to Angela.

"You can come, if you'd like. To the wedding."

"Oh, I would love that!" Angela exclaimed.

Mona wrote down her address and the time of the wedding on a notepad by the door.

"I'm really happy you'll be there," she said as she put the pen down. "It'll be nice to have more family."

"I wouldn't miss it for the world."

Mona gave her one last hug before bouncing

down the stairs with a skip in her step that felt so similar to Clare's, I had to catch my breath.

"I'll see you both soon," Angela called from the door before going back inside.

I climbed into Mona's car and buckled myself in.

"I don't know how today happened," Mona said, taking the time to look at me before putting her key in the ignition. "But thank you."

"You're not mad at me for reading your journal?"

"To be honest, I'm kind of glad you read it. There's so much I've wanted to explain and not known how. Maybe this was just God."

"Do you really believe in God?" I asked her. "I mean, after everything that's happened?" How could so many bad things happen if God really existed, or cared about me? But then again, who else could have pulled this all off?

"That's exactly why I believe in him," she said, starting the car. The engine revved beneath us. "After everything that's happened, and we're both still here. That's somewhat miraculous, don't you think?"

"Yeah," I answered. "I guess it is."

Chapter Twenty-Six

The warehouse was even more full of activity than it had been for the prior two rounds of the competition. More local television crews than ever surrounded the room, pointing cameras in each contestant's face. I'd had to give several quick interviews already, repeating the same answer time and time again.

I stood at my station and smoothed my hands over my jeans. I hadn't initially wanted to enter the competition, but now that I was here, I really wanted to win. I didn't know what the last round would entail, but whatever it was, I was ready for it.

"Boo," a voice said behind me, grabbing my shoulders as I jumped in surprise.

"Cameron," I said, turning to find him smiling down at me.

"You ready?" he asked.

"I am," I said confidently.

"Good. Because you're better than everyone else here."

I laughed. "You're just saying that."

"Maybe, but that doesn't mean it's not true. Besides, the other two left are old, and I think someone young who can really take advantage of the prize should win."

"Cameron, these people are *not* old."

"Whatever. Older."

I looked past his shoulder and my mouth dropped open as a familiar face popped into the room.

"Shut up!" I yelled.

Olivia bounded toward me, her arms open wide as we crashed into each other. I picked her clean off the floor and we spun around like the final couple at the end of *Love Island*.

"What are you doing here?" I practically squealed in her ear as I put her down but still held her close, my arms wrapped around her shoulders.

"Your Mona called. Can you believe I got

flewed out for the first time?" She wiggled her hips. "Anthony better step his game up."

"God, I love you so much."

"Well, of course." She lowered her sunglasses down her nose. "But enough about me, who is that looking at you like you're the cherry on top of a banana split?"

"Oh, that's Cameron." I didn't even have to turn around to know who she was talking about. The obsession was real, but it went both ways.

"Cutie," she said. "He's giving shy but assertive. Yeah, I'll give him a ten."

"Stop it, he'll hear you," I warned her.

"Oh, I heard her," Cameron said.

I introduced them and Olivia held on to his hand as she sized him up.

"Oh, you are definitely a good fit for my girl here." She smiled. "With a strong handshake."

"Olivia!" I screeched.

"What?" she said, shrugging, but Cameron just laughed and wrapped his arm around me. I surprised myself by not stepping away, leaning my weight more into him. It felt nice.

"I'm going to find a good seat," Olivia said, turning to peruse her options.

"I meant to ask you, what are you wearing

to the wedding?" Cameron asked, dropping his arm to walk me back to my station.

"I don't think I'm going to make it to the wedding," I told him.

"You sure about that?"

"Yeah?" I swung my arm around the room, indicating where we were. The round hadn't even started yet and it was already ten a.m. Unless we were making Pillsbury cookies for round three, this was going to take at least three hours, and the wedding was at noon.

"Hmm," he muttered, placing his hand on his chin.

"What did you do?"

"I didn't do anything." He shrugged. "I just know something you don't."

"And what is that?"

He gave me a conspiratorial smile.

"I think these belong to you," Taylor said behind me.

I spun around. Gaby, Frankie, and Mona stood beside her, looking around the room in awe.

"What are y'all doing here?" I asked them in disbelief, surprised at how happy I was to see them. But their wedding was in two hours and they were in jeans, not a bridal updo to be found.

"Well, we thought it was more important to be here," Mona said.

"We texted everyone and told them the ceremony would actually start later, at five. So as long as you're done a little bit before then..." Gaby added.

"Why would you do that for me? You've been planning this day since before I got here."

"You're more important to us," Gaby said.

"Contestants, can you go to your stations now so we can get started?" Mrs. Forrester asked from the front of the room.

"Well, I have to go," I told them. They each gave me a hug, Mona's still a little stiff, as I pointed them toward Olivia in the audience. "Hey, Cameron," I called to him as he moved to sit beside Taylor. "My dress is maroon."

He gave me a smile and a wink before sitting down.

My station was ready for me as I got myself situated. I looked up into the risers to see a whole row dedicated to me. They all shot me thumbs-ups and fist pumps as the cameras began to roll and Mrs. Forrester began explaining this round of the competition.

"We are so excited to have you all for the

finale of this year's baking competition. The three of you are the best of the best, but after today's round, one of you will reign supreme. Today's competition will have you baking something familiar and figuring out how to make it spectacular."

A crew member came out with a towering cake—a wedding cake, in fact. Its white frosting glistened under the lights. Irony really was a hell of a thing.

"You three are tasked with creating a four-tier cake. But not just any cake. We want your cake to stand out, so you're going to have to pay extra attention to your decorations. In addition to the design blowing us away, you must also blow us away with flavor and texture. So don't sacrifice style for substance. You will have three hours to complete your cakes. Get ready, get set, go."

I stared at the ingredients in front of me and drew a blank. Cake was simple, but making a cake *spectacular* was not. I wasn't much of a decorator. And did I go for spectacular design or spectacular flavor? Mrs. Forrester said both were important, but I could excel at one or just do so-so all around.

I glanced back at my row of friends and

family. I didn't just want to win for myself. I wanted to win for all the people who'd showed up for me today. Flew halfway across the country or delayed their wedding. I wanted to win for Taylor, who'd spent hours in the bakery helping me get to this point. I wanted to win for Cameron, who had become my rock, supporting me every step of the way and believing in my abilities when I didn't even believe in them myself.

As I took them in, I suddenly knew exactly what I was going to make. Style-wise, I didn't think it'd be anything spectacular, but I knew I could make it taste good. I'd done it a million times. I looked up to the ceiling with a smile.

"This one's for you, Dad."

And then I started to bake.

Chapter Twenty-Seven

Olivia zipped up the back of my dress as we got ready in my room. I'd successfully washed off the sugar and flour from today's competition, and now it was time to party. I could hear the violinist play from my window, and I slid the windowpane up to let in more of the music. I was surprised to hear an orchestral version of Stevie Wonder's "Isn't She Lovely." Dad's favorite song. If that wasn't a sign that he was here with me, then I didn't know what was.

"You look hot," Olivia said as she finalized my makeup look. In addition to Olivia being one of the best artists in Austin, she also knew how to beat the hell out of a face. But I guessed a face wasn't too different from canvas—it was all just a blank slate on which you could make something beautiful.

I leaned out the window as I put in my earrings and found Cameron looking back up at me. He looked amazing in his black suit and maroon tie, which matched my dress perfectly. I didn't know how he got the color exactly right, but I suspected Gaby had something to do with it.

"So you really like him?" Olivia asked as she took a seat on my bed. Her dress was a flouncy floral masterpiece that sat beautifully on her tan skin. Something only she could pull off. Her straight now-black hair was pulled into a high bun that she smoothed down with the Eco styling gel I usually used on my baby hairs.

"I really do." I smiled shyly, dropping my face down so that she couldn't see the warmth in my cheeks.

"Love that for you. You seem so different."

"What do you mean? Like in a bad way?"

"God, no. I mean, more relaxed, maybe? Sometimes it felt like you thought you needed to take care of everyone. But now it's like you're letting people take care of you. You're in your 'soft girl' era and we love to see it, is all."

"I've grown to appreciate this place. I mean,

it's not the same without Dad, and I wish more than anything that he was here. But if I have to start over somewhere, this hasn't been the worst place."

"It's done you right. I mean, a baking competition? I never thought I'd see you really put yourself out there like that. It was incredible."

"I lost," I reminded her. Beaten by a four-tier cake designed to look like the Parthenon.

"Yes, you did. Badly." She laughed. "But I think you won so much more in the end. I mean, did you think you'd have everyone you love all in one place today?"

"I definitely did not." And she was right. Other than Dad, everyone I'd ever cared about was in that warehouse cheering me on. And even though he couldn't physically be there, the outpouring of love made him feel more present than he had since the car accident. Like the universe had taken his love for me and split it among them.

"Sky, are you ready?" Gaby called from downstairs.

"Yeah!" I yelled back, smoothing my hand over my dress.

"Are you?" Olivia asked me as she followed me down the stairs.

I stopped at the bottom and turned back to her. "I really am."

"And I'm really proud of you," she said, giving me a hug before she disappeared out the back door to snag a good seat.

Gaby came out of the kitchen with a blue Popsicle in her mouth. Her white sleeveless dress fit her in all the right places before flaring out like a mermaid tail. But man, was she brave to bring blue raspberry anywhere near it.

"Wow, Gaby, you look incredible," I told her.

"I do, don't I?" she said with a laugh as she nudged a piece of Popsicle out of the plastic and into her mouth.

"Aren't you worried you're going to spill that?" I asked.

"You know something I learned in this whole fiasco?" she asked as she finished off the Popsicle and sucked up all the excess juice. "I was so worried about something going wrong with this wedding, but in reality, nothing could go wrong. I'm renewing my vows with the love of my life, and I have my family here to support me this time." She reached for my hand. "All of my family."

She pulled me toward her and gave me a hug.

At this point, I was practically hugged out for today, but I let her hold on as long as she wanted.

"Let's rock and roll," she said as she pulled away.

Frankie was standing by a man who looked like a bald, older version of Gaby. I suspected it was her dad as he took her arm in his.

"Frankie, you have the rings?" Gaby asked him.

Frankie nodded enthusiastically and took one box out of each of his pockets.

"Good boy," Gaby crooned. "You're going to walk out with Sky."

As Gaby walked toward the back door and paused, Frankie grabbed my hand and pulled me down so my ear was next to his mouth.

"What's up?" I asked him.

"I'm happy you're my sister now," he said with a smile.

"I'm happy you're my brother," I told him.

He gave me a wide, toothless smile, having lost three teeth this summer. I led him in front of Gaby, and awed silence overtook the backyard. The violinist began to play again, this time "Heaven Sent" by Keyshia Cole. Okay, slay.

I led Frankie out the door and into the backyard, following the makeshift aisle that went between the two rows of chairs. Cameron winked at me as I caught his eye, and I winked back. Frankie walked beside me, giving the crowd a smile so wide I was sure his cheeks would be aching later. I spotted Angela on the same side as Cameron, Taylor, and the Forresters. She gave me a smile as I passed her, and I nodded in return.

Then there was Mona.

She stood at the end of the aisle in a white tux that looked so good on her she should have been on the cover of a magazine. I could practically hear Dad's wolf whistle. For the first time since I'd been here, I gave her an unguarded smile. She'd made a lot of mistakes, but she was not a bad person. Dad had loved her, and maybe over time, I would too. For now, I didn't hate her, and that felt like progress.

Gaby came down the aisle like an ethereal being. I glanced over at Mona and saw that she was crying. I was glad that Gaby had pushed so hard for this wedding. Their love deserved to be celebrated.

After their vows, there wasn't a dry eye in the yard. When the officiant, a friend from Gaby's pottery class, finally declared them wife and wife again, they shared a delicate kiss as Mona held Gaby's face with gentle fingers. If she hadn't married my dad, she might never have been able to find this for herself.

Gaby turned to everyone seated and waved her bouquet in the air. She raised Mona's hand in hers like she had won the greatest prize. Her mascara had smudged at the corners of her eyes as it mixed with her tears, but she still looked flawless.

"Who's ready to party?" she yelled.

It required an almost Herculean effort to switch the chairs over to reception tables with intricate flower centerpieces. Cameron, Taylor, and Olivia volunteered to help while Gaby, Mona, Frankie, and I went off to take photos, followed by a happy hour in the house for the thirty invited guests.

"Skylar?" Angela said when we finally had time to grab a snack. I stuffed a bacon-wrapped shrimp in my mouth and tried to swallow it down before she got to me. "I'm so sorry, dear, caught you right in the middle of eating. I just wanted to express how lovely today was."

"Thank you so much for coming. I know it means a lot to Mona. And thank you, again, for, you know, the puff pastry. I'm sorry I lost. You probably would've won the whole thing."

She waved her hand dismissively. "Like I said, I'd do it again." She glanced at everyone here who'd also been at the competition. "Besides, look at all of these people you brought together because of it. You made something very beautiful, both in competition and in life."

"I think you may be my guardian angel," I told her.

"No," she said. "I think you've got one of those already." She placed her hand on my cheek gently before swaying away to the canapés.

By the time the reception started, the backyard had been completely flipped. I was impressed at how different it could look after just one hour. Flowers and vines hung from the tent poles, and the tables were covered with flower petals, the centerpieces full and blooming in their gold vases.

My cake, the tower of strawberry shortcake I made for the competition, sat on a table with the official carrot cake they had ordered. Sliced strawberries made a detailed and decadent design along the sides and on the top of the four tiers.

Even though it wasn't a winner, I was still proud of it, and I knew Dad would be too.

Gaby and Mona took to the dance floor for their first dance as a twice-married couple, but just a few minutes in, they invited other couples to join them.

"Wanna dance?" Cameron asked me.

I wasn't much of a dancer, but I felt like I was entering my "yes" era.

I let Cameron guide me from the table to the dance floor. His hands rested on my waist as my arms encircled his neck.

"I didn't get to tell you how beautiful you look," he said.

"You look pretty dapper yourself," I told him.

"So what's the final verdict on Virginia? Still hate it?"

I looked back at my table of friends, both old and new. Mona caught my eye as she twirled Gaby in a circle and smiled. Frankie bounced past me with a slice of each cake. Dad might not have been here, but I felt like he'd left me in good hands.

I smiled up at Cameron and laid my head on his chest.

"I think it's given me every reason to stay."

Acknowledgments

To say the completion of this book relied on a heap of faith and even more patience would be an understatement. Losing my grandmother in the middle of its drafting (if you read *Love Times Infinity* or know me at all, then you know this is basically the most devastating thing that could have happened) and then having my daughter just a month later (again, if you know me at all, then you know this is basically the best thing that could have happened) is the kind of emotional whiplash that makes life a little too chaotic.

To my agent, Peter Knapp, and his team (Stuti, Jalynn, Danielle, and others who I'm sure my lizard mom brain is forgetting but not because they are forgettable)—I can't even begin to imagine how much work you did behind the scenes to keep this book on the rails. Thank you, seriously.

To my editor, Alex Hightower—if there were a Nobel Prize for patience, I would move heaven and earth for you to get it. Thank you for having my back through an incredibly harrowing process. I self-appointed myself as your biggest PITA author a long time ago, but it's pretty much solidified now. You are the best out there. To the rest of the Little, Brown Books for Young Readers team—you all have my eternal thank-you. Thank you to Amanda Gaglione for a great suggestion that forever changed Ma. Thank you to Jake Regier, Barbara Perris, Brandy Colbert, and Su Wu for getting this book in tip-top shape and fixing every instance in which I simply could not count the number of participants left in the cooking competition from one page to another (but you guys…it's a trunk!). Thank you to Jill De Haan and Gabrielle Chang for the most adorable book cover. Thank you to Martina Rethman, Stefanie Hoffman, Isabella Friedman, Savannah Kennelly, Maggie Montgomery, Hannah Klein, and Victoria Stapleton.

To Alex and Amanda—thank you for all the baby time you put in so that I could meet at least one of many missed deadlines. Thank you for showing up for me time and again through the highest and lowest points of my life. To Abby—thank you for being the best babysitter and playing with my child so I could, again, meet at least one of many missed deadlines.

To G—thank you for calling me an artist, even if you were pandering to the audience and reminding me constantly that I could do this. Love you lots.

To Grandma—God, I miss you. Life is not nearly as good without you.

To C—thank you for giving me a reason.

Nohelia Valentin

LANE CLARKE

is an author of young adult contemporary books. When she's not watching *One Tree Hill* or *My Wife and Kids* on repeat, she can be found experimenting with dairy-free recipes. Lane lives in Virginia with her husband, daughter, and fur babies. She invites you to visit her online at laneclarkewrites.com and on Instagram and TikTok @lanewriteswords.

CELEBRATING 100 YEARS OF PUBLISHING

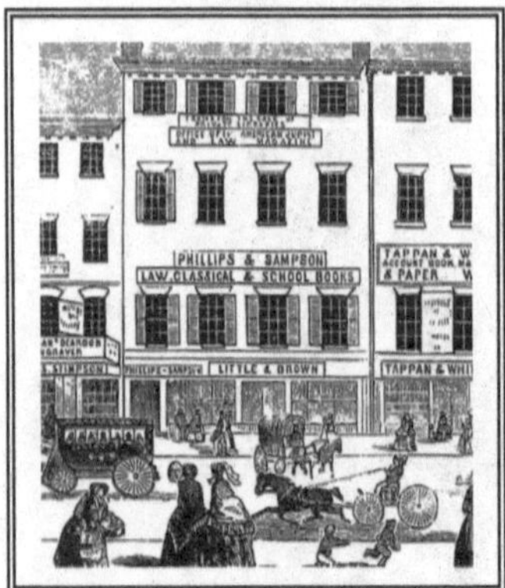

Dear Reader,

You may have noticed the words "Little, Brown and Company" on the title page of this book and wondered what they mean. Well, Charles C. Little and James Brown were the founders of this publishing house, and the "and Company" is all the editors, designers, marketers, publicists, salespeople, and more who help produce each book and bring it to readers like you. Little, Brown was founded in Boston, Massachusetts, in 1837, and some of its early publications included *The Writings of George Washington* and *The Works of Benjamin Franklin*. The catalog grew to feature works by Emily Dickinson and Louisa May Alcott, among many other notable authors. In 1926, recognizing that the literature we read when we are young has a deep and lasting influence and requires expert curation, the company appointed an editor to lead a dedicated children's department.

In 2026, Little, Brown Books for Young Readers celebrates one hundred years of excellence in publishing. Today, we are a division of Hachette Livre, the third-largest publisher in the world, and we are based in New York City. Our staff has grown from a team of two to more than one hundred people. And with the changes in technology, our books are read by more readers, in more ways, and in more countries than ever before. However, one thing has not changed: our commitment to providing a supportive home for all creators and superb stories for all readers. Thank you for being one of them.

Megan Tingley
President and Publisher

To learn more about Little, Brown's history, authors, and books, please visit LBYR.com.

www.ingramcontent.com/pod-product-compliance
Lightning Source LLC
LaVergne TN
LVHW030018300626
842253LV00039B/581